LOVE OF THE LAW . . .

Longarm hauled out his .44 and slid over to the doorway, standing well to one side as he asked softly, "Who's there?"

"It's me, Mabel Hanks! I've been so worried! I heard there was a shooting, and—"

"Nobody hurt, ma'am. I'm pure sorry we couldn't have dinner and all but having folks shooting at me goes with the job."

"May I come in for a moment?"

"Ma'am, I ain't decent. I just took off my britches."

She laughed softly and asked coyly, "Not even a shimmy shirt? I can't sleep and, well . . ."

Longarm considered, then he decided, what the hell, he'd *told* her, hadn't he, and unlocked the door.

Mabel Hanks slipped in and shut the door behind her, turning her eyes away from his long, naked legs as she murmured, "You must think me shameless."

He did. She'd let her long brown hair down and was wearing a long nightgown. "I'll snuff the candle so's we can talk without fluster," he said. "You must have something pretty important on your mind . . ."

Also in the LONGARM series from Jove

LONGARM

TABOR EVANS

JOVE BOOKS, NEW YORK

LONGARM

A Jove Book / published by arrangement with
the author

PRINTING HISTORY
Jove edition / October 1978

ISBN: 0-515-08965-6

Jove Books are published by The Berkley Publishing Group,
200 Madison Avenue, New York, New York 10016.
The name "JOVE" and the "J" logo
are trademarks belonging to Jove Publications, Inc.

PRINTED IN THE UNITED STATES OF AMERICA

20   19   18   17   16   15

Chapter 1

One gray Monday morning it was trying to rain in Denver. A herd of warm, wet Texas clouds had followed the Goodnight Trail north, tripped on the Arkansas Divide, and settled down to sweat itself away in the thin atmosphere of the mile-high capital of Colorado.

In the Union Yards a Burlington locomotive sobbed a long, lonesome whistle as Longarm awoke in his furnished room a quarter of a mile away.

For perhaps a full minute, Longarm stared up from the sagging brass bedstead at the smoke-begrimed plaster ceiling. Then he threw the covers off and swung his bare feet to the threadbare gray carpet and rose, or, rather, *loomed* in the semidarkness of the little corner room. Longarm knew he was tall. He knew he moved well. He didn't understand the effect his catlike motions had on others. His friends joshed about a man his size "spooking livestock and making most men thoughtful, with them sudden moves of his." But Longarm only thought it natural to get from where he'd been to where he was going by the most direct route. He was not a man who did things by halves. A man was either sleeping or a man was up, and right now he was up.

Longarm slid over to the dressing table and stared soberly at his reflection in the tarnished mirror. The naked figure staring back was that of a lean, muscular giant with the body of a young athlete and a lived-in face. Longarm was still on the comfortable side of forty, but the raw sun and cutting winds he'd ridden through since coming west as a boy from West-by-God-Virginia had cured his rawboned features as saddle-leather brown as an Indian's. Only the gunmetal blue of his wide-set eyes, and the tobacco-leaf color of his close-cropped hair and longhorn moustache gave evidence of Anglo-Saxon birth. The stubble on his lantern jaw was too heavy for an Indian, too. Longarm ran a thumbnail along the angle of his jaw and decided he had time to stop for a professional shave on his way to the office. He was an early riser and the Federal Courthouse wouldn't open until eight.

He rummaged through the clutter atop the dresser and swore when he remembered he was out of soap. Longarm was a reasonably clean guy who took a bath once a week whether he needed it or not, but the sociable weekend activities along Larimer Street's Saloon Row had left him feeling filthy and his mouth tasted like the bottom of a birdcage. He picked up a half-filled bottle of Maryland rye and pulled the cork with his big ivory-colored teeth. Then he took a healthy slug, swished it around and between his fuzzy teeth and cotton tongue, and let it go down. That took care of dental hygiene this morning.

He poured tepid water from a pitcher into a cracked china basin on a nearby stand. Then he spiked the water with some more rye. He dipped a stringy washrag in the mixture and rubbed himself down from hairline to shins, hoping the alcohol would cut the grease enough to matter. The cold whore-bath stung the last cobwebs from his sleep-drugged mind and he felt ready to face another week working for Uncle Sam.

That is, he was ready, but willing was another matter. The new regulations of President Hayes's Reform Administration were getting tedious as hell, and lately, Longarm had been thinking about turning in his badge.

He scowled at himself in the mirror as he put on a fresh flannel shirt of gunmetal gray and fumbled with the foolish-looking shoestring tie they had said he had to wear, these days. Back when U.S. Grant had been in the catbird seat, the Justice Department had been so surprised to find a reasonably honest lawman that they'd been content to let him dress any old way he pleased. Now the department was filled with prissy pink dudes who looked like they sat down to piss, and they said a Deputy U.S. Marshal had to look "dignified."

Longarm decided that the tie was as pretty as it was likely to get and sat his naked rump on the rumpled bed to wrestle on his britches. He pulled on a pair of tight, knit cotton longjohns before working his long legs into the brown tweed pants he'd bought one size too small. Like most experienced horsemen, Longarm wore neither belt nor suspenders to hold his pants up. He knew the dangers of a sweat-soaked fold of cloth or leather between a rider and his mount moving far or sudden. By the time he'd cursed the fly shut, the pants fit tight as a second skin around his upper thighs and lean hips.

He bent double and hauled on a pair of woolen socks before grunting and swearing his feet into his low-heeled cavalry stovepipes. Like the pants, the boots had been bought a size too small. Longarm had soaked them overnight and put them on wet to dry as they'd broken in, molding themselves to his feet. Like much of Longarm's working gear, the low-heeled boots were a compromise. A lawman spent as much time afoot as he did in the saddle and he could run with surprising speed for a man his size in those too-tight boots.

In boots, pants, and shirt he rose once again to lift the gunbelt from the bedpost above his pillow. He slipped the supple cordovan leather belt around his waist, adjusting it to ride just above his hip bones. Like most men who might be called upon to draw either afoot or mounted with his legs apart, Longarm favored a cross-draw rig, worn high.

It hardly seemed likely that his gun had taken it upon itself to run low on ammunition overnight, but Longarm had attended too many funerals of careless men to take such things for granted. He reached across his buckle for the polished walnut grip and drew, hardly aware of the way his smooth, swift draw threw down, instinctively, on the blurred image in the mirror across the room.

He wasn't aiming to shoot himself in the mirror. He wanted to inspect one of the tools of his trade. Longarm's revolver was a double-action Colt Model T .44-40. The barrel was cut to five inches and the front sight had been filed off as useless scrap iron that could hang up in the open-toed holster of waxed and heat-hardened leather.

Swinging the gun over the rumpled bed, Longarm emptied the cylinder on the sheets, dry-fired a few times to test the action, and reloaded, holding each cartridge up to the gray window-light before thumbing it home. Naturally, he only carried five rounds in the six chambers, allowing the firing pin to ride safely on an empty chamber. More than one old boy had been known to shoot his fool self in the foot jumping down off a bronc with a double-action gun packing one round too many.

Satisfied, Longarm put his sixgun to rest on his left hip and finished getting dressed. He put on a vest that matched his pants.

Those few who knew of his personal habits thought Longarm methodical to the point of fussiness. He considered it common sense to tally up each morning just what he was facing the day with. Before bedding down he'd spread the contents of his pockets across the top of the dresser. He made a mental note of each item as he started stuffing his pockets with a calculated place on his person for each and every one of them.

He counted out the loose change left from the night before, noting he'd spent damned near two whole dollars on dinner and drinks the night before. The depression of the '70s had bottomed out and business was starting to boom again. He was overdue for a raise and prices were getting outrageous. A full-course meal could run a man as much as seventy-five cents these days and some of the fancier saloons were charging as much as a nickel a shot for redeye!

He dropped the change in his pants pocket and

picked up his wallet. He had two twenty-dollar silver certificates to last him till payday unless he ran into someone awfully pretty. His silver federal badge was pinned inside the wallet. Longarm rubbed it once on his woolen vest and folded the wallet. Then he slipped on his brown frock coat and tucked the wallet away in an inside pocket. He wasn't given to flashing his badge or his gun unless he was serious.

He dropped a handful of extra cartridges into the right side pocket of his coat. The matching left hand pocket took a bundle of waterproof kitchen matches and a pair of handcuffs. The key to the cuffs and his room went in his left pants pocket along with a jack-knife.

The last item was the Ingersoll watch on a long, gold-washed chain. The other end of the chain was soldered to the brass butt of a double-barrelled .44 derringer. The watch rode in the left breast pocket of the vest. The derringer occupied the matching pocket on the right, with the chain draped across the front of the vest between them.

Longarm tucked a clean linen handkerchief into the breast pocket of his frock coat and took his snuff-brown Stetson from its nail on the wall. He positioned it carefully on his head, dead center and tilted slightly forward, cavalry style. The hat's crown was telescoped in the Colorado rider's fashion, but the way he wore it was a legacy from his youth when he'd run away to ride in the war. Longarm "disremembered" whether he'd ridden for the blue or the gray, for the great civil war lay less than a generation in the past and memories of it were still bitter, even this far west. It didn't pay a man to talk too much about things past, out Colorado way.

Ready to face the morning, Longarm let himself out silently, slipping a short length of wooden matchstiek between the door and the jam as he locked up. His landlady was supposed to watch his digs, but the almost invisible sliver would warn him if anyone was waiting for him inside whenever he returned.

Longarm moved through the dark rooming house on silent, booted feet, aware that others might still be sleeping. Outside, he filled his lungs with the clean, but oddly-scented air of Denver, ignoring the slight drizzle that he knew would blow over by noon.

His furnished digs lay in the no-longer-fashionable quarter on the wrong side of Cherry Creek, so Longarm crunched along the damp cinder path to the Colfax Avenue Bridge. He noticed as he crossed it that Cherry Creek still ran low and peaceable within its adobe banks. He hadn't thought the unusual summer rain was worth his yellow oilcloth slicker. It figured to last just long enough to lay the dust and maybe do something about that funny smell.

Longarm prided himself on his senses and liked to *know* what he was smelling. He could sniff a Blue Norther fixing to sweep down across the prairie long before the clouds shifted. He could tell an Indian from a white man in the dark and once he'd smelled lightning in the high country just before it hit the ridge he'd just vacated. But he'd never figured out why, in winter, spring, summer, or fall, the town of Denver always smelled like someone was burning autumn leaves over on the next street. He'd seldom *seen* anyone burning leaves in Denver. Aside from a few planted cottonwoods in the more fashionable neighborhoods there were hardly enough trees in the whole damned town to matter. Yet there it was, even now, in the soft summer rain. That mysterious smell was sort of spooky when a man studied on it.

On the eastern side of Cherry Creek the cinder pathways gave way to the new red sandstone sidewalks they were putting down along all the main streets these days. Colfax Avenue had gas illumination, too. The town was getting downright civilized, considering it had been just another placer camp in the rush, less than twenty years before.

Longarm came to an open barber shop on a corner and went in for a shave and maybe some stink-pretty.

His superiors had taken to commenting on a deputy who reported to work smelling like Maryland rye, and the bay rum George Masters, the barber, splashed over a paying customer didn't cost extra.

He saw that the barber already had a customer in the chair and sat down to wait his turn. A stack of magazines was piled next to him and, deciding against Frank Lesley's *Illustrated Weekly,* he picked up a copy of Ned Buntline's *Wild West* magazine. Longarm didn't know what the people who put it out had in mind, but he considered it a humorous publication.

He saw that there was another yarn in this month's issue about poor old Jim Hickock. Old Jim had died in Deadwood damned near five years ago, but they still had him tearassing around after folks with a sixgun in each hand. For some reason they kept calling Old Jim "Wild Bill."

There was a comical article about crazy Jane Canary, too. The writers called her "Calamity Jane" and had her down as Jim Hickock's lady love. Longarm chuckled aloud and wet his thumb to turn the page. The last time he'd seen Hickock alive he'd been a happily married man, and the last gal on earth Jim or any other sane man would mess with was Jane Canary. If anyone really called her "Calamity," it was probably because they knew she'd been tossed out of Madame Moustache's parlor house in Dodge for dosing at least a dozen paying customers with the clap!

Longarm saw that the barber was about finished with the first customer and he put the magazine aside. As the other man rose from the chair, George whipped the barber's cloth aside and Longarm saw that the customer's right hand was on the butt of the Walker-Colt riding his right hip!

Longarm crabbed to one side. His own gun appeared in front of him as if by magic, trained on the stranger's bellybutton. Longarm said, "Freeze!" in a soft, no-nonsense tone.

George was already well to one side with a swiftness

gained from cutting hair this close to the Larimer Street deadline. The man half out of the barber's chair snatched his hand from the butt of his holstered revolver as if it had suddenly stung him and his face was chalky as he gasped, "Mister, I don't even *know* you!"

"I ain't sure as I've seen you before, either, old son. You got a *reason* for coming up out of that chair grabbing iron, or were you just born foolish?"

"I don't know what you're talking about! I was just shifting Captain Walker, here, to ride more comfortable-like!"

"Well, that old hog leg's a heavy gun and what you say's almost reasonable, but hardly common sense. If you aim to wander through life with that oversized sixgun dragging alongside, you'd best learn not to make sudden moves toward it around grown men!"

The other, perhaps ten years younger than the deputy, licked his lips and said, "Mister, I have purely learnt it! I swear I never saw a gun-slick draw so fast before! I don't know who you are, but you must surely have one dangerous job!"

"The name is Custis Long and I'm a Deputy U.S. Marshal, which I'll allow can leave a man thoughtful. Where've I seen *you* before, friend?"

The youth moved clear of the barber chair, keeping his hands well out to both sides as he smiled and answered, "I doubt as you've seen me at all, Marshal. My handle is Jack Robinson and I just came up from Texas. I'm riding for the Diamond K, just outside of town, these days. And that sixgun trained on my middle is making me a mite skittish, dang it!"

Longarm nodded thoughtfully. Then he lowered the muzzle to his side as he asked the barber the price of the cheroots in the open cigar box on the marble counter. George said they were a nickel each, so Longarm said, "Have a smoke on me, then, Tex. I'll allow we was both still half asleep, so let's part friendly and forget it, hear?"

The cowhand clumped over to the counter and

helped himself to a cheroot, saying, "That's right neighborly of you, Marshal. Am I free to mosey on?"

"Sure. You don't aim to give me a shave, do you?"

They both laughed, and as Longarm took his place in the chair, the younger man left. Longarm stared after him thoughtfully until his booted footfalls faded up the walk outside. The barber brought a hot towel, but Longarm motioned it away and said, "Ain't got much time, George. Just run your blade through this stubble and I'll be on my way. Don't want to report in late again and I ain't had breakfast yet."

The barber nodded and started to swivel the chair around to face the mirror. Longarm shook his head and said, "Leave her facing the doorway, George."

"You still edgy about that young cowboy, Mister Long? He looked harmless enough to me."

"Yeah. He said he was from Texas, too. I'll take this shave sitting tall, if it's all the same to you."

The barber shrugged and went to work. He knew the deputy wasn't a man for small talk in the morning, so he lathered Longarm silently, wondering what he'd missed in the exchange just now. The barber was still stropping his razor when the open doorway suddenly darkened. The youth who'd apparently left for good was back, with the Walker-Colt gripped in both hands and his red face twisted with hate.

Longarm fired three times as he rose, pumping lead through the barber's cloth from the short muzzle of the .44 he'd been holding in his lap, as the barber dove for cover.

When George Masters raised his head, Longarm was standing in the doorway, the cloth still hanging from his neck and the smoking .44 in his big right fist as he stared morosely down at the figure sprawled on the wet sandstone paving in the soft summer rain. Masters joined the lawman to stare down in wonder at the death-glazed eyes of the stranger who'd left his Walker-Colt inside on the tiles as he fell. Masters gasped, "How did you *know*, Mister Long?"

13

Longarm shrugged and said, "Didn't, for certain. He's changed a mite since I arrested him down in the Indian Nation four or five summers back. He shouldn't have said he was from Texas. It came to me who he was as he was walking away. He was wearing high plains spurs. That's how he come back so quiet. Most Texans favor spurs that *jingle* when they walk. His hat was wrong for Texas, too."

"My God, then you was ready for him all the time!"

"Nope. Just careful. Like I said, it was a good five years back and I could have been wrong. A man in my line arrests a lot of folks in five years."

Their discussion was broken off by the arrival of a uniformed roundsman of the Denver police department. He elbowed through the crowd of passersby now gathering around the body on the walk and sighed, "I hope somebody here has an explanation for all this."

Longarm identified himself and explained what had happened, adding, "This here's what's left of one Robert Jackson. He'd changed his name bass-ackwards to Jack Robinson but he hadn't learned much since I beat him to the draw a few years back. He'd gunned a Seminole down in the Indian Nation and was supposed to be doing twenty years at hard labor in Leavenworth. I don't know what he was doing in Denver, but, as you see, he don't figure to cause nobody much bother."

"You're going to have to come down to the station house and help us make out a report, Deputy Long. I hope you don't take it personal. I'm just doing my job."

"I know. I got a job to do myself, so let's get cracking. The boss is going to cloud up and rain all over me if I come in late again this morning."

The sky had cleared by the time Longarm left the police station and resumed his walk up Colfax Avenue. Up on Capitol Hill the gilded dome of the Colorado State House glinted in the rain-washed sunlight, but the civic center, like the rest of Denver's business district, nestled in the hollow between Capitol Hill to the east

14

and the Front Range of the Rockies, fifteen miles to the west.

Longarm came to the U.S. Mint at Cherokee and Colfax and swung around the corner to walk to the federal courthouse. He saw he was late as he elbowed his way through the halls filled with officious-looking dudes waving legal briefs and smelling of macassar hair oil. He climbed a marble staircase and made his way to a big oak door whose gold leaf lettering read, *UNITED STATES MARSHAL, FIRST DISTRICT COURT OF COLORADO.*

Longarm went inside, where he found a new face seated at a rolltop desk, pounding at the keys of a new fangled engine they called a typewriter. Longarm nodded down at the pink-faced young man and said, "You play that thing pretty good. Is the chief in the back?"

"Marshal Vail is in his office, sir. Whom shall I say is calling?"

"Hell, he knows who I am. I only asked was he *in.*"

Longarm moved over to an inner doorway, ignoring the clerk as he bleated, "You can't go in *unannounced,* sir!"

Longarm opened the door without knocking and went in. He found his superior, Marshal Vail, seated behind a pile of papers on a flat-topped mahogany desk.

Vail looked up with a harassed expression and growled, "You're late. Be with you in a minute. They've got me buried under a blizzard that just blowed in from Washington!"

Longarm sat on the arm of a morocco leather chair across the desk from his superior and chewed his unlit cheroot to wait him out. It seemed that all he ever did these days was wait. A banjo clock on the oak-paneled wall ticked away at his life while Longarm counted the stars in the flag pinned flat on the wall over Vail's balding head. Longarm knew there were thirty-eight states in the Union, these days, but his eyes like to keep busy and the marshal wasn't much to look at.

15

In his day, Marshal Billy Vail had shot it out with Comanche, Owlhoots, and, to hear him tell it, half of Mexico. Right now he was running to lard and getting that baby-pink political look Longarm associated with the Courthouse Gang. There was something to be said for working in the field, after all. Vail wasn't more than ten or fifteen years older than Longarm. It was sobering for Longarm to think that *he* might start looking like that by the turn of the century if he wasn't careful about his personal habits.

Vail found the papers he was looking for and frowned up at Longarm, saying, "You've missed the morning train to Cheyenne, God damn your eyes! What's your tall tale this time, or did you think this office opened at noon?"

"You know a feller called Bob Jackson, supposed to be doing time in Leavenworth?"

"Oh, you heard about his escape, eh? He's been reported as far west as here and I've got Collins and Bryan looking for him on the street."

"You can tell 'em to quit looking. He's bedded down peaceable in the Denver morgue. I shot him on the way to work."

"You *what*? What happened? Where did you spot him?"

"I reckon it's fair to say he spotted me. He must have taken it personal when I arrested him that time, but I can't say his brains or gun hand had improved worth mentioning. The Denver P.D.'s doing the paper work for us. What's this about a train to Cheyenne?"

"Slow down. You're going to have to file a full report before you leave town on the escaped prisoner you just caught up with."

"All right, I'll jaw with that jasper you have playing the typewriter out front before I leave. Who are we after in Wyoming Territory?"

Vail sighed and said, "I'm sending you to a place called Crooked Lance. Ever hear of it?"

16

"Cow town, a day's ride north of the U.P. stop at Bitter Creek? I've seen it on the map. I worked out of Bitter Creek during the Shoshone uprising a few years back, remember?"

"That's the place. Crooked Lance is an unincorporated township on federally owned range in West Wyoming Territory. They're holding a man with a Federal want on him. His name's Cotton Younger. Here's his arrest record."

Longarm took the sheet of yellow foolscap and scannned it, musing aloud, "Ornery pissant, ain't he? Says here Queen Victoria has a clain on him for raping and killing a Red River breed. What are *we* after him for, the postal clerk he gunned in Nebraska or this thing about deserting the Seventh Cav during Terry's Rosebud Campaign against the Dakotas?"

"Both. More important, Cotton Younger is reputed to be related to Cole Younger, of the James-Younger Gang. Cole Younger's salted away for life after the gang made a mess of that bank holdup in Minnesota a couple of years back. Frank and Jesse James are still at large, and wanted for everything but leprosy."

Longarm hesitated before he nodded and said, "I can see why you'd like to have a talk with this Cotton Younger, Chief, but does picking up and transporting a prisoner rate a deputy with my seniority?"

"I didn't think so, either, at first. You know Deputy Kincaid, used to work out of the Missouri office?"

"Know him to say howdy. He working this case with me?"

"Not exactly. Like you said, it seemed a simple enough chore for a new hand. So I sent Kincaid up there two weeks ago."

"And?"

"That's what I want you to find out. I can't get through to Crooked Lance by wire. Western Union says the line is down in the mountains and both Kincaid and his prisoner are long overdue."

Longarm consulted his watch and said, "I can catch

the afternoon Burlington to Cheyenne, transfer to the transcontinental U.P. and maybe pick up a mount before I get off at Bitter Creek. Who do I report to in Crooked Lance?"

"Wyoming Territory was sort of vague about that. Like I said, the settlement's in unincorporated territory. Apparently a local vigilance committee caught Cotton Younger riding through with a running iron in his saddle bags and ran him in as a cow thief. They were holding him in some sort of improvised jail when they asked the territorial government for a hanging permit. Wyoming wired us, and from there on you know as much as I do."

"Vigilantes picked him up, you say? He's lucky if he's still breathing regular. I don't care all that much for vigilantes. Not many left, these days."

"I gathered the folks in Crooked Lance are leery of lynch law, too. I'd say their so-called committee is just an *ad hoc* bunch of local cowmen. The town itself is a handful of shacks around a post office and general store. I don't know how in the hell Kincaid could have got lost up there."

Longarm got to his feet and said, "Only one way to find out. If the wire's up when I get there I'll let you know what happened. If it ain't, I won't. Figure on me being back in about a week. I'll need some expense vouchers and a railroad pass, too."

"My secretary will take care of that before you leave. Would you like to take a couple of extra hands with you?"

"I work as well alone, Chief. No sense getting spooked till we find out what happened. Kincaid and his prisoner might well be on their way this very minute and I'd play the fool tearassing in at the head of a posse for no good reason."

"You handle it as you've a mind to, but for God's sake, be careful. I don't aim to lose *two* deputies to . . . to whatever!"

As Longarm was leaving, Marshal Vail called after

him, "Damn it, son, you might have offered me an educated guess to chew on while I'm waiting here!"

Longarm turned the doorway to say, "If I knew any more than you I'd likely be able to save myself the trip, Chief. You ain't paying me to guess. As I see it, I'm to go and fetch them two old boys."

"I'm going to be sweating bullets anyway, until you come back with some reasonable explanation. You said a week, right? What am I to do if you *don't* come back in a week?"

Longarm considered before he shrugged and said, "Don't know, but it won't be my problem, will it?"

"What do you mean, it won't be your problem? Are you saying you'll be back in a week unless you're no longer alive?"

Longarm didn't answer. That was the trouble with men who worked behind an office desk. Instead of thinking, they got into the habit of asking all sorts of foolish questions.

Chapter 2

Longarm sat along on a greenplush seat near the rear of the passenger car of the U.P. local-combine. Somewhere up ahead the Wyoming sun was going down. He smoked a cheroot and stared out the dirty window with one booted foot braced against the cast-iron frame of the empty seat facing him. The train was climbing the Rocky Mountains, but you couldn't tell. The sunset-tinted scene outside seemed gently rolling prairie, for the snow-clad spine of the Continental Divide dipped under a vast mountain meadow near South Pass. Some accident of geology had left an annex of the high plains cattle country stranded in the sky.

The Indians had found this easy way through the Shining Mountains long before they'd shown it to the mountain men, who'd mapped it for the covered wagon trains and, twenty years later, the transcontinental railroad.

Longarm wasn't crossing the continent. He was about an hour and a half from the jerkwater stop at Bitter Creek, at the rate they were moving. He hoped there'd be a tolerable hotel in Bitter Creek; he planned on a good night's sleep between clean sheets, and if possible, a bath, before he spurred a horse for Crooked Lance. He was hoping someone there might know where the fool town was; Longarm had a War Department survey map saying it was one place, while the map he'd asked the land office for had it in another. Either way, it was a good distance to ride on a fool's errand.

A voice pitched high, with a slight lisp, asked, "Are

you a cowboy, mister?" and Longarm swung his eyes from the window to stare morosely at what had climbed up on the seat facing him. It had long blond curls, but was wearing a velvet Little Lord Fauntleroy suit, so it was probably a boy. Longarm remembered seeing the child get on with a not-bad-looking gal in a feathered hat at Medicine Bow, so the sissy-looking kid was liable to be hers. Longarm decided the father had to be damned ugly, if that pretty little thing down at the other end of the car had given birth to anything so tedious to look at.

The prissy little boy repeated his question and Longarm, remembering his manner, smiled crookedly and answered, "I'm sorry, sonny. But I ain't a cowboy. Ain't no Injun, either."

"You look like a cowboy. We saw some cowboys riding horses back near that last town. My name is Cedric and I'm almost seven and when I grow up I'm going to be a cowboy!"

Longarm's face softened, for he'd been seven once, so he nodded soberly and said, "You look like you have the makings of a top hand, Cedric. You ever ride a bronc?"

"Well, I used to have a pony, before my daddy had to go away with the angels of the Lord."

"Oh? Well, I'm purely sorry about that, sonny. It's been nice meeting up with you, but don't you think you'd better go back and keep your mother company?"

Cedric pulled his tiny feet up on the green plush, stood on the seat, and shouted down the length of the car, "Mommy! Mommy! Can I stay here and talk to this cowboy?"

Heads turned and a rustling of soft laughter filled the car as Longarm wondered if crawling under the seat might seem too obvious a way to vanish. Only half the seats were filled, this far out on the local run, but everyone on earth seemed to be looking his way.

Before the brat could yell again, the woman seated near the front of the car got up and moved their way, her pretty face mortified under the bouncing feathers of her black-veiled hat. Longarm now noticed that she was wearing black widow's weeds and that she moved nicely, edging around the potbellied stove in the center of the car. As she came nearer, the deputy rose from his seat, took the cheroot from his mouth and tipped his Stetson, murmuring, "Your servant, Ma'am."

"I'm terribly sorry, sir," she replied, as Longarm tried to decide if she was blushing or just glowing prettily in the red light of evening.

She took Cedric by the shoulder and shook him gently, as she warned him in a low tone, "I've told you a hundred times it's not *refined* to *shout* like that, darling!"

"Aw, hell, Mom, I was just talking to the cowboy!"

A few seats away a man tried not to laugh out loud and failed, and this time the woman seemed really flustered. Longarm pointed at the seat across from his and muttered, "Why don't we all set? We'll be stopping soon and your Cedric ain't fretting me all that much."

The woman hesitated, then took a seat by her noisy darling, not looking at Longarm as she murmured, "I'm not in the habit of speaking to strangers, sir, but . . . oh, Cedric, what am I to *do* with you?"

Privately, Longarm had considered a good sound birching as good a way to start as any. Aloud, he said, "I know I'm a stranger, ma'am, but if it's any help to you, I'm a Deputy United States Marshal, so it ain't like you've fallen in with thieves, should anyone ask."

Cedric chortled, "Oh, boy, a *sheriff!*"

More to shut him up than with any idea that it might be of interest, Longarm corrected, "No, sonny, a marshal ain't no sheriff. You'll understand it better when you grow up." He didn't add, "*if.*" The poor young widow woman had enough on her plate as it was.

The lady pursed her lips as if coming to a brave decision before she said, "Allow me to introduce myself to you, Marshal. I am Mabel Hanks, widow to the late

22

Ruben Hanks of Saint Louis. You've met my son, Cedric, to my considerable mortification."

"Well, I'm Custis Long and pleased to meet you both and he'll likely outgrow it, ma'am. Are you getting off at Bitter Creek?"

"Yes, my late husband has a sister there. Or, rather, she and her husband live just north of there, at a place called Crooked Lance."

"Do tell? I hope somebody's meeting you, then. Crooked Lance is more than a day's ride from where we're all getting off."

Mabel Hanks looked stricken as she flustered, "Oh, dear, I had no idea! How on earth will we ever get there? You don't suppose I'll be able to hire a hansom cab in Bitter Creek, do you, Mister Long?"

"Not hardly. Don't your kinfolks know you're coming?"

"I'm not sure. My sister-in-law was very gracious to invite us to come and live with her, and frankly, we have little other choice right now. We, ummm, were not left in very gentle circumstances by my late husband's unexpected passing."

"My daddy made beer in Saint Louis," Cedric offered in a piping voice, adding for the whole car to hear, "The angels of the Lord took him when a streetcar ran over him one morning."

"Cedric, dear heart, will you please be still?" the mother gasped. She looked as if she were about to cry. Longarm quickly cut in with, "You say you're coming out invited, ma'am. Can I take it you wrote your kin what train they could expect you to arrive on?"

"Of course. The railroad was a bit hazy on just when, but I sent them a telegram by Western Union when we boarded at Omaha."

"You sent the wire to Crooked Lance, ma'am?"

"Of course. Western Union says there's an office there. Is something wrong? Forgive me for presuming, but I seem to detect an odd look in your eye, sir."

23

Longarm shrugged and said, "May as well come right out and say it, then. The telegraph line's been down for some time, ma'am."

"You mean they couldn't have gotten my message? They won't be waiting for us? Oh, dear! Oh, what are we to do? What's to become of us?"

Longarm could see more heads turning as the widow matched her infernal brat's damned noise with considerable attention-getting near-hysterics of her own. He quickly soothed, "Now simmer down, ma'am. It's not all that big a shucks! Your kin will be there. Crooked Lance is only out of touch, not swallowed up by wolves!"

"Yes, but they won't be waiting for us at the station in Bitter Creek, and you say there are no cabs, and . . . oh, Lord, I don't know what we're to *do*!"

"Well, now, let's just eat the apple a bite at a time, ma'am. I'll help you get your things from the station to the hotel once we arrive, which shouldn't be all that long now. Once you've et, and bedded down Cedric here, we can ask about Bitter Creek for friends of your kin or something. Shucks, there's a chance someone from Crooked Lance will be there."

"But what if—"

"Don't cross your bridges before you come to 'em, ma'am. At the very worst, you'll arrive in Bitter Creek unexpected and have to spend a day or so at the hotel till your kinfolks know you're there and send a buckboard to fetch you. As to *how* they'll know, I'll tell 'em. I'll be riding to Crooked Lance come sunup, and if you give me a message for anyone in Crooked Lance, I'll likely deliver it within a day or so."

Cedric grinned and asked, "Can't we go to see Aunt Polly with *you*, Mister?"

It was a fool question, but Longarm saw that the widow seemed to think the kid's question made sense, so he shook his head and said, "Not hardly. The army mount I borrowed from Fort Laramie is alone with my saddle and trail gear in the freight section behind us.

24

Don't seem likely the three of us would fit comfortably in a McClellan saddle, and if we could, the old army bay couldn't carry us far enough to matter." To the widow he added, "I've already thought of a hired buckboard, ma'am, and I'd be proud to give you a lift, if I had any idea where the town was and how much trouble I'd have getting there."

He saw the hope in her eyes as she insisted, "Forgive my boldness, but, as you see, I'm desperate. We'd be willing to take our possible discomforts with good grace, if only—"

"*You* might be, but I wouldn't, ma'am," Longarm, cut in explaining, "You see, I'm not paying a social call in Crooked Lance. I'm on U.S. Government business and, while I'll be pleased to tell your kin where to find you, there's no way I could see fit to expose you and the boy here to possible danger."

"Danger?" she gasped, "I had no idea! Are you going to Crooked Lance to *arrest* someone?"

"Let's say I'm just having a looksee, ma'am. I don't mind talking about my self, but Uncle Sam's business is sort of private. No offense intended, but we do have these fool regulations."

"Oh, I understand, sir. Forgive my stupidity! I never meant to pry!"

The conductor saved Longarm from having to think up a gracious answer as he came through the car, calling out, "Next stop Bitter Creek, folks! We'll be pulling in about ten minutes from now. Please have your selves ready to detrain sudden, as we ain't stopping to jerk water on the downgrade!"

"We'd better go back to our seats," the widow said, but she didn't seem to be moving. She licked her lips and, not looking at him, asked, "Is, uh, this hotel in Bitter Creek liable to be expensive, sir?"

"Don't know. Never stayed there before."

"You don't suppose they'd charge more than a dollar a night, do you?"

"Dollar a night's pretty steep, for a trail town hotel. Might be less. Can't hardly be much more, ma'am."

"Oh. You're sure you'll be able to reach Crooked Lance within two days at the most?"

"No, ma'am, I said I aimed to try."

"Oh, dear."

If she'd been leading up to it, she was pretty slick. He stared at her for a long hard minute, then he shrugged and said, "If you need a loan, just till I can get word to your kinfolks . . ."

"Sir!" she gasped. "Whatever are you suggesting?"

"Ain't suggesting. Offering. Seems to me you and the boy, here, are in a pickle. I won't insult no lady with numbers, but if you'll let me put a few day's room and board on my own tab . . ."

"That's out of the question, sir! I can see you are a gentleman and I understand your offer was meant in kind innocence, but, *really* . . . !"

"Let's say no more, then, ma'am. It was a fool thing to say to a lady."

For the first time she smiled at Longarm, lighting up the dusk-filled space between them a bit, as she said, "On the contrary, it was . . . well, I'd hardly call it gallant, but I understand, and I think you're a very sweet person, Mister Long."

Longarm looked out the window, redfaced, and said, "I see some lights up ahead. We're pulling in to Bitter Creek. Would you be likely to cloud up and rain all over me if I helped you with your things?"

This time she laughed, a pretty skylark laugh, and said, "I'd be honored if you escorted us to the hotel, Mister Long."

Longarm got to his feet to follow as she rose and moved back to her own seat for their luggage, with little Cedric in her wake between them. Longarm noticed that she had a nice, trim waistline too. If only she didn't have that ugly little kid with her . . .

Under his breath, he muttered to himself, "Now just you back off, old son! They didn't send us up here to

26

spark a widow woman, ugly kid or no! How are you going to get them, their luggage, and your own mount and gear unloaded without losing more'n half of it? Damn that prissy kid. What's he gotten you into, anyway? Don't you know better than to talk to strangers on a train?"

Chapter 3

The hotel in Bitter Creek wasn't much, but it was the only one they had. After checking the widow and her son into one room and himself into another, and ignoring the leer in the old desk-clerk's eye, Longarm went out, leaving her and the boy at the hotel and his army bay in the livery stable next door. It was still early evening and the streets of Bitter Creek were crowded, not because there were a lot of people in town but because the town was so small.

Nobody around the hotel had ever heard of the Widow Hanks or her in-laws at Crooked Lance. It was hard enough to find someone who'd admit there might *be* a place called Crooked Lance, "a day or so up yonder."

That wasn't much help.

Longarm strode down the plank walks until he came to the town marshal's office and went in. The deputy he found seated at a packing-case desk seemed impressed by his federal badge and willing to help. So Longarm hooked his rump over the corner of the improvised desk and asked where in thunder Crooked Lance might be, adding, "This place I'm looking for is downright spooky, Deputy! If you tell me it's been shifted again . . ."

"Hell, we got it on a map over on the wall, Deputy Long. You wouldn't be the one they call Longarm, would you?"

"You can call me that. You can call me anything but late for breakfast if you'll answer some questions.

"I figured you was Longarm. That jasper they're holding up in Crooked Lance must be somebody important, huh?"

"You know about Cotton Younger up in the Crooked Lance jail?"

"Sure. All sorts of people have been coming through here looking for him. I've been showing 'em the same map you see on yonder wall. Seems like a lot of fuss and feathers over a cow thief, if you ask me!"

"Did another Deputy U.S. Marshal pass this way, asking for directions to wherever?"

"Sure, couple of weeks back. You looking for *him,* too?"

"Maybe. Was his name Kincaid?"

"Yep, now that you mention it, that's who I think he said he was."

"All right. We know Kincaid got as far as here and was last seen headed up to Crooked Lance. Who were these others you say were interested in that old boy they have up there?"

The deputy considered before he replied, "Don't remember the names. There was a feller from the Provost Marshal's Office, War Department, I think he said he rode for. Then there was this lawman from Missouri, county sheriff I think. Oh, yeah, and there was one real funny lookin' jasper in the damndest looking outfit you ever saw. Had on a red jacket. I mean *blinding* red! Ain't that a bitch?"

"Northwest Mounted Police?"

"Don't think so. He said he was from Canada. What in hell did that poor cow thief up there *do?*"

"Enough to get a lot of folks riled at him. Funny nobody seems to have gotten to him, though! Tell me what you know about Crooked Lance."

The other lawman shrugged and said, "Ain't much to tell. Just a two-bit crossroads. Ain't hardly a proper town, like Bitter Creek."

"It's my understanding this Cotton Younger's being held by a vigilance committee. How does your boss feel about vigilantes operating in his neck of the woods?"

"Don't make no nevermind to us. Crooked Lance is a long, hard ride from here. Besides, they ain't what you'd call *mean* vigilantes. Just some old boys who keep an eye out for road agents, cow thieves, and such. They've never given folks hereabouts no trouble."

"Do you know who runs things up there?"

"Hell, nobody runs Crooked Lance. It's just a wide spot in the road. There's a post office and the storekeeper tends the wire for Westen Union, when the line's up. There's no schoolhouse, no city hall or nothing. It's just sort of where the stockmen shop a mite and get together to spit and whittle of a quiet afternoon."

"How come it rates a telegraph office, then?"

"That's easy. The stockmen have to keep in touch about the price of beef. They ship beef here at Bitter Creek, but they have to know when to herd it down out of the high country."

"Makes sense. Got any ideas on why that wire's down?"

"Ain't got idea one. Some fellers from Western Union rode out a few days ago to fix it. Next night it went out again. Likely high winds. This whole country's halfway to heaven, you know. Hardly a month goes by without at least some snow in the high passes, hereabouts."

"Been having summer blizzards this year?"

"No, not real blizzards. But, as you'll likely see when you study yonder map, there's some rough country between here and Crooked Lance. Wire could get blowed out a dozen ways in as many stretches of the trail. The valley Crooked Lance sets in is lower and warmer, half the year. But it's sort of cut off when the weather turns ornery."

"Telegraph office open here in Bitter Creek?"

"Should be. Doubt you'll get through to Crooked Lance, though. Feller I know with Western Union says they've given up for now. Said they'd wait till the company decides on a full reconstruction job. Figures they're wasting money fixing a line strung on old poles through such wild country. Said they'd likely get around to it next year or so."

"I'll get Western Union's story later. You know any names to go with the folks up in Crooked Lance?"

"Let's see, there's the Lazy K, the Rocking H, the Seven Bar Seven . . ."

"Damn it, I ain't goin' up there to talk to *cows*! Who in thunder owns them spreads up there?"

"Folks back east, mostly. The town's hardly there to mention, but the outfits are big whopping spreads, mostly owned by cattle syndicates from Chicago, Omaha, New York City, and such. I understand the Lazy K belongs to some fellers in Scotland. Ain't that a bitch?"

"I know about the cattle boom. Let's try it another way. You say they ship the beef from here. Don't somebody *drive* them herds to Bitter Creek?"

"Well, sure. Once, twice a year they run a consolidated herd over the passes to our railroad yards. The buyers from the eastern meat packers bid on 'em as they're sorted and tallied in the yards. Easier to cut a herd amongst corrals and loading shunts, so . . ."

"I know how to tally cows, damn it. Don't any of the Crooked Lance riders have names?"

"Reckon so. Most folks do. Only one springs to mind is the one they call Timberline. He's the tally boss. I disremember what the others are called. They mostly go by Billy, Jim, Tex and such."

"Tally boss is usually a pretty big man in the neighborhood, since the others have to elect him. You know this Timberline's last name?"

"Nope. But you're right about him being *big*. Old Timberline's nigh seven feet tall in his Justins. Seems to be a good-natured cuss, though. The others hoo-rah him about having snow on his peak, ask him how the weather is up yonder around his nose and stuff like that, but Timberline never gets testy."

31

"But he's in charge when the Crooked Lance hands are in town?"

"If anybody is, it's him. He's the ramrod of the Rocking H, now that I think on it. I think it was Rocking H hands who caught that cow thief of yours." He paused to think, then nodded, and added, "Yep, it's comin' back to me now. They found him holed up in the timber with a running iron on him. Dragged him into town for a necktie party, only some of the folks up there said it wasn't right to hang a stranger without a trial. From there on you know as much as myself."

Longarm saw that they were tracking over the same ground again, so he got to his feet and said, "I'll just have a look at your survey and be on my way, then."

He strode over to the large, yellowed map nailed to the wall and studied it until he found a dot lettered "Crooked Lance." It was nowhere near the locations given by the conflicting government surveys, but Longarm opined that the folks here in Bitter Creek had the best chance of being right. He ran a finger along the paper from Bitter Creek to Crooked Lance, noting forks in the trail and at least three mountain passes he'd have to remember. Then he stepped back for an overall view.

The sudden movement saved his life.

The window to his right exploded in a cloud of broken glass as what sounded like an angry hornet hummed through the space he'd just occupied to slam into the far wall!

As Longarm dropped to the floor, the deputy marshal rolled backwards, bentwood chair and all, and from where he lay on his back, shot out the overhead light as another bullet from outside buzzed in through the broken window. Meanwhile, Longarm had crabbed sideways across the floor to another window, gun in hand.

As he risked a cautious peek over the windowsill the other lawman crawled over to join him, whispering, "See anything?"

"Nope. Everyone outside's dove for cover. There's light in the saloon across the street, so they ain't in there. You move pretty good, Deputy."

"I've been shot at before. You reckon they're after you or me?"

"I'd say it's on me, this time. How do you feel about that narrow slit between the east end of the saloon and the blank wall over there?"

"That's where I'd be, if I was shooting at folks hereabouts. I'll scoot out the back way and circle in while you mind the store, savvy?"

Longarm considered it before he answered. He was the senior officer and it was his play. On the other hand the local lawman knew the lay of the land and it was pretty dark out there. Longarm said, "Go ahead. I'll try to make up something interesting to keep 'em looking this way."

As the deputy crawled away in the dark and Longarm heard the creak of an invisible door hinge, he moved to one side and gingerly raised the sash of the other, unbroken window. Nothing happened, so he risked another peek.

Then he swore.

The street was filled with people now, and a burly figure with a tin star pinned to his chest was clumping right toward him, gun in hand, and shouting, "Hey, Morg! You all right in there, son?"

Longarm got to his feet and stood in a shaft of light from outside, holstering his own gun as the door burst open. What was obviously the missing deputy's superior officer froze in the doorway, his gun pointed at Longarm, and asked, "You have a tale to tell me, Mister?"

"Deputy Morgan and me are friends, Marshal. He's out trying to get behind somebody who just busted your window. He should be back directly."

"I heard shots and come running. What's it all about?"

"Don't know. Them who did the shooting never said.

33

By the way, your young sidekick's pretty good. He had the light out before they'd fired twice. Sounded like they was after us with a .30-30."

"Old Morg's good enough, I reckon. How'd you get so good at reading gunshots, Mister? I disremember who you said you was."

Longarm introduced himself and brought the town marshal up to date. By the time he'd finished, the marshal had put his gun away and Deputy Morgan had crossed the street to rejoin them.

Morgan nodded to his boss and said to Longarm, "Long gone, but you figured right about that alleyway. Way I read the signs, it was one feller with a rifle. Had on high-heel, maybe Mexican, boots."

The deputy held out a palm with two spent cartridges as he added, "Looks like he packs a bolt-action .30-30. Funny thing to use in a gun fight, ain't it?"

Longarm shrugged and said, "I'd say he was out for sniping, not fighting. The heel marks over there say much about the size and weight of anybody?"

"Wasn't anybody very big or very small. I'd say, aside from the fancy boots and deer rifle, most any hand for miles around could be made to fit. Dirt in the alleyway was packed hard. Feller in army boots like yours wouldn't have left any sign at all."

The older Bitter Creek lawman said, "Whoever it was has likely packed it in for now. The whole town's looking for him. Morg, you'd best start cleaning up this mess in here. I'll mosey around town and see if anybody spied the cuss. They'd remember a stranger in Mexican heels."

Longarm asked, "What if one of your local townsmen walked past in three-inch heels, maybe with a rifle in hand?"

"Don't think so. Folks don't take much notice of folks they know."

"I'd say you're right. How many men in town would you say could fit the bill?"

"Hell, at least a baker's dozen. Lots of riders wear

34

Mexican heels and half the men in town own deer rifles. But I'll ask around, anyway. There's always a chance, ain't there?"

Longarm nodded, but he didn't think the chances were good. By now, if anyone in Bitter Creek had any suspicion of who'd shot out their own town marshal's window, they'd have come forward.

Unless, of course, they knew, but didn't aim to say.

Chapter 4

The clerk at the Western Union office gave Longarm much the same tale about the line to Crooked Lance as the deputy had. Longarm took advantage of the visit to wire a terse report to Marshal Vail in Denver. He brought his superior up to date and added that the big frog in the Crooked Lance puddle seemed to be a very tall rider called Timberline. It was the only information Vail might not have about the murky situation. They knew in Denver that Kincaid had gotten this far. At a nickel a word it was pointless to verify it.

Leaving the Western Union office, Longarm headed for the hotel the hard way. The sniper with the .30-30 *could* have been after the local law, but he doubted it. If someone was trying to keep him from getting to Crooked Lance, it meant they knew who he was. If they knew who he was, they might know he was staying at the hotel.

So Longarm followed the cinder path between the railroad tracks and the dark, deserted cattle pens until he was beyond the hotel entrance on Main Street. He found a dark side street aimed the right way and followed it, crossing Main Street beyond the last lamppost's feeble puddle of kerosene light. He explored his way to the alley he remembered as running through the hotel's block, then, gun drawn, moved along it to the hotel's rear entrance.

The alley door was unlocked. Longarm took a deep breath and opened it, stepping in swiftly and sliding his back along the wall to avoid being outlined against the

36

feeble skyglow of the alley. He eased the door shut and moved along the pantryway to the foot of the stairs. Beyond, the shabby lobby was deserted, bathed in the flickering orange glow of a night lamp. The room clerk was likely in his quarters, since there'd be little point in tending the desk before the next train stopped a few blocks away.

Longarm climbed the stairs silently on the balls of his feet and let himself into his rented room with the hotel key he'd insisted on holding on to. He struck a match with his thumbnail and lit the candle stub on the dressing table. There was no need to fret about the window shade. He'd chosen a side room facing the blank wall of the building next door and had pulled the shade before going out. But a man in his line of work had to consider everything, so he picked up the candlestick and placed it on the floor below the window. There was no chance, now, of its dim light casting his shadow on the shade, no matter how he moved about the room.

The room was tiny, even for a frontier hotel. The bed was one of those funny contraptions that folded up into the wall. Longarm opened the swinging doors and pulled the bed down, sitting on it to consider his next move.

His keen ears picked up the sound of voices from the head of the fold-down bed. The widow and little Cedric were in the next room and the partition between the folding beds was a single sheet of plywood. Be interesting, Longarm thought, to stay in this hotel when honeymooners were bedded down next door. The widow was talking low to her son, likely telling him a bedtime story. When one of them moved he could hear their bedsprings creak.

He remembered saying something about having a bite with the woman and her child. But it was later than he'd figured on and it didn't make much sense to take a lady to dinner with a rifleman skulking around out there. It sounded like they were in bed, anyway. He had the names of her Crooked Lance kin written down on an

37

envelope she'd given him, so there was no sense pestering her further.

Longarm looked at his pocket watch. It was getting on toward nine o'clock. He put himself in the boots of the rifleman and studied hard. If the sniper still meant business, he'd be likely to wait around until . . . midnight? Yeah, midnight was a long, lonesome stretch and it would be cold as hell out there by then, at this altitude. Sensible move for the sniper would be to hole up for a while and make another try at sunup. He'd told lots of folks he was riding out at dawn. The livery stable? It would make more sense for him to be waiting up the trail to Crooked Lance, where nobody in town would hear a gunshot. The sniper would want to be there first, so . . . yes, he knew what to do, now.

Longarm stood up and got undressed, spreading his clothes and belongings with care, to be ready to move out suddenly after a few hours of rest. He was down to nothing but his flannel shirt when someone rapped softly on his door.

Longarm hauled out his .44 and slid over to the doorway, standing well to one side as he asked, softly, "Who's there?"

"It's me, Mabel Hanks! I've been so worried! I heard there was a shooting, and—"

"Nobody hurt, ma'am. I'm purely sorry we couldn't have dinner and all, but having folks shooting at me goes with the job."

"May I come in for a moment?"

"Ma'am, I ain't decent. I just took off my britches."

She laughed softly and asked, coyly, "Not even a shimmy shirt? I can't sleep and, well . . ."

Longarm considered, then he decided, what the hell, he'd *told* her, hadn't he, and unlocked the door.

Mabel Hanks slipped in and shut the door behind her, turning her eyes away from his long, naked legs as she murmured, "You must think me shameless."

He did, since she'd let her long, brown hair down and was wearing a long pink cotton nightgown and fluffy bedroom slippers, but he said, "I'll snuff the candle so's we can talk without fluster. You must have something pretty important on your mind."

As he crossed the room to drop gingerly to one naked knee and pinch out the candle with his fingertips, he noticed that she'd taken a seat on the foot of his bed. It was getting pretty difficult to take this situation in any way but a pretty earthy one, but in country matters, as in all others, Longarm moved cautiously. There was always that one chance in a hundred that a gal was simply stupid about menfolks. She didn't *look* like a loose woman.

He stood over her in the almost total darkness, putting his gun away as he asked, "What's little Cedric up to at the moment, ma'am?"

"He's fast asleep, the poor darling. I'm afraid the long trip tired him."

"*You* ain't tired all that much, eh?"

"I'm afraid I'm not. It's difficult to fall asleep in a strange place . . . alone." Then she blurted out, "Heavens, what am I saying? I didn't mean that the way it sounded!"

Longarm moved over to the door and locked it.

She gasped, "What are you doing, sir?"

"Just making sure we don't get shot. The key's in the lock, when you're ready to leave, Ma'am."

"Oh, I thought . . ."

"What can I do for you, ma'am? You're purely beating about the bush like you thought a wounded grizzly was holed up in it."

"I've been thinking about your offer of . . . well, help. This is terribly embarrassing, but I just counted out our remaining funds and, and, oh, Lord, this is all so sordid!"

Longarm fumbled for his pants and fished out a pair of ten-dollar eagles. He handed them to her in the dark, noticing how smooth her fingers were, as she suddenly took his hand in both of hers and pressed a cheek to it,

39

sobbing, "Oh, *bless* you! I simply didn't know what we were going to do!"

"Heck, it ain't like I'm sending little Cedric through college, Ma'am. You can pay me back whenever you've a mind to. I don't reckon there's anything else you need, huh?"

Her voice was blushful in the dark as she said, "There *is* one thing more, but I just can't bring myself to ask it—Custis."

"You just ask away—Mabel. It pleasures most gents to be of service to a pretty gal."

"Well, you know I'm a recent widow and . . . this is just terribly embarrassing, but my late husband used to help me out of my, um, corset."

"Oh? Didn't know you had one on. Not that I looked too close before I snuffed the candle."

She got to her feet, her scented hair near Longarm's nostrils as she murmured, "I can't get at the laces without help. It's a new model with steel stays instead of whalebone and it's cutting me in two! Would you think me shameless if I asked you to unlace me from the back?"

"I could give it a try, but I ain't had much experience with such things. I've never worn one, myself." He hesitated, wondering why his mouth felt so dry as he added, "Uh, how do I git at it?"

Mabel Hanks slipped the nightgown off over her head and dropped it on the bed, saying, "Don't worry, I'm wearing a shift under the corset so it's not as if . . . isn't this silly? We've hardly met and here you are undressing me! Whatever must you be thinking?"

Longarm didn't think it would be polite to say, so he kept his mouth shut as he ran his suddenly too-thick fingers along her spine, feeling for the knot of her corset laces. He noticed that her breathing had become rapid and shallow. He found the slip knot and untied it. She reached behind herself to guide his wrists as he unlaced her. The tight corset suddenly snapped free and fell to the floor. She took a deep breath and gasped,

40

"Oh, that feels so *good!*" A woman really needs a man if she intends to dress fashionably, don't you think?"

Longarm ran his hands up to her bare shoulders, turned her around, and hauled her in for a blindly aimed kiss. He missed her mouth on the first try, but she swung her moist lips to his, and for a long moment they just stood there, trying to melt into one another in the dark.

Then he picked her up and put her gently across the mattress, dropping himself alongside her as, still kissing, he ran his free hand down the front of her thin silk shift to the warm moisture between her trembling thighs. She tried to mutter something between their pressed-together lips as Longarm parted her knees with his own. And then he was in her, his bare feet on the rug and her hips almost hanging over the edge of the mattress as he drove hard and deep. She gasped and moved her face to one side, sobbing, "Whatever are you *doing* to me?" as her legs belied her protest by rising to lock firmly around the big man's bouncing buttocks.

He came fast, stayed inside her, and moved them both farther onto the bed for a more comfortable second encounter, taking his time now, as their heaving flesh got better acquainted. She suddenly moaned and raked her nails along his back, almost tearing his shirt as she sobbed, "Oh, God! Oh, Jesus Christ! It's been so *long!*"

She'd dropped her expected modesty completely now and was responding like a she-cougar in heat, digging her nails in and raising her knees until her heels were crossed behind Longarm's neck. He was hitting bottom with every stroke, and eased off a bit, aware that he could be hurting her, but she pumped hard to meet his thrusts and growled, "All of it! I want it all inside me! Oh, Jesus, it's coming again!"

He didn't know which of them she meant, but it didn't seem important as, this time, they had a long, shuddering mutual orgasm and she suddenly went limp. Longarm knew he was heavy, so after lying there long

41

enough to catch his breath, he shifted his weight to his elbows and eased off a trifle.

She sighed, "Don't move. Just let it soak inside me till we can do it some more. You're still nice and hard. My, there certainly is a *lot* of you, isn't there?"

"It's been a while for me, too, Mabel."

"I'm so happy, darling. I know you think I'm an absolute hussy, but I don't care. I don't care if you think this is what I had in mind all the time!"

"Didn't you?"

She hesitated, then answered roguishly, "You know damned well I did, dear heart. Women may not be supposed to want such things, but I was married for nearly eight years and, well, I don't care if you think I'm bawdy!"

"Hell, gal, what's sauce for the goose is sauce for the gander. There's nothing to be ashamed of. We just done what's natural."

"Can we do it again? This time I want to do it naked, with me on top!"

Longarm rolled off her, slipped out of his shirt, and lay back, spreadeagled, as she tore off her last shreds of silk, and giggling like a naughty schoolgirl, climbed above him, with a knee by each of Longarm's hip bones. She toyed with his moist erection, guiding herself onto it with her hands. He sighed with pleasure as she suddenly dropped her pelvis hard, taking it deep with a breathless hiss of her own.

And then she was moving. Moving up and down with amazing vigor as she leaned forward, swinging her nipples across Longarm's face as she almost shouted, "Suck me! Suck my titties!"

He did, but not before he softly warned, "Take it easy! You'll wake the kid! That partition between our rooms is paper-thin!"

"I don't care. He's too young to kno what we're doing and he's a sound sleeper anyway. Oh, dear God, isn't this *lovely*?"

Longarm allowed that it was, but as he lay there,

holding a nipple between his lips as she went wild, he heard a soft plop above the louder creaking of the bed springs. Longarm's keen ears were educated. So he knew what it was. The key he'd left in the door had just fallen on to a sheet of paper!

Longarm ran a big hand under each of Mabel's thighs and heaved, catapulting her up over him to crash, screaming, against the plywood partition at the head of the fold-down bed. At the same time, Longarm rolled off the mattress, grabbed the bed frame, and lifted hard, folding the bed, with Mabel in it, up into the wall.

Stark naked, he moved toward the door, snatching his .44 as he passed his gunbelt hooked over a chair. He heard running footsteps from the other side of the door, so he opened it and leaped sideways into the hallway, facing the stairwell in a low crouch for a split second to see nothing there, then pivoting fast to train his gun down the other end of the hallway. He saw that the door to Mabel Hanks's room was ajar, spilling candle-light across the shabby carpeting. Longarm made the door in two bounds, hit it with a free elbow, and landed in the center of the room, back to the wall and facing the other fold-down bed.

The bed was empty. It figured. Longarm grabbed the metal footrail of the bed and slammed it up into the wall. Then he covered the small, froglike figure who'd been hiding under it with the muzzle of his sixgun and said, "All right, you little son of a bitch, on your feet and grab some sky!"

Little Cedric without his blond wig was even uglier, and his voice was deeper as he got to his little feet, saying, "Take it easy, Longarm. I'm a lawman, too!"

"Let's talk about it in my room. Your . . . mama is standing on her head against the wall. *She's* likely got something to tell me, too!"

He frogmarched the midget out to the hall as the hotel's desk clerk appeared at the far end, asking, "What in hell's going on up here?"

Then he saw a full-grown naked man holding a .44

on what looked like a little boy in a velvet suit and decided to go away.

Longarm herded the creature called Cedric inside and slammed the door. Covering his odd captive as he bent to retrieve the doorkey from where it had landed on a sheet of newspaper, he shook his head and said, "Serves me right. I should have known better. Anybody can fox a key out of the inside keyhole to land on a paper shoved under the door. What were you fixing to do once you pulled it through on the paper, Cedric? You don't look big enough to whup me with your fists. No offense, of course."

"How'd you get on to us, Longarm?"

"Let's see what you're packing in that sissy little suit before we talk. Unless that's a cow I hear bellowing inside the wall, your partner's likely anxious to rejoin us."

He frisked the midget, relieving him of a man-sized S&W Detective Special .38 and saying, "Shame on you, sonny!" before he motioned the dwarf to a seat in a far corner and, still covering him, relit the room's candle. Then he went over to where Mabel Hanks was yelling curses through the mattress and pulled down the folding bed.

The naked woman rolled out of the wall and sat up, staring wildly around through the hair hanging over her face as she gasped, "What in the hell's *happening*?"

The she spotted the midget in the corner and sighed, "Oh, shit!"

"Let's talk about it," Longarm suggested. He saw the girl moving as if to get to her discarded nightgown and said, flatly, "You just stay put, honey. It ain't like we're strangers and have to be formally dressed. Either one of you can tell me who the hell you are, as long as *somebody* says something sudden."

The one called Cedric said, "We're private detectives. Our badges are in the other room. You want to see 'em?"

"I'll take your word for it. Why were you detecting *me*? I don't remember being wanted anywhere. Last time I looked, I was toting my own badge for Uncle Sam."

Cedric said, "Hell, we know that. We're out here after the reward."

"What reward would that be, friend?"

"The one on Frank and Jesse James, of course. Our agency works for the railroad and the James-Younger Gang has been playing hell with their timetables. We was on our way to Crooked Lance, same as you, to fetch that Cotton Younger back to Missouri."

"Don't you mean to make a deal with him? Maybe a deal to spring him loose in exchange for Jesse James's new address?"

The midget detective shot a weary glance at his naked female partner and sighed, "I *told* you they said he was a smart one, Mabel. Look what your hungry old snatch has gotten us into, *this* time!"

"Oh shut up, you little pissant! It's not *my* fault! I told you you were overplaying your part!" She smiled timidly at Longarm and added, "You might as well know the truth. I'll admit I did try to find out what you might know about Cotton Younger and the odd situation up in Crooked Lance. You see, one of our agents came out here a week ago and—"

"Spare me the details. I know something in Crooked Lance seems to eat lawmen fer breakfast. As to overplaying parts, I'm sort of interested in why Cedric, here, was trying to creep in on us just now."

"I done no such thing!" the midget protested, adding, "I had my ear against the plywood when all hell busted loose out there! I can see someone was using the old paper trick, but, honest Injun, you are barking up the wrong tree."

"Why were you hiding under the bed, then?"

"Hell, I was scared! I heard running in the hall, cracked open the door, and saw you bounce out stark naked with a full-grown gun in your fist! Before you could turn and blow my fool face off I dove for cover. You know the rest!"

45

"You're likely full of shit, but saying you ain't, did you get a look at anyone attached to them running footsteps?"

"No. Whoever it was made the stairwell before I got to the door. Ain't you aiming to put that gun away?"

"Maybe. Tell me something a man with his head against that plywood might have heard."

"What are you talking about? All I heard was you an' Mabel—you know."

"I don't know. I know what she was saying as I heard the key hit paper. If your ear was next to that plywood, you must have heard it, too."

The woman blushed, for real this time, and stammered, "Longarm, you're being nasty!"

But Longarm insisted, "Cedric?" and with a malicious grin at the naked woman on the bed, the midget said, "She said what you were doing to her was just lovely."

Longarm lowered the muzzle of his .44, nodded at the woman on the bed, and said, "You can get dressed now."

Mabel Hanks leaned over, grabbed up her nightgown and put it on, gathering the other things in one hand. He saw she was looking at the two gold eagles lying on the rug near the foot of the bed and said, "Leave 'em be, honey. I don't know what I owe you, but twenty dollars seems a mite steep, considering."

"You—you son of a bitch!"

"Will you settle for two bucks? I understand it's the going price, these days. I don't hold it against you that we never finished the last time."

She swept grandly out, too mortified to answer. The midget dropped off the chair with a smirk and edged his way for the door, saying, "I'd be willing to split that reward, if you want to talk things over."

"You talked just enough to save your ass, old son. And by the way, you need a shave. You and your Mama hit Crooked Lance with that stubble on your

46

pretty little chin and there might be some who haven't my refined sense of humor!"

Cedric hesitated in the doorway with a sly smile on his ugly little face as he asked, "You don't aim to give our show away, Longarm?"

The big lawman laughed good-naturedly and asked, "Why should I? I've enjoyed the show immensely!"

Chapter 5

The sky was a starry black curtain fading to gray in the east as Longarm reined in on the Crooked Lance Trail and sat his mount for a time, considering the ink blots all around them. He'd slipped out of the hotel a little after three in the morning, gotten his borrowed army bay from the livery without being seen, and was now a distance from the town that he judged about right for a bushwhacking.

In the very dim light of the false dawn he could just make out a granite outcropping, covering the trail. Longarm clucked to the bay, eased him around to the far side, and tethered him to one of the aspens growing there. He slid the Winchester .44-40 from its boot under the saddle's right fender and dismounted. He soothed the bay with a pat and left it to browse on aspen leaves as he climbed the far side of the outcropping. He knew the treetops behind him would hide his outline against the sky as the light improved. He lay atop the rock, levered a round into the Winchester's chamber, and settled down to wait. If he'd timed it right, the sniper with that .30-30 deer rifle would be getting up here just about now, and if the rifleman knew the lay of the land along this trail he'd have a hard time picking a better place to set his own ambush.

A million years went by, and the sky was only a little lighter. Longarm was used to waiting, but he'd never liked it much. The stars were going out one by one from east to west, but the sniper seemed to be taking his own good time. What was the matter with the fool? He wasn't dumb enough to stake out the front of the damned hotel, was he?

He wondered if Kincaid or any of the other missing lawmen had run into this situation. It made more sense than a town where they shot strangers on sight. Kincaid or any of the other missing men could be buried anywhere for a full day's ride or so. The folks in Crooked Lance, for all he knew, could be just as puzzled as everyone else. With the wire down, they were cut off, so nobody there would know who was coming or when.

He took a cheroot from his vest pocket and put it between his teeth, not lighting it, as he studied what he knew for sure.

It wasn't much, but he could assume the hands who'd captured Cotton Younger and locked him up were acting in good faith. If they'd been on the outlaw's side, they never have captured him. If they hadn't wanted the law to know they had him, they'd have just killed him and kept still about it. Could it be an escape plot?

Maybe, but not on the part of the folks in Crooked Lance, for obvious reasons. The most likely candidates to plot an escape would be friends of Cotton Younger, and if it was true he was tied in with Frank and Jesse James . . . possible, but wild. None of the James-Younger Gang had ever operated this far west, and if it was them, they were acting differently than they'd ever acted before. He'd studied the working habits of the James-Younger Gang. They were given to moving in fast, hitting hard, and moving out even faster. Cotton Younger was being held in a log jail, probably loosely guarded by simple cowhands. If the James-Younger Gang had ridden out here to spring him, he'd have been long gone by now and there'd be no need for all this skullduggery.

On the other hand, the gang had been badly shot up in Minnesota and were scattered from hell to breakfast. If a lone member of the old clan was trying to help his kinsman . . . that might fit.

Behind him in the fluttering aspen leaves a redwing

49

awoke to announce its undisputed ownership of the grove. It sounded more like a wagonwheel in need of grease than a bird, and it meant the sun was getting ready to roll up the eastern side of the pearling sky. Longarm could see the trail he was covering more clearly, now. In less than an hour things would have color as well as form down there. His sniper was either a late riser or stupid. Or he'd given up for now.

Longarm decided to wait it out till full light. Half the secret of staking-out lay in waiting out that last five minutes. It was tedious as hell, but he'd made some good arrests by simply staying put a little longer than common sense seemed to call for. It was a trick he'd learned as a boy from a friendly Pawnee.

Another bird woke up to curse back at the redwing and a distant peak to the west was pink-tipped against the dark blue western horizon as it caught the sunrise from its greater altitude. Innocent travelers would be taking to the trail soon. Where in thunder was his sniper?

Longarm's eyes suddenly narrowed and he stopped breathing as his ears picked up the distant scrape of steel on rock. He saw two blurs moving into view up the trail. What he'd heard was a horseshoe on a lump of gravel.

He could see who it was, now. A lone rider on a big black plowhorse, with a teammate tagging along behind like an oversized hound. As the odd group came nearer Longarm saw that the man on the lead mount was carrying a rifle across his knees. He was riding bareback, his long legs hanging down to the end in big bare feet. The top of him was clad in patched, old-fashioned buckskins, a fur hat made of skunk skin with two feathers cocked out of one side, and a long, gray beard covering the upper third of his burly chest.

He was peculiar looking, but Longarm decided he was likely not his man, as he studied the weapon the rider was packing. It was an old Sharps .50. Single-shot and wrong caliber. The lack of high heels, or even

50

boots, was comforting, too. Longarm flattened himself lower against the granite to let the stranger pass without needless conversation. The odd old man and his pets passed by the lawman's hiding place without looking up and vanished on up the trail. Longarm stretched to ease his cramped muscles, then settled down to wait some more.

It was perhaps five minutes before he noticed something else, or, rather, noticed something missing.

The birds had stopped singing.

Longarm rolled over and up to a sitting position, his rifle across his knees, as he faced away from the trail into the aspen grove his mount was tethered in. The old man in the feathered fur hat was stepping out from between two pale green aspen trunks, the battered Sharps pointing up the slope at Longarm.

Longarm nodded and said, " 'Morning."

The other called out, "By gar, M'sieu, she must think she's vairie clevaire, him! Myself, Chambrun du Val, she has the eyes of the eagle!"

"I wasn't laying for *you,* Mister du Val. My handle's Long. I'm a U.S. Deputy Marshal on government business and I'd take it kindly if you'd point that thing someplace else."

"Mais non! You will throw down your weapon at once! Chambrun du Val she's demand it, him!"

"Sorry, I don't see things quite that way. You got the drop on me and I got the drop on you. If there's any edge, it's on my side. You got one round in that thing. I got fifteen in this Winchester."

"Bah, if Chambrun du Val she shoot, it is all ovaire!"

"You fire, old son, and you'd best do me good with your one and only try, for I can get testy as all hell with a buffalo round in or about my person! But I don't see this as a killing situation. I'd say our best play would be to talk things over before this gets any uglier."

"What is M'sieu's explanation for making the ambush, eh?"

51

"I told you, I'm a lawman. I was staked out here for a bushwhacker who took a shot at me in Bitter Creek last night. What's your tale?"

"Chambrun du Val she is going to Crooked Lance to kill a beast, he."

"Feller named Cotton Younger?"

"Exactement! How does M'sieu know this thing?"

"Cotton Younger's wanted in Canada, and if you ain't a French Canuck you sure talk funny for Wyoming. Are you a lawman or is your business with Cotton Younger more personal?"

"The animal, she is murdaire mon petite Marie Claire! Chambrun du Val she swear on the grave revenge!"

"Well, you can stop aiming at *me,* then. We're on the same side. My boss sent me up here to carry Cotton Younger in for a hanging. Along with what he did up Canada way, he's killed a few of our folks, too."

"Bah! Hanging, she is too good for this Cotton Younger! It is the intention of Chambrun du Val to kill him in the manner of les Cree!"

"You'll likely have to settle for a hanging. One of your own Northwest Mounties is up in Crooked Lance ahead of us both. There's a sheriff from Missouri and at least a brace of private detectives working for the railroads, too. At the rate it's going, he'll be long hung before either of us gets there, so do you reckon we should shoot each other or get on up to Crooked Lance some time soon?"

"M'sieu knows the way?"

"More or less, don't you?"

"Mais non, Chambrun du Val, she is, how you say, looking for Crooked Lance."

"Well, I see the man I was laying up here on these rocks for don't seem anxious to show his face, so I'll be neighborly and carry you there if you'll promise not to shoot me."

The old *voyageur* lowered the muzzle of his buffalo gun, so Longarm swung his own muzzle politely to port arms and slid down the granite to join him. As they walked together to where all three horses were munching aspen leaves, Longarm asked, "How well do you know Cotton Younger, Mister du Val?"

"Chambrun du Val, she's nevaire see the beast, but she will know him. It is said the animal is big and very blond. They call him Cotton because his hair, she is almost white. Also, she is now in the jail at Crooked Lance, and, merde alors, how many such createures like this can there be in any one jail, ah?"

"They say he's related to some who rode with the James-Younger gang a few years back. You hear anything about that, up Canada way?"

"Mais non, this createure rode alone through the Red River du Nord Countrie. Chambrun du Val was off on the traplines when he murdaire mon petite Marie Claire. Mon merde on what he do down here in les States. He shall die, most slowly, for what he do to Marie Claire!"

Longarm untethered his bay and swung up in the saddle, slipping the Winchester into its boot as he led off without comment. Behind him, the old man leaped as lightly as a young Indian aboard the broad back of his huge black gelding, calling its mate to heel with a low whistle.

The French Canadian waited until they were free of the trees and out on the trail before he called out, cheerfully, "M'sieu has not considered Chambrun du Val just had the opportunity to shoot him in the back?"

Not turning his head, Longarm called back, "You don't look stupid. You've got enough on your plate without gunning a U.S. lawman for no reason this far south of the border."

"M'sieu is a man who misses little, ah?"

Longarm didn't answer. What the man had said was the simple truth. The oldtimer's eyes were sharp as hell and, together, they stood a better chance of riding into Crooked Lance alive.

Once they got there, Chambrun du Val would be one

more headache. He'd want to kill the prisoner. The other lawmen ahead of Longarm would doubtless argue over who had first claim on Cotton Younger, too. In fact, by now, it was a pure mystery what the owlhoot was *doing* in that jail up ahead. The Mountie, the Missouri sheriff, or *some* damned lawman must have gotten through by now. Anyone riding in would be packing extradition papers, so why wasn't anyone riding *out* with Cotton Younger?

Longarm leaned forward and started to urge his mount to a faster pace. Then he eased off and shook his head, muttering, "Let's not get lathered up, old son. We've a long ride ahead and farther along we'll know more about it. Riding ourselves into the ground ain't going to get us there, so easy does it. Whatever in thunder is going on has been going on for weeks. It'll keep a few more hours."

Chapter 6

The Crooked Lance Trail was longer and rougher than Longarm had anticipated. He and his fellow traveler rode through old burns where charred lodgepole trunks and fetlock-deep ashes obscured the trail. They crossed rolling meadowlands frosted with sweet-smelling columbine and climbed through steep passes where patches of dusty snow still lay unmelted and the air was thin, cold stuff that tasted like stardust. They forded whitewater streams and rode gingerly over vast stretches of frost-polished granite, keeping to the trail by reading sign. The seldom-used trail vanished for miles at a time under new growth or windblown forest duff, but a mummified cow pat or the bleached, silvery pole of the telegraph line led them to the next stretch of visible trail. Longarm noticed that the single line of copper wire was down in more than one place as they passed a telegraph pole rotted away at its base. He couldn't really tell whether the line had been torn up by the harsh winds of the high country or by someone intent on silencing it. You could read it either way.

The journey ended when they rode down into a flat-bottomed valley cradled among high, jagged peaks. Longarm reined in, and as the Canadian paused beside him, he studied the cluster of log buildings down the slope. He counted a dozen or so buildings surrounded by corrals, near an elbow of the sluggish stream draining the valley bottom. It looked peaceful. He saw some ponies hitched in front of some buildings and figures moving quietly along one unpaved street. Two of them appeared to be women in gathered print skirts and sun bonnets. A cluster of men were sitting on the boardwalk in front of a larger building, their boots stretched before them in the street, as they talked quietly or just sat there waiting for something to happen, as men tend to do in small towns.

Longarm said, "Let's ride in," and ticked the bay gently with a heel, loping slowly down the slope with du Val following.

He made for the building with the most people around it and reined in again. Nodding down at the quartet of cowhands in front of what he now saw was the general store, he said, "Howdy."

Nobody answered, so Longarm said, "Name's Long. U.S. Deputy Marshal. This other gent's called du Val."

One of the men looked up and stared soberly for a time before he asked, "Is that a McClellan saddle?"

"Yep. They tell me there's a Federal prisoner being held here in Crooked Lance."

"Maybe. How do you keep from bustin' your balls on that fool saddle? You couldn't *give* me one of them durned fool rigs to ride!"

There was a low snickering from the others as Longarm stared at the one who'd voiced the comment. Longarm said, "I ride a government saddle because I ride on government business and because a McClellan's easy on a horse's back. So, now that I've answered your question, friend, suppose you answer mine?"

The village jester turned to one of his cronies and asked, innocently, "Did you hear him ask a question, Jimbo?"

"Can't say. He talks sort of funny. Likely on account of that ribbon-bow round his neck, don't you reckon?"

The French Canadian swore, swinging his Sharps around as he roared, "Sacre God damn! You make the jest at Chambrun du Val?"

The one called Jimbo snickered and said, "Hell no, Pilgrim, we're making fun of your funny-looking side-

56

kick, here. Where'd you ever find him? He looks like a whisky drummer. Hey, do you sell whisky, boy?"

"What did you say?"

"I asked if you sold whisky, boy."

Longarm dismounted, ominously, and strode over to the one called Jimbo as the latter got to his feet with a smirk. Longarm said, "Asking a man what he does for a living is reasonable. Calling hira a boy can get him testy."

"Do tell? What do you do when you gets *testy*, boy?"

Longarm's sixgun appeared in his right hand as he kicked Jimbo in the kneecap, covering him and anyone else who wanted a piece of the action as Jimbo went down, howling in agony.

The first lout who'd spoken leaped to his own feet, gasping, "Are you *crazy*, mister?"

"I could be. But now that we've changed *boy* to *mister*, let's see what else we can work out. As I remember, I was asking some fool question or other, wasn't I?"

Jimbo rolled to a sitting position, grasping his injured knee as he moaned, "God damn it, fellers, *take* him! He's busted my fucking leg!"

One of the cooler heads among the Crooked Lance crowd sighed, "*You* take him, if you've a mind to. This is gettin' too serious for funning. The man you want is across the way in yonder log house, lawman."

"Now that's more neighborly. Who do I see about taking him off your hands?"

There was a moment of silence. Then the informative one shrugged and said, "You'd have to clear it with Timberline, I reckon. He ain't here."

"He's the ramrod of the Rocking H, right?"

The other nodded and Longarm asked, "Who's guarding the prisoner over there, right now?"

"I reckon it's Pop Wade. Yeah, it's Pop's turn over to the jail. Pop won't give him to you, though. Nobody does anything hereabouts 'less Timberline says they can."

Longarm saw that the Canadian had swung his big

gelding around and was heading for the jailhouse. He trotted after du Val and called out, "Slow down, old son. I know what you're thinking, but don't try it."

Du Val ignored him. The Canadian crossed the open stretch just ahead of Longarm and pounded on the plank door, shouting curses in French. Longarm took him by the elbow and swung him around, trying to disarm him as gently as possible. But gentleness wasn't effective. The old man was redfaced with rage and Longarm's English wasn't making any impression on his hatefilled mind. So as the others ran across the street toward the jail, he tapped du Val with the barrel of his .44, hitting him just below the ear.

Du Val collapsed in the dust like a rag doll as the jailhouse door flew open and a worried, middle-aged man peered out. One of the hands from the general store looked soberly down at the unconscious man and opined, "You *do* be inclined to testiness, by God! Was you birthed this ornery, mister? Or is it something you et?"

Longarm handed the unconscious Canadian's weapon to the jailer, saying, "You're best put this away. This old boy rode all the way from the Red River of the North to gun your prisoner. I'd like a look at him myself."

The jailer hesitated. One of the town loafers suggested, "You'd best let him, Pop. This one's a purely ornery cuss!"

"Timberline ain't going to like it," the jailer said, as he stood aside to let Longarm enter.

The interior was divided into two rooms. The rearmost room was closed off by a door of latticed aspen poles and barbed-wire mesh. As Longarm's eyes adjusted to the gloom he saw a tall, blond man standing just inside the improvised cell, staring at him with a mixture of hope and utter misery. As the jailer followed him across the room, Longarm nodded to the prisoner and said, "I'm from the Justice Department, Mister Younger."

The prisoner shook his head and said, "That well may be, but I ain't Cotton Younger! I keep telling everyone I ain't, but will they listen?"

Pop Wade snorted, "Listen to the jaybird, will you? The son of a bitch was catched fair and square stealing Lazy K cows and he matches them reward posters to the T!"

"I never stole cow one! Where in hell would I *go* with a stolen cow?"

"You saying you never had that running iron in your possibles, Son?"

"All right, I did have a length of bar-iron I sort of picked up along the way. That don't prove all that much!"

"It proves you had the tools of the cow thief's trade, God damn your eyes!"

Longarm had heard this same discussion almost every time he'd talked to a man in jail and it was tedious every time. He said, "What you done hereabouts ain't the question, Mister Younger. I'll be taking you to Denver to talk to the judge about some other matters."

"God damn it, I ain't Cotton Younger! My name is Jones. Billy Jones from Cripple Creek!"

"Jesus H. Christ, son, can't you do better than Jones?"

"Hell, *somebody* has to be named Jones, don't they?"

"How about James? Ain't the Younger and the James boys kin?"

"How should I know? I ain't kin to nobody named James *or* Younger. I'm jest Billy Jones, from Cripple Creek, and ever'body hereabouts is crazy!"

"Well, then, you got nothing to worry about when I carry you back to Denver, have you?"

"Why in hell do I want to go to Denver? I was on my way to Oregon when these crazy folks hereabouts damn near killed me and started callin' me an outlaw! I don't want to go to Denver!"

" 'Fraid you're bound there, just the same. You answer the description and I'm just the errand boy, not the judge." He turned to the jailer and said, "I got his papers right here. You want me to sign for him, Mister Wade?"

Pop Wade said, "Can't let you have him. It ain't my say who goes in or out of here, mister."

"What are you talking about, you can't let me have him? I'm a U.S. Deputy Marshal with a Federal Warrant on this cuss, God damn it!"

"I don't doubt that for a minute, mister. There's a Canadian mountie, a Missouri Sheriff, and a whole posse of other lawmen over at the hotel who say the same thing. The committee says it ain't made up it's mind yet."

"What committee, what mind, and about what?"

"Vigilance Committee of Crooked Lance. This here Cotton Younger is their prisoner until they says different. Ain't nobody taking him no where till Timberline and the others say it's fitting."

Longarm considered.

He could take Younger away from the elderly jailer easily enough, and the hands out front would likely crawfish back long enough for the two of them to ride out. On the other hand, it was a long ride to the nearest place he'd be able to hold him safely.

Longarm shrugged and said, "I'd better have a talk with those other lawmen and this big hoo-rah called Timberline."

Chapter 7

The hotel in Crooked Lance wasn't as fancy as the one in Bitter Creek. It wasn't a hotel, in fact. The family who owned the general store and ran the post office and telegraph outlet had a livery shed and an extra leanto partitioned into tiny, dirt-floored cubicles they rented to those few riders staying overnight in town. The family's name was Stover and they were inclined to take a profit wherever one could be found. The so-called hotel had a sort of veranda facing the muddy banks of the valley stream, on the far side from the one street. There, Longarm found another quartet of moody men, seated on barrels, or in one case, pacing up and down. The man on his feet wore the scarlet tunic of the Northwest Mounted Police, trail-dusty and worn through at one elbow. The other three wore civilian clothes, but one had a tin star pinned to his lapel. As the storekeeper introduced Longarm to his fellow lawmen, the Mountie asked, "Are you the person who just beat up a Canadian citizen?"

" 'Fraid so. Where'd they put old du Val? By the time I came out of the jailhouse they'd carried him off."

"He's inside, with a concussion. They told us you'd beaten him unconscious. I'd say you owe me an explanation, since I'm here on Her Majesty's business and . . ."

One of the others said, "Oh, shut up and set down, dammit. You know he's a U.S. Marshal!" To Longarm he added, "I'm Silas Weed, from Clay County, Missouri. This here's Captain Walthers from the U.S. Army

61

Provost Marshal's office, and the gent with the big cigar is a railroad dick called Ryan."

Longarm nodded and hooked a boot over the edge of the veranda as he said, "My outfit's missing a deputy called Kincaid. Any of you met up with him?"

There was a general shaking of heads, which didn't surprise Longarm. He turned to the one called Ryan and asked, "Are you from the same detective agency as a funny couple called Hanks, Mister Ryan? They said one of their agents was missing, too."

Ryan grimaced around the stub of his cigar and growled, "Jesus. Are you talking about a female traveling with a dwarf?"

"Sounds like the same folks. You with their outfit or not?"

"God, no! Cedric Hanks and his wife work alone! They're bounty hunters, not detectives! Where'd you run into them?"

"Bitter Creek, headed this way. You say the gal's his *wife*?"

"Yeah, when he ain't pretending to be her little kid. Ain't that a bitch? They run con games when they're not hunting down men with papers on 'em. If you met up with that pair you're lucky to have the fillings in your teeth!"

"They were likely lying about having a partner up here, too, then. What's the story on that prisoner over yonder, gents? I take it all of us rode up here on the same errand."

The man from the provost office snapped, "The army has first claim on him. He's not only wanted on a hanging military offense, but I was here first!"

Sheriff Weed said, "The hell you say, Captain! Clay County's papers on him have seniority. We've been after him a good six years!"

The Mountie wheeled around and challenged, "Not so fast! Your own State Department has honored Her Majesty's warrant for the murder of a British subject!"

Longarm smiled crookedly at the railroad detective,

who smiled back and said, "That's half of the problem. The other half is the Crooked Lance Vigilance Committee. They say they're holding Cotton Younger for the highest bidder."

"The *what?* These cowpokes hereabouts are holding a man for ransom with four—make that *five*—lawmen in town?"

"They don't see it as ransom. It's all the damn paper Cotton Younger and his kin have out on 'em. He's worth five hundred to the railroad I work for. Clay County, there, says he's worth about the same to Missouri. Queen Victoria ain't been heard from, but she'd likely pay some damn thing, and Army, here, says the standing offer for deserters runs three to five hundred, depending. I'd say Army was low bidder, up to now. How much is he worth to the Justice Department?"

"Don't know. My boss never mentioned a reward."

"There you go, old son. You just made last in line!"

Longarm stuck a cheroot between his teeth and thumbnailed a match as he gathered his thoughts. Then he shook his head and said, "I don't see it that way, gents. Justice Department outranks all others."

"All but Her Majesty's Government!" the Mountie amended.

"No offense to your Queen, but her writ doesn't carry much weight in U.S. Federal territory, which Wyoming happens to be. Before we fuss about it further amongst ourselves, what's keeping the five of us from at least getting back to the rails and telegraph with the prisoner? Seems to me it'd make more sense to let our superiors fight it out, once we had him locked in a civilized jail."

The Missouri sheriff asked, "The jail in Bitter Creek?"

"Why not? It's got bars and a telegraph office we can get to."

"Town marshal down there's sure to want a split on the reward."

Longarm snorted, "Oh, for God's sake, this is the

dumbest situation I've ever been in, and I've been in some pissers! We're talking about a shiftless thief with a lousy five hundred on him, and—"

"No, we ain't," the railroad dick cut in, "We're talking about *ten thousand* dollars, no questions, cash on the barrelhead!"

Longarm frowned and snapped, "Ten thousand dollars, on that tall drink of water over yonder?"

"Hell, no, on his kinfolks, Frank and Jesse James! Between the state of Missouri, The Pinkertons, and a dozen small banks and such, either one of the James boys is worth at least that, dead or alive. Should any man nail both, he'd collect more like twenty!" He shrugged and added, "I ain't that greedy, myself. I'd settle for either."

"Yeah, but the prisoner here ain't Frank or Jesse James. When I just talked to him, he denied even being Cotton Younger."

"What else did you expect, Longarm? Once he's getting fitted for that hemp necktie, he'll talk, all right."

Sheriff Weed chimed in, "That's for damn sure. Our only problem seems to be just who gits him, and how to convince the locals who caught him that they'll have a share in the reward."

"Ain't everyone counting unhatched chickens, gents?"

Weed nodded and said, "Sure they are. That's what's holding up the parade. Nobody here can promise a reward for a James boy still at large. Getting some of these dumb cowboys to see it that way can be a chore. All of us have tried, one time or another."

Longarm muttered, "I don't believe this! There's five of us, damn it! If any *two* of you would back me, I'd be riding out of here with Cotton Younger within the hour!"

He waited to see if there were any volunteers. Then he asked Weed, "How about it, Sheriff?"

"Would you turn him over to me as soon as we rode free?"

"God damn it, you're obstructing justice!"

"No, I ain't. I came all the way out here from the County of Clay to arrest that boy and that's my aim. That's my only aim. I don't pull chestnuts out of the fire for other lawmen."

Longarm looked at the army agent, who shrugged and said, "I have my orders."

"How about you, Mountie? You up to backing my play?"

"On the condition I take him back to Canada? Of course."

Longarm knew better than to ask the railroad dick. He took a drag on his cheroot and said, "Somebody, here, has to start thinking instead of being greedy! How long do you all figure we can just sit here, stalemated, like big-ass birds?"

The railroad dick said, "I got time. I'll allow it's a Mexican standoff now, but sooner or later somebody has to cave in. I don't mean for it to be me!"

Captain Walthers said, "I sent a telegram to the War Department. I'm waiting for further instructions."

Sheriff Weed said, "I got some old Missouri boys riding out to back my play."

The Mountie said nothing. His service was only a few years old, but Longarm had heard about their motto.

Turning to Weed, he said, "You've come from the owlhoot's old stamping grounds, Sheriff. Before we get ourselves in any deeper, is there a chance that pissant over at the jail could be telling the truth? We're gonna look silly as all hell if it turns out he's *not* the Cotton Younger all of us are fighting over."

Weed said, "It's him, all right. How many tall, skinny owlhoots with a wispy white thatch like his can there be?"

The railroad dick nodded and said, "I've seen photographs of the kid, sitting next to his cousin Cole Younger, and Frank James. He's older now, and his hair's gone from almost white to pale yellow, but it's him."

The army man smiled a bit smugly and said, "At the risk of finding something to agree on with the rest of you, I have his army records and they fit him like a glove. He deserted from Terry's column as a teenaged recruit. He's no more than twenty-five now. He's a few pounds heavier, but the height is right on the button. They let me measure him. It would be possible to make an error of half an inch, but his records don't. He's exactly six-foot, six and three-quarter inches. He tried to tell me he'd never been in the army, too."

Longarm nodded, satisfied at least with the identification of the prisoner, if nothing else. Before he could go into it further, the door to the hotel banged open and Chambrun du Val came out loaded for bear. He scowled at Longarm and roared, "Salud! Por quoi you hit Chambrun du Val? Where is mon rifle? Sacre! I think she will kill you, me!"

As the burly older man lurched across the veranda at Longarm, the railroad dick put out a boot and tripped him, sending du Val sprawling on his hands and knees as Longarm stepped clear with a nod of thanks. Before du Val could rise, Longarm snapped, "Now listen, old son, and listen sharp! Your war is over. You ain't going to harm a hair on Cotton Younger's head. I ain't asking you, I'm telling you."

"I kill him, but first, by gar, I kill you!"

"Oh, shut up, I ain't finished. You ain't going to kill me because I don't aim to let you. On the other hand, I can't watch you around the clock and still get anything done, so I'm counting on your good sense about the prisoner over at the jail house. You gun that old boy and you can say goodbye to breathing. Forgetting me and these four other lawmen, he's worth God knows what to a whole valleyful of vigilantes, and if they decide to string you up for murdering their prisoner, I for one wouldn't stop 'em!"

"Chambrun du Val, she fears nothing, him!"

66

"Maybe, but you think on it before you make any more sudden moves." The Mountie came over to help the old man to his feet, saying, "I'll take over, Longarm."

He took the old man by the arm and walked him off for a fatherly talk. Longarm noticed the Mountie was speaking French, but a few paces off the old trapper laughed and swore, "Merde alors! M'sieu speaks like a Paris pimp! The English of Chambrun du Val, she is more betaire than these strange noises M'sieu regards as French!"

The laugh was a good sign. Longarm decided the old man would be all right for now and turned back to the other three on the veranda, saying, "It's early yet. I'm going to have a talk with this Timberline everyone in Crooked Lance looks up to. Any of you know how I can find him?"

Sheriff Weed said, "He'll likely be riding in later. He's the foreman of the Rocking H, about six miles down the valley."

"He comes to town every night? Don't they have a bunkhouse at his spread?"

"Sure, but he's interested in our stalemate, here."

The railroad dick added, "Interested in Kim Stover, too. Her spread's just outside of town, behind them trees to the north."

"I'll bite. Who's Kim Stover? Any kin to the rascal who owns this hotel and everything else in town worth mention?"

"Old Stover's her father-in-law. Miss Kim's the widow of his late son, Ben. They tell us he was run over by the trail herd, summer before last. Matter of fact, she don't seem to get along good with her in-laws."

Captain Walthers sniffed and chimed in, "Who could blame the poor woman? You saw the unwashed lout who's taking advantage of us at two bits a night. The Stovers are white trash!"

Longarm didn't ask if the widow was good-looking. She had the la-di-da young officer defending her and the big froggy of the valley courting her. He blew a thoughtful smoke ring. "Like I said, it's still early. I'll just mosey out to the Rocking H this afternoon and see what this Timberline gent has to say about the burr he's put under my saddle."

Longarm walked around the building to where he'd left his bay in the livery shed. As he was saddling up, the others drifted in and started untethering their own mounts.

The railroad dick said, "The boys and me will just tag along to sort of keep you company, all right?"

"You trust each other as much as you trust me?"

Sheriff Weed grinned and said, "Not hardly," as the Mountie and du Val came in from their stroll. The older man's two big black geldings were the only ones not in the livery shed. Du Vall let them run free like old hounds, but Longarm knew they'd come when he whistled. He led his own mount out from under the low overhang and waited politely as the others saddled up. There was no sense trying to get a lead on them. Wherever he went, it seemed likely he'd have company.

Chapter 8

As it turned out, it wasn't a long ride. The railroad dick had fallen in beside Longarm's bay as the federal man led off. They were passing a windbreak of lodgepole pine and the detective had just said, "That cabin over there's the Lazy K, Kim Stover's place," when they both spied two riders swinging out to the main trail from the modest spread.

One was a hatless woman with a halo of sunset-colored hair and buckskin riding togs. She rode astride, like a man. She sat her mount well, though.

The rider to her left was a man in a mustard Stetson and faded blue denim, on a gray gelding almost as big as one of du Val's plow horses. The man needed a big mount. He was at least a head taller than any human being should have been. Longarm didn't ask if he was Timberline. It would have been a foolish question.

The two parties slowed as they met on the trail.

Since all of them except Longarm had been introduced, the railroad dick did the honors. Timberline smiled, friendly enough, and said, "Glad to know you, Deputy. Like I always say, the more the merrier!"

The girl was less enthusiastic. She nodded politely at Longarm, but sighed, "Oh, Lord, another lawman is all we need!"

The others had told him the big ramrod was sparking the widow, so Longarm swung in beside Timberline as the entire group headed back to Crooked Lance. He explained his mission as Timberline listened politely but stubborn-jawed. The leader of the local vigilantes was maybe thirty, with coal-black sideburns, and clean-shaven. He sat his gray with the relaxed strength of a man used to having horses, and men, do just about anything he wanted them to.

He heard Longarm out before he shook his head and said, "If it was up to me you could have the rascal, Deputy. Hell, I was for just stringing him up the afternoon we caught him skulking about this little lady's spread."

"Yeah, I heard you found him with a running iron on him."

"Well, to tell the truth, I can't take all the credit. Miss Kim, here, spied him hunkered down near the creek in some brush as me and a couple of my hands rode up to her front porch. Had not ladies been present, that would have likely been the end of it. The skunk lit out when he saw us coming. Windy Dawson, one of my hands, made as nice an overhand community-loop as you've ever seen and hauled the thief off his pony at a dead run. Miss Kim, here, said not to kill him right off, so Windy dragged him into the settlement and we threw him in the jailhouse."

He swung around in his saddle to say to the girl on his far side, "You see why we shoulda strung him up that first day, honey? I *told* you he was a mean-looking cuss, and now we even have a *federal* lawman up here pestering us for him!"

The widow said, "Nobody's getting him until they do right by the folks up here!" and Longarm saw he'd been barking up the wrong tree. The lady might not be related by blood to the money-hungry Stover family, but she'd surely picked up some bad habits from her in-laws!

Speaking across Timberline, Longarm said, "What you're doing here ain't legal, ma'am."

Behind him, Sheriff Weed called out, "Save your breath, Longarm. I've laid down the law till I'm blue in the face and nobody hereabouts seems to know what law *is*!"

Longarm ignored him and explained to the determined-looking redhead, "You're holding that Cotton Younger on a citizen's arrest, which is only good till a legally appointed peace officer can take him off your hands."

Kim Stover's voice was sweetly firm as, not looking his way, she said, "The Crooked Lance Committee of Vigilance was elected fair and square, mister."

"I hate to correct a lady, but, no, ma'am, it wasn't. Crooked Lance ain't an incorporated township. The open range hereabouts ain't constituted as a county by Wyoming Teritory. So any elections you may have held are unofficial as well as unrecorded. I understand the position you folks are taking, but it's likely to get you all in trouble."

For the first time she swung her eyes to Longarm, and they were bitter as well as green when she snapped, "We're already in trouble, mister! You see a schoolhouse hereabouts? You see a town hall or even a signpost telling folks we're *here*? Folks in Crooked Lance are *poor*, mister! Poor hard-scrabble homesteaders and overworked, underpaid cowhands without two coins to rub together, let alone a real store to shop in!"

"I can see you're sort of back in the nothing-much, ma'am, but I fail to see why you're holding it against me and these other gents."

"I never said it was your fault, mister. We know who's fault it is that Crooked Lance gets the short end every time! It's them durned big shots out in the country you all rode in from. The cattle buyers who shortchange us when we drive our herds in to Bitter Creek. The politicians in Cheyenne, Washington, and such! They've been grinding us under since I was birthed in these mountains, and now we mean to have our own back!"

Timberline noted the puzzled look in Longarm's eyes and cut in to explain, "When Miss Kim's husband, Ben,

71

was killed, them buyers over to the railroad tried to get her cows for next to nothin'! Luckily, me and some of her and Ben's other friends made sure they didn't rob her before Ben was in the ground. We drove her herd in with our others and all of us stuck together on the price of beef."

Kim Stover added, bitterly, "A little enough herd it was, and a low enough price, after all the hard work my man put into them durned cows!"

Longarm nodded and said, "I used to ride for the Jingle Bob and a couple of smaller outfits, ma'am. So I know how them eastern packers can squeeze folks, dead or alive. But Uncle Sam never sent me here to bid on beef. I'm packing a federal warrant on that owlhoot you folks caught, and I mean to ride out with him, one way or another."

"Not before we settle on the price," Kim Stover snapped.

Timberline added, still smiling, "Or whup damn near every rider in this valley, fair and square!"

"There's five of us, Timberline."

"I know. I can likely scare up thirty or forty men if push comes to shove. But I don't reckon it will. These other four gents and me have had more or less this same conversation before you got here. And, by the way, in case you ain't asked, the five of you ain't together. We figure you'll be bidding against one another before Cotton Younger leaves this valley."

Sheriff Weed called out, "I've told you I'll split the reward with you all, Timberline. This federal man aims to carry him to Denver, where they'll likely hang him without even asking about Frank and Jesse James!"

There was an angry muttering from the other lawmen and du Val spat, disgusted. The railroad dick laughed and told Longarm, "Ain't this a caution? We get into this fix every time we talk to these folks. My own bid's highest of all, but nobody listens. If you ask me, they're just funning us. I'm getting to where I wouldn't be surprised if that jaybird in the hoosegow wasn't in on it with these valley folks!"

Longarm considered the idea seriously for a moment. It made as much sense as anything else he'd heard that afternoon. He asked Timberline and the girl, "Have you folks thought about the *who* as much as the how much?"

Kim Stover asked what he meant. Longarm said, "The reward might have greeded you past clear thinking. I, for one, could promise all the tea in China, were I a promising sort. But, on the hoof, your prisoner's worth two hundred and fifty to you, period, and assuming you can take the word of whoever among us you turn him over to."

Timberline began, "The reward on the James Boys—"

Longarm cut in to insist, "Cotton Younger ain't no James. He's small fry. So the most he's worth in *any* place is maybe five hundred, split with the arresting officer. That is, with *some* arresting officers."

Sheriff Weed said, "Damn it, Longarm!" But Longarm ignored him to go on, "County officers are allowed to accept rewards. Federal officers ain't. If either of you can count, you'll see I've just eliminated one temptation."

The army man, Captain Walthers, cried out, "Hold on there! I'm a federal officer, too!"

Longarm nodded and said, "I'll get to you in a minute, Captain. I'm trying to cut the sheriff out of the tally at the moment!"

Weed yelled, "I told 'em I'd let 'em have the whole reward, God damn your eyes!"

"Well, sure, you *told* 'em, Sheriff. Likely, if you was to double-cross these folks out here in Wyoming, the folks in Missouri would vote against you, next election, too."

He saw the widow Stover's eyes were going *tick-tick-tick* in her pretty but bitter-lipped face, so he dropped the attack on the sheriff to say, "The railroad dick, here, is a civilian who's working for the reward and

73

nothing else. If he double-crossed you . . . well, being in the cattle business, you must know how fair a shake you'll get from the courts, against the railroads and such."

The railroad dick sighed and said, "Next time that French Canuck tries for you . . ."

"It was ornery, but you just tried to outbid the rest of us. Like I was saying, a U.S. Deputy Marshal ain't allowed to accept rewards. So if I agreed to forward such rewards as was due . . ."

"I can see what you're trying to pull," snapped Kim Stover. "It won't work. We know better than to trust any of you to send us the money!"

Timberline laughed and said, "I keep telling you we've been over this same ground, Longarm. You'd best see if Uncle Sam's ready to pay that ten thousand. We ain't piggy. We'll sell the owlhoot to you for half what both James Boys is worth, and if anybody gets the other ten—"

"Back up, Timberline. You're starting to talk about the national debt again. Number one, we don't know whether Cotton Younger knows where either Frank or Jesse James are hiding out. Number two, we don't know whether he'll be willing to tell us, if he does."

Timberline shrugged and said, "I could get it out of him in five minutes if the little lady here would let me talk to him my own way!"

Kim Stover shook her head and insisted, "I said there'd be no hanging and no torture and I meant it. We're poor but decent folks in Crooked Lance." Then she spoiled it all by adding, "Besides, they'll have ways of getting him to talk, once they pay us for him. I reckon once they've paid us the ten thousand, they'll get him to say whether he knows or not!"

By now they were moving down the main street of the settlement and further argument was broken off as the railroad dick groaned, "Oh, no, that's all we need!"

A buckboard was parked in front of the general store. A woman in a canvas dust smock and feathered hat was being helped down from her seat by a midget dressed in dusty black. Little Cedric had abandoned his disguise and was puffing a two-bit cigar under his black porkpie hat.

Timberline choked and asked, "Jesus! What is it?"

Longarm said, "Meet Mister and Mrs. Hanks, but don't play cards with them."

As Mabel looked up at the party reining in around them, Longarm touched the brim of his Stetson and said, "Evening, ma'am. I see you got here after all. I asked around for your kin, but nobody here seems to know 'em."

Cedric Hanks said, "Oh, stuff a sock in it, Longarm. We're here fair and square with an honest business proposition."

Before they could go further into it, the Northwest Mountie moved up beside Longarm and asked, "Did you see where du Val was heading, Deputy?"

Longarm twisted around in his saddle to count heads as he frowned and replied, "Never saw him drop out. Not that I was watching."

The army agent said, "I was, but I didn't think it was important when he dropped back. Who cares about the old drifter, anyway?"

"I do!" snapped Longarm, kicking his bay into a sudden lope as he tore over to the jail and slid from the saddle, drawing as he kicked in the door. The startled jailer, Wade, jumped up from his seat with a gasp, even as Longarm saw the jail was empty except for Pop Wade and the prisoner.

Longarm put his sidearm away with a puzzled frown, explaining, "That old Canuck is up to something. I thought he was heading for here."

He stepped back to the doorway as the Mountie and Sheriff Weed came in, guns drawn. Longarm shook his head and said, "Nope. We were wrong. You think he's in the hotel?"

Weed said, "Not hardly. His two geldings ain't in sight, neither. You reckon he's lit out?"

Longarm said, "Maybe. But why?"

"He was a funny old cuss. Said he'd come to gun this jasper, here. Likely he saw there was no way he could, and—"

"After riding all the way from Canada, without even saying adios? I rode in with him. Du Val didn't strike me as a man who makes sudden moves without a reason."

The prisoner bleated, "You fellers got to protect me! I don't like all this talk about my getting gunned!"

Ignoring him, the Mountie said, "The reason I was keeping an eye on him is that there's something very odd about that man. For one thing, I don't think he's a Red River breed."

"You waited till now to tell us? *I* took him for a Canuck."

"No doubt, but then, you don't speak Quebecois."

"You mean when you and him were talking French and he said yours was sissy?"

"Yes, he said I spoke with a Parisian accent. My mother was named DeVerrier. My Quebecois is perfectly good.

"Why in thunder didn't you say so?"

"Like you others, I've been playing my own hand for Her Majesty. I knew he was an imposter, but I didn't know why. I still don't know why, but, under the circumstances—"

The railroad dick came over to join them, saying, "He ain't anywhere near the general store or hotel, gents. What do you reckon his play might be?"

Longarm said, "He's either lit out for good, or he wants us to think he's lit out for good."

"Meaning another play for our prisoner, come dark?"

Longarm moved over to the cage and asked the prisoner, "You have a friend with a long gray beard and a passable Canuck accent?"

"I never saw the varmint! Pop, there, told me about him trying to bust in, but—"

76

"Or bust you out," Longarm cut in, turning away. He didn't expect the prisoner to confirm his suspicion, but it was worth thinking about.

Sheriff Weed said, "We'll have to take turns tonight, keeping an eye peeled for the hombre."

Longarm stared morosely at him for a moment before he shook his head and said, "That's doing it the hard way. Why sweat him out when I can *ask* him what he's up to?"

"Ask him? How do you figure to ask that old boy word one, Longarm? None of us knows where he *is!*"

"Not right now, we don't. But there's a good hour's daylight left and I know where he turned off the trail."

"Hot damn! You reckon you can track him down before sunset?"

"I aim to give it one good try."

Chapter 9

Longarm rode his bay slowly through the crack-willow on the wrong side of the creek, snorting in annoyance as he spotted another big hoofprint in a patch of moist earth. The man calling himself du Val was wasting their time and getting himself brush-cut for nothing. There was little use taking to the tall timber to hide your trail when you traveled with two big geldings wearing over-sized draft shoes. The sun was low and he was well clear of the settlement, now. The evening light made the occasional hoofprint easy to read in the orange, slanting rays. In fact, aside from the way du Val had vanished and the odd tale the Mountie told, the signs read as if the oldtimer was simply heading for Bitter Creek Crooked Lance without taking too many precautions about his trail. Longarm considered that as he rode on. Was du Val setting him up for a bushwhacking, or had he simply given up?

Longarm ducked his head under a low branch and, as he rode out into a clearing, spied one of du Val's pets, grazing quietly in thè gauzy light. The other was outlined against pale aspen trunks across the clearing. Neither mount had a rider.

Longarm reined back into the shadows of the tree-line, sweeping the far side cautiously with his eyes. He slid the Winchester from its boot as he dismounted.

He circled the clearing instead of crossing it, clucking to the gelding near the treeline as he approached it. Neither plowhorse paid much attention to him. They were tired and settled in for the evening. They were either stupid, even for farm animals, or nothing very exciting was about to happen.

Longarm saw a human knee sticking up out of the long grass near the grazing animal he was approaching. He froze in place to study it, then moved closer, his Winchester at port-arms. The man lying in the grass on his back groaned. Longarm dropped to one knee, raising the barrel of his rifle and feeling with one hand under the long beard as he said, "Evening, du Val. Where'd they hit you?"

"Lights and liver, I reckon," the old man sighed, his French Canuck accent missing. Longarm's hand came out wet and sticky as the dying man complained, "He didn't have to do it. I'd never have told."

Longarm wiped his fingertips on the matted beard, then lifted it away from the old man's chest which was tattooed with a panoramic scene of a once-important sea battle. Someone had put a rifle bullet right between the Monitor and the Merrimac. Why he was still breathing was a mystery. He was one tough old man.

Longarm asked, "Who bushwhacked you, Sailor?"

"You figured out who I am, huh? You're pretty sharp, Longarm."

Longarm cursed himself for offering a digression and insisted, "Who did it? It ain't like you owe him loyalty."

"He must have thought I was on your side. We rode in—"

And then the old man was gone. Longarm cursed and got back to his feet, gazing about for sign. It was getting too dark to track, and the two tame geldings told him no strangers were about. They knew him as well as they had known their dead master. He'd noticed they were shy of others.

Longarm circled back to where he'd left his own mount. The body would keep for now in the chill night air and it might be sort of interesting to keep the others in the dark for now. Nobody but the one who'd killed the man who'd called himself du Val knew who he was, or where, right now.

Despite the roundabout path the old man had taken, it was only a short ride back to Crooked Lance. The sun was down by now but the sky was still lavender with one or two bright stars as Longarm rode in. The settlement was crowded with shadowy figures, mounted or afoot, and as Longarm passed a knot of horsemen he heard a voice mutter, "That's the one who kicked old Jimbo."

Ignoring them, Longarm rode first to the log jail, meaning to have a discussion about the bearded mystery man with the prisoner. But he didn't. A quartet of cowhands stood or squatted by the doorway, and as Longarm dismounted, one of them waved his rifle barrel wildly and said, "No you don't, stranger. Our orders are to hold Cotton Younger tight as a tick and that's what we aim to do."

"Hell, I wasn't fixing to eat him. Just wanted to ask him some more questions."

"You ask your questions of the Vigilance Committee, hear? Go along now, friend. Windy, here, was tellin' us a funny story and you're spoiling the ending."

Longarm led his bay by the reins to the livery, peeled off the McClellan and bridle, and rubbed the horse's brown hide dry with a handful of straw before bedding it for the night in a stall.

He went around to the hotel, where he found the others in the so-called dining room, pinned to the back of the general store. The table was crowded but Sheriff Weed made room for him on one of the bench seats, asking softly, "Find anything?"

"Read some sign. The old man's gone," Longarm replied. He counted noses, saw that the other lawmen and the Hankses were at the table, and asked, "Where's Timberline and the gal?"

"Likely spooning. Saw Kim Stover talking to some hands around the jailhouse just before they rang the dinner bell. I hope you ain't hungry. Considering we're paying two bits a day for room and board, this grub is awful."

Someone dropped a tin plate in front of Longarm. He glanced up and saw it was one of the storekeeper's womenfolk. It was either his wife or his daughter. It hardly mattered. Both were silent little sparrows. The storekeeper himself wasn't at table. Longarm put a cautious spoonful of beans between his lips and saw why. He helped himself to some coffee from the community pot, to wash the beans down. With plenty of sugar and a generous lacing of tinned milk it was just possible to drink the coffee.

The others were hungrier, or maybe didn't have spare food in their bed rolls, so they ate silently, as people who live outdoors a lot tend to do. The only conversationalist at the table was Mabel Hanks, down at the far end. She was buttering up Captain Walthers. She'd likely sized him up, as Longarm had, as a man with an eye for the ladies. Her midget husband ignored her play, spooning his beans more directly to his mouth, since his head rode lower above the table. A picture of the two of them in bed rose unbidden to Longarm's mind and he looked away, shocked a bit at his own dirty imagination.

One of the sparrowlike Stover women brought an apple pie in from the kitchen next door and when Longarm smiled at her she blushed and scooted out. He decided she was the daughter. They were both ugly, had heads shaped like onions, buck teeth, and mousy brown hair rolled up in tight buns. The best way to tell them apart was by their print dresses. The mother wore white polkadots on blue and her daughter's print was white on green. The older mountain woman had likely given birth at sixteen or so, because there wasn't a great gap in their ages. They both looked forty and driven into the ground.

Longarm gagged down half the beans and helped himself to a slice of pie, which turned out to be another mistake. He was glad he had packed some pemmican and baker's chocolate. Glad he wasn't a big eater, too.

He saw that the railroad dick was getting up from the

table, either in disgust or to relieve himself outside. Longarm pushed himself away from the table to follow, catching up with the detective near the outhouse.

"Call of nature?" grinned the railroad dick, holding the door of the four-holer politely. Longarm said, "Social call. Go ahead and do whatsoever. I want to talk to you."

The detective stepped back outside, saying, "It'll keep. What's on your mind, Longarm?"

"Got a deal for you. You got any papers on a Missouri owlhoot called Sailor Brown?"

"Hell yes, I do! He rode with James and Younger when they robbed the Glendale train!"

"Good reward on him?"

"A thousand or more. You know where he is, Longarm?"

"Yep. The reward is dead or alive, ain't it?"

"Of course. What's the play?"

"I'm sending you into Bitter Creek with his body, which I'm giving you as a gift in exchange."

"Exchange for what? You say his . . . body?"

"Yeah. That old man calling himself du Val was really Sailor Brown. He likely heard they had a friend of his here and rode in with that fool tale to see if he could bust the boy out. I got him on ice for you in a place we'll discuss if you're willing."

"Willing to what?"

"Drop out of this game. You must know your chance of taking Cotton Younger away from the vigilantes and us other real lawmen ain't so good. On the other hand, you've come a long way, so you've been waiting, hoping for a break. All right, I'm giving you one. You carry Sailor Brown to the U.P. line and telegraph at Bitter Creek and collect the bounty on him. How does that strike you?"

"Strikes me as damn neighborly. Naturally, you're expecting a cut."

"Nope. Can't take any part of the reward. It's all

yours. I'm going to tell you where the body is and then I'll expect you to be long gone."

"Leaving you with one less rival to deal with, eh? All right. I'm a man who knows enough to quit whilst he's ahead. You got a deal. Who killed the Sailor, you?"

"Nope. Don't know who bushwhacked him. That's why, if I was you, I'd pick him up tonight and scoot. I'll ride up the mountain with you to help you pack him on a horse, and to make sure you get away safe. The one who shot him might have other ideas on the subject."

"Jesus. You reckon they'll have the body staked out?"

"Doubt it. Looks like somebody just shot him down like a dog and left him for the crows. You'd best take that piss, now. I'd like to get the two of you off my hands before bedtime."

The detective laughed and said, "I admire a man who thinks on his feet, and you do think sharp and sudden. How'd you know *I* wasn't the killer?"

"You, Weed, and the Mountie are the only ones who couldn't be."

"And I'm the one without a real badge. All right, you've gotten rid of me. How do you figure to get rid of the others?"

"It ain't your worry, now. I eat the apple one bite at a time. So take your piss and let's get cracking."

Chapter 10

By eight-thirty the railroad dick was packing the dead outlaw over the mountains to the transcontinental railroad and Longarm was getting off his bay in front of Kim Stover's cabin.

Light shone through the drawn curtains and somewhere inside a dog was yapping, so Longarm wasn't surprised when the door opened before he'd had a chance to knock.

Kim Stover peered out at him, the lamplight making a red halo of her hair, as Longarm said, "Evening, ma'am. You folks rode off before I could get around to asking one or two more questions."

"Mister Long, if you've come to make your bid for Cotton Younger—"

"Uncle Sam don't work that way, ma'am, but let's leave your odd notions aside for now. You see, there seems to be more'n one outlaw working this neck of the woods. He took a shot at me in Bitter Creek the other night, and tonight I learned he wasn't funning. I thought we might talk about it."

"Are you suggesting one of my friends took a shot at you?"

"No, ma'am. I think you and yours are just being surly. You see, somebody came up here to bust Cotton Younger out of your so-called jail. Somebody else gunned him. But that's all been looked after. What I wanted to ask you about was new faces in the valley."

"You mean since we captured Cotton Younger? You've met them all by now."

"How about before your friends caught the boy skulking round? You have any new hands on the spreads, hereabouts?"

She shook her head and said, "No. Everyone I know in Crooked Lance has been here for some time."

"How much time is some, ma'am?"

"Oh, at least five years. Wait a minute. Timberline did hire some new hands when they made him ramrod of the Rocking H. The cattle company that owns it has expanded in the last few years. There's Windy Dawson, came to work two, maybe three years ago—"

"He's that short, fat feller who throws good?"

"Yes, Windy's one of the best ropers in the valley."

"I took him for a top hand. I'd say he was a cowboy, not a train robber. Anyone else you can think of?"

"Not really. Windy's the newest man in the valley. There's Slim Wilson, but he was hired earlier and, like Windy, is considered a hand who knows his way around a cow. I'd be very surprised to learn that Slim wasn't a man who started learning his skills early, and he's no more than twenty-odd, right now."

"What about Timberline?"

"Are you trying to be funny? He's cowboy to the core, and was one of the first men hired by the Rocking H."

"Just asking. A man his size stands out in a crowd, too, and I don't have anything like him on any recent flyers. You mustn't think I'm just prying for fun, ma'am. It's my job to put all the cards out on the table for a looksee. I'd say what we have here is a lone gunman who hides good on the ridge lines, or somebody playing two-faced."

"Your killer has to be one of the men on your side, then. What was that you said about an attempted jailbreak?"

Longarm hesitated. Then he said, "I reckon it's all right to level with you, ma'am. That old French Canuck I rode in with wasn't. He made that fool play at the jailhouse door to get a look at the prisoner and maybe

85

slip him a word or two. But he wasn't out to kill Cotton Younger. He was sent, or came here on his own, to set a kinsman free."

"And you saw through his scheme? You do know your job, don't you?"

"Well, it was the Mountie that made him for a fake Canuck. Who gunned him, or why, is still pure mystery. From the few words I got out of him before he died, he seems to have had a misunderstanding with someone, and I know it wasn't the man you have locked up; they never got to see each other."

"Oh, that must mean there's another member of his gang here in Crooked Lance! But why are you telling me all this? I thought you were cross with me and mine."

"I am, a mite. You see, ma'am, this notion you have on holding our prisoner for some sort of fool auction is getting serious. You folks in Crooked Lance are playing cards for high stakes with professionals, and—no offense intended—some of your cowhands could get hurt."

"You know our stand about the money, durn it."

"Yep, and it's getting tedious. You ain't a stupid woman, Miss Kim. You must know time is running out on you. Any day now, the army will send in a troop of cavalry to back Captain Walthers, or a team of federal officers will be coming to see what's keeping me. If I was you, I'd go with the Justice Department. One feller just made himself a modest bounty tonight, by cooperating with me."

"Could you give me something in writing, saying we were due the reward on Younger and his gang, whenever they're caught?"

"I could, ma'am, but it wouldn't be worth the paper it was written on. You see, Cotton Younger has to stand trial before it's legal to hang him, and there's always that outside chance some fool jury might set him free. The reward's for capture and *conviction*. As to Frank and Jesse James, us federals might make a deal with

Younger and we might not. I could put in a good word for you if it was a federal man that caught them rascals, but there's others looking. So the James boys might get caught by other folks. They might get turned in for the reward by anybody. They might never be caught at all, since nobody's seen hide nor hair of either one for a good two years or more. You see how it is?"

She signed and said, "At least you're likely more honest than some of the others. Sheriff Weed's promised us the moon, but he gets cagey every time I ask him to put it in writing."

"You're not likely to get anything on paper, and if you do, it won't be worth all that much. The position you've taken just won't wash, ma'am. The longer you hold that prisoner, the more riled at you his rightful owners are going to get."

She hesitated. Then, with a firmer tilt to her head, she said, "I have to think about it. You've got me mixed up, as you doubtless intended."

Longarm believed in riding with a gentle hand on the reins, so he tipped his hat and said, "I'll just let you sleep on it, then. Good night, ma'am. It's been nice talking to you."

They were waiting in the shadows as Longarm rode out to the main trail. He saw they weren't skulking, so he didn't draw as Timberline and another tall man fell in on either side of him as he left the redhead's property. Longarm nodded and said, " 'Evening, Timberline."

"What was you pestering Miss Kim about, Longarm?"

"Wasn't pestering. Wasn't cutting in on you, either. As she'll likely tell you, it's no secret I was asking questions."

He turned to the other rider and asked, "Would you be Slim Wilson?" The youth didn't answer. Timberline said, "A stranger could get hurt, messing about my intended, Mister."

"I gathered as much, but like I said, that ain't my

87

play with the widow. I only want what's mine. That owlhoot you and she are holding in defiance of the law."

"Oh, hell, that pissant's caused more trouble than he's worth! If she'd just let us string the rascal up and have done with him, the valley could get back to its business, raising cows!"

"Why don't you just let me take him off your hands, then? We'd all ride out and you could be free to pick posies for your gal, Timberline."

"It's tempting, but she'd never talk to me again. You may have noticed Kim Stover is a stubborn woman, Longarm."

"I did. You really want to marry up with her?"

"Hell, yes, but she's stubborn about that, too. Says she has to know me better. Hell, I've known her half a dozen years already, but she's skittish as a colt about a second try." Timberline's voice dropped lower as he confided, "That Ben Stover she was married to was a mean-hearted little runt, just like his father over to the general store."

"I noticed his old woman and the gal look tuckered, some. Haven't had more'n two words with the storekeeper. Seems a moody cuss."

"He is. Beats both his wife and the girl. Ben Stover used to whup Miss Kim when they first married up. That is, he did until me and him had a friendly discussion on his manners."

"I take it you've always been right fond of Kim Stover."

"You take it right, pilgrim. And don't think I can't see that you're a good-looking man, neither. You see where this friendly talk is taking us?"

"Yep. We're almost to the store, too. Look, Timberline, I said I ain't sparking the widow and I don't lie any more'n most gents. I got enough on my plate, without fighting over women."

"All right, I'll let you off this time, boy."

Longarm's .44 was suddenly out and almost up Timberline's nose as he reined in, blocking the bigger man's mount with his own as he purred, "You did say *mister,* didn't you?" He saw the one called Slim about to make a foolish move and quickly added, "Stay out of this, Slim. You make me blow his face off and you figure to be next, before you can clear leather!"

Timberline kept his free hand well clear of his holstered hogleg as he gasped, "You hold the cards, Longarm! What in thunder's got into you?"

"I don't take kindly to being bullied and I don't like being talked down to. You may have taken the simple truth as crawfishing, but let's get one thing straight. I ain't been riding you, so I don't mean to be rode. You got that loud and clear?"

"Mister, you have made your point, so point that thing somewheres else."

Longarm said, "*Mister* is all I was after," and lowered the Colt, holding it down at his side as he added, "I reckon this is where we say good night, don't you?"

Timberline nodded and said, "Yep, and I'll be parting friendly for now, since I suspicion we understand one another."

Longarm sat his mount quietly as the other two swung around and rode back toward Kim Stover's spread. He didn't know if Timberline had been calling or just watching. It wasn't really his business. The big ramrod and the stubborn redhead were welcome to one another.

But he couldn't help wondering, as he rode to the hotel, what that sulky little spitfire would be like in bed.

Chapter 11

Longarm awoke in the pitch-black little room, aware that he was not alone. He pretended another snore as his right hand slid under the cornhusk pillow for his derringer. He'd left his room key there, too, this time. Wasn't it safe to sleep *anywhere* in Crooked Lance?

He flinched as cool fingers brushed his naked shoulder and a soft whisper sighed, "Oh, pretty! So pretty!"

"Mabel?"

"Hush! Oh, do be still! He'll hear us and he can be so cruel!"

Longarm felt the shabby blanket lift as a cool, nude body slid into bed with him. He moved over to make room on the narrow little cot as his mystery guest flattened small, firm breasts and a work-hardened, almost boyish body against his warmer flesh. As she buried his face in loose, fine hair and began to nibble his collar bone, Longarm folded her in his big arms and muttered, "Did you lock the door behind you, ma'am?"

She placed a palm over his mouth and hissed, "Yes! Oh, don't make a sound! His ears are sharp and his temper's not of this world!"

She waited until she saw he wasn't going to say anything, then slid the hand, moist from his lips, down the front of his body. All the way.

Longarm lay there, as puzzled as he was aroused as she took his penis in her hand and began to play with it, whispering, "Oh, so pretty. I want! I need!"

And then she'd forked a thigh over and was on him, riding him as if in the saddle, astride a trotting pony.

Longarm tightened his buttocks and drove up to meet her as she ground her pubic bone against his, hissing like a pleasured cat with each movement. He ran his hands up and down her spine, noticing how the bones rode under her tight, smooth skin like those of a half-starved Arapahoe camp dog. Then, wider awake and getting more interested, he got a firm grip on each of her small, lean buttocks and started helping her on the downstrokes. She was good, damned good, whoever she was, and she pleasured him the first time fast. As he gasped in enjoyment she kept going, sliding and moaning her own pleasure as the wetness seemed to add to it.

Longarm was still able to serve her, but the first flush had cleared his mind enough to wonder what in hell was going on. This hellcat rutting with him wasn't Mabel; she moved no way at all like this one. It couldn't be Kim Stover, could it? Nope, there was more *to* the redhead than this skinny little bundle of pure lust. That left . . . hell, *that* hardly seemed likely!

And then she shuddered, stiffened, and fell forward, kissing him full on the lips as she ran her tongue between them. It was old Stover's wife or daughter, sure enough. Both of them had buck teeth.

Longarm was a gentlemen of the old school, so he didn't laugh. The poor, ugly little brute had done her best to please him, and in the dark, kissing her chinless little face wasn't all that bad. She nestled into him like a lost kitten, kissing him over and over as Longarm felt warm wetness on his cheek and knew she was crying.

He rolled her over to his side and cuddled her, kissing the tears from her eyelids gently as he petted her trembling, nude flanks, as if he were calming a spooked pony or a kicked dog. She buried her face in the hollow of his neck and whispered, "Oh, you're so nice. So very nice. I knowed it when first I seen you!"

Longarm frowned in the darkness, trying to see his way out of this mess. How was a gent supposed to deal with a lovesick critter like this? Good God! How was he going to explain it? He could already see the jeering looks of the others at the breakfast table. Both mother and daughter were ugly as sin, and come to think of it, which of the damn fool Stover women had he just laid?

Longarm started exploring her flesh gently with his free hand, looking for wrinkles, stretch marks, or some such sign. There wasn't a fold of loose skin clinging to her thin, muscular body. Her skin was smooth and nice to feel. He tried to picture the two worn-out looking women who'd served dinner. Both had been skinny and scared-looking. Scared little sparrows that never looked a man in the eye. He was hoping like hell it was the older one. She moved like a gal who knew the facts of life, and Jesus H. Christ, if it was the unwed daughter . . . !

The woman took his explorations to mean desire and responded with caresses of her own. She suddenly slid her hips from the cot and trailed her unbound hair down Longarm's belly, grabbing him again and kissing his semi-erect penis teasingly. Longarm sighed and let her give him a French lesson, for he was in as much trouble already as he was likely to be.

She got him back in the mood amazingly fast, considering her buck teeth and all, so Longarm pulled her up from where she was kneeling and climbed aboard to do it right. Her legs locked around him and she started wagging her tail like a happy puppy. It was a funny way for a gal to move herself, but it was pure heaven, and in the dark it was easy to forget what she looked like in broad daylight.

They made love, wildly and as silently as church mice, for perhaps a full hour. Then she suddenly leaped up, unlocked the door, and was gone without a word.

Longarm made sure the door was locked again, then sank back on the cot, puzzled. It wasn't as if he'd never had anything as good, but it hadn't been bad, considering. You never could tell, just by looking at a woman, could you?

He stretched out on the moist blanket, suddenly grinning as the old trail song sprang to mind.

. . . I humped her standin' and humped her lying . . .
If she'd had wings I'd have humped her flying!
Come a ti-yi-yippee all the way, all the way,
Come a ti-yi-yippee all the way!"

Then he frowned and muttered, "It ain't funny, you
damn fool stud! How is God's name are you ever
gonna face that gal at breakfast, and more important,
which of them Stover women was it?"

Breakfast came like death and taxes and there was no
way to get out of biting the bullet. So, although he took
his time getting dressed, Longarm finally went in to join
the others around the plank table, braced for damned
near anything.

All but the railroad detective were there ahead of
him, of course. One of the Stover women came out of
the kitchen and put a tin plate of buckwheat cakes in
front of him without comment. Longarm watched her
back, saw the gray in her tied-up hair, and decided it
couldn't have been the mother.

The midget, Cedric Hanks, called down the table,
"Where's that dick, working for the railroad? Anybody
seen him this morning?"

Longarm broke into the puzzled murmurings to announce, "I sent him to Bitter Creek. Don't seem likely
he'll be back."

The Mountie smiled thinly and asked, "So you've
eliminated one of us? How do you propose to get rid of
me, Longarm?"

"Don't know. Still thinking about it."

Captain Walthers said, "I warn you, Deputy, you'll
have the War Department to answer to if you try to
. . . whatever you did to that other man!"

"Don't get spooked, Captain. I didn't use nothing but
sweet reason on him. It ain't my way to threaten. Ain't
my way to brag, neither. Speaking of which, is there any
chance some of your friends at the War Department
might be sending in a squadron or so of cavalry? I just

counted heads across the street. There's a good two dozen cowhands and such loafing around the log jail. Don't know if they're fixing to lynch the prisoner, run us out of town, or both."

Sheriff Weed said, "I moseyed over to jaw with that Timberline just now. They seem more cautious than unruly. Timberline says since you rode in, some of the vigilance committee's getting anxious."

"Could be. Timberline tried to crawfish me, last night."

"Do tell? What happened?"

"I didn't crawfish worth mention. He's likely surprised to meet up with somebody who ain't afraid of him."

Weed laughed and agreed, "That's the trouble with growing as big as a moose. Most fellers leave their brains behind once they top six feet. Get used to having their own way without the effort the rest of us have to put out. You been following that trouble they've been having down in New Mexico Territory, Longarm?"

"Lincoln County War? Last I heard, it was over. New governor cleaned out both factions' friends in high places and appointed new lawmen. What's Lincoln County to do with hereabouts?"

"Just thinking about a matter of size they got mixed up on down there. You ever hear of Kid Antrim?"

"Billy the Kid? Sure, he's called Kid Antrim, Billy Bonney, Henry McCarthy and God knows. There's a federal warrant on him for killing an Indian agent, but other deputies are looking for him. I take it you don't know where Kid Antrim's hiding, these days?"

"No, I was talking about his size. Kid Antrim can't be more'n five foot four, and he's killed more men than men like Timberline ever even have to punch. You see my point?"

"Saw it long before you took us all over the Southwest Territories to say it. When folks crowd me, I just crowd back. I didn't have to spin no yarns to Timberline. I suspicion we've got it straight, about now."

The daughter came in from the kitchen with a fresh pot of coffee and placed it on the table, looking neither at Longarm nor at the others as she scooted out again. Weed said, "Ain't they something? Act like they expected one of us to grab 'em and run off to the South Seas or a Turkish harem with 'em."

"Mountain folks are bashful, " Longarm said, feeling much better.

The storekeeper, Stover, came in to glare down at everyone and ask, "Is everything to your pleasure, gents? Excuse me—*lady* and gents?"

Mabel Hanks dimpled prettily and said, "My husband and I were just admiring your cutlery. Wherever did you get such a splendid service? It's so—so unusual."

Stover said, "It's odd stock from a bankrupt mail-order house, mostly, ma'am. I reckon some it it's all right. We don't stint on guests in Crooked Lance."

Stover saw there were no complaints forthcoming, so he went back to tend his other enterprises as Captain Walthers smiled at Mabel knowingly. The army man was wrapped about her finger, right enough. But how was a U.S. Deputy to use that? Longarm knew the woman could be bought, but the captain didn't look like a man who would desert in the middle of a mission.

After breakfast they all filed out back to walk by the creek or sit on the veranda, waiting for something, anything, to break the deadlock, as what promised to be another tedious day settled in.

Longarm managed to get the army man aside as the latter was checking out his own big walking horse in the livery. Longarm watched Walthers clean the walker's frogs with a pointed stick for a time before he cleared his throat and asked, "Would you be willing to take a federal prisoner back to Bitter Creek for me, seeing as we're both federal officers?"

"You mean Cotton Younger? Of course, but how are we to get him away from those crazy cowboys across the way?"

"Wasn't talking about him. As I see it, we're stuck in

95

this bind with the vigilantes till somebody sends help or they come to their senses I'd say that could take at least a week. Meanwhile, I'm figuring to make an arrest. I mean, *another* arrest."

"Oh? You mean you've identified someone here in Crooked Lance as a wanted man?"

"Ain't rightly sure just *what* he's up to, but I got a charge that will stick, if I could get him before a judge."

"I see. And you think I'd be fool enough to transport him back to civilization, leaving you with one less of us to contend with?"

"Hell, you're not about to get Cotton Younger. Why not take in at least *some* damn prisoner and let me share the credit with you?"

"Longarm, you really should have gone into the snake oil business! Are you telling me any truth at all? I'll bite. Who's our suspect, and when are you going to arrest him?"

"Pretty soon. Are you aiming to help?"

"Help you arrest a man on a federal charge, certainly. Transport him out of here for you? Never!"

"Well, it was worth a try. Make sure you get that hind shoe. It looks like your walker's picked up a stone."

As he stepped outside, Walthers followed. "Not so fast. I'd like to know what you're up to."

"Since you ain't helping, it ain't your nevermind, Captain."

"You intend to take him alone?"

"Generally do. We'll talk about it after."

Leaving the army man watching, bemused, Longarm hunted down the Mountie and repeated his request. The Canadian lawman's response wasn't much different. He was willing to back a fellow officer's arrest, but he had no intention of leaving Crooked Lance without Cotton Younger. Longarm decided he'd never met such stubborn types.

He strolled back to the veranda and hunkered down, sitting on the edge, as he pondered his next move. He knew he didn't intend to ride out with any prisoner but the one they'd sent him for. On the other hand, he couldn't just let his intended victim run free much longer. The man was dangerous, and Longarm had no idea what his play was. You eat an apple a bite at a time, and the prisoner in the jail would likely keep for now.

He saw that the midget detective and his wife were over by the stream-side. Cedric, for some reason, was skipping rocks across the water. Likely it came from pretending to be a little boy most places they went.

Sheriff Weed was seated in a barrel chair down at the far end, smoking a cigar and digesting his cast-iron buckwheats. Longarm half turned, still seated, and said, "I've been going over what you said about Kid Antrim, Weed."

"Do tell? Thought you said you wasn't after him right now."

"Ain't. I've been counting strikes. I'd say knowing one of Billy the Kid's less written-up handles makes it strike three. You mind telling me who the hell you are?"

Weed suddenly rose from the chair, frowning through a cloud of tobacco smoke as he asked, "Strike *what*? What in tarnation's got into you? I told you I was Sheriff Weed of Clay County, Missouri!"

"That was strike one. I didn't see why a county sheriff would ride all the way out here in person, 'stead of sending a deputy, in an election year. But, like I said, that was just strike one. You coulda been a *dumb* sheriff from Missouri."

"I don't like being called dumb, but have your full say, son."

"All right. Last afternoon, over by the jailhouse, you called Chambrum du Val an *hombre*. That was strike two, Weed. Folks from Missouri don't call men hombres. That's Southwest talk. Maybe Texas or New Mexico. But, what the hell, you could have picked it up from Ned Buntline's magazine or somebody you rode

97

with one time, and anyway, you don't call a man out on two strikes, so I waited till you let that slip about the Lincoln County War, down in the Southwest—"

The man calling himself Sheriff Weed went for the S&W at his side. He didn't make it. Longarm fired, sitting, with the derringer he'd been holding in his lap, then dove headfirst and rolled across the grass, whipping out his sixgun as he bounded to his feet, dancing sideways as he trained it at the end of the veranda.

Then he stopped and lowered the unfired .44, knowing he didn't have to use it now. The man called Weed was spreadeagled in the dust beyond the end of the planks, his heels up on the veranda with his hat between them. As Longarm moved over to stare soberly down at the glazed eyes staring sightlessly up at him, he was joined by the other two lawmen and the odd detecteve team.

Captain Walthers gasped, "My God! Did you have to kill him?" and the Mountie shouted, "You can't be serious! I know that man! He's the sheriff of Clay County, Missouri!"

Longarm shook his head and said, "Not hardly. Maybe something on him or in his possibles can tell us who he really was."

As Longarm knelt to go through the dead man's pockets, a bunch of local cowhands and Kim Stover ran around the corner of the building. The storekeeper, himself, came out, cursing, but with neither his wife nor his daughter in evidence.

At the same time, Timberline rounded the cluster of buildings on the far side, gun in hand. He slowed down as he took in what had happened and approached the crowd around Longarm saying, "What did he do, Longarm? Call you a *boy*?"

Captain Walthers said, "Longarm, I hope you had a federal charge against that man. As the senior federal officer here—"

"Oh, don't tell us all you're dumb, Captain. Let us figure some things out for ourselves. Of course I had a charge. It's a federal offense to impersonate an elected official, which a sheriff is. This badge he had pinned on his vest says 'Sheriff,' but it don't say what county, Clay or otherwise. Man can pick a toy badge up in most any pawnshop. He's got nothing with a name on it in his wallet. What's this?"

Longarm unfolded a sheet of stiff paper he'd taken from the dead man's breast pocket and spread it on Weed's chest. Kim Stover gasped and said, "Oh, dear, it's got blood on it."

"Yes, ma'am. Bullet went through it. It's a telegram, federal flyer sent to every law office worth mention a week or more ago. This particular one's addressed to the Territory of New Mexico, Santa Fe. Likely where this feller stole it."

Walthers blustered, "Damn it, man, what does it say?"

"What we all know. That Cotton Younger's been picked up as a cow thief, here in Crooked Lance."

"But if he intercepted it in Santa Fe . . . what do you make of Weed, a bounty hunter?"

"That's a likely guess. Since Lew Wallace cleaned up New Mexico the territory's filled with unemployed guns. From the way he spoke at the breakfast table, I'd say he rode with one side or the other in the Lincoln County War and has been looking for a new job. He heard about the folks here holding Cotton Younger, heard about the herd of rewards it might lead to, and was playing Foxy Grandpa. He did make you the best offer for your prisoner, didn't he, Miss Kim?"

The redhead grimaced, not looking at the body, as she nodded and turned away. Longarm decided to push her further off balance by observing, brutally, "Yep, no telling how many bounty hunters we'll have riding up here before long. Might even have the James and Younger Gang paying us a visit, as word of your hospitality gets around. You folks might as well know, one of Cotton Younger's old sidekicks has already come and gone."

Timberline blinked and said, "The hell you say. Who *was* the varmint?"

The midget, Cedric, chortled, "The railroad dick! I knew it!"

Longarm shook his head and continued searching the corpse. "Nope. He's taking Sailor Brown in for me. The Mountie, here, gets credit for unmasking him. He was that oldtimer pretending to be a Canuck."

Timberline asked, "Who shot him, you or the feller working for the railroad?"

"Don't know who shot him. I suspicion it was the same one that shot Deputy Kincaid, the man from my outfit who never got here. Kincaid was from Missouri, so he might have known members of the James-Younger Gang on sight. I suspicion that's why he was kept from getting here. Though, now that I think on it, my own reception in Bitter Creek wasn't all that friendly."

Timberline said, "Hot damn! I see it all, now! This feller you just gunned down was pretending to be a Missouri Sheriff! Don't that mean—"

"Slow down. It don't mean more than another cud to chew, Timberline. Weed, here, couldn't have shot the old man. Anybody could have done whatever to my partner, Kincaid. This situation's getting more wheels within wheels than an eight-day clock."

He found a pocket watch with an inscription and read, " 'To Alexander McSween on his fifth wedding anniversary.' Looks like real silver, too."

"You reckon that was the jasper's real name, Longarm?"

"Not hardly. Alexander McSween was on the losing side of the Lincoln County War. They gunned him down with his wife watching, a couple of summers ago. I'd say this bounty hunter was one of them that did the gunning. No wonder he was so interested in Kid Antrim. The Kid rode for McSween. He made a bad slip by calling Billy the Kid *Antrim* instead of *Bonney*. Nobody aside from a few federal officers knows that name, outside Lincoln County."

Kim Stover's face was pale as she asked, "Do you think there's a chance Billy the Kid could be headed this way, Mister Long?"

Longarm considered nodding, but thought honesty was perhaps the best policy when a lie might sound foolish. He shook his head and said, "Doubt it. Kid Antrim's likely in Mexico, if he's got a lick of sense. He's a gunslick, not a bounty hunter. No way a wanted man could collect a reward. Unless, like this jasper, he figured to dress up like a lawman."

He saw her relieved look and quickly shot it down by repeating, "All we have to worry about is Frank and Jesse James and company."

Someone asked about the disposal of the remains and Stover quickly said, "I'll bury him right decent for ten dollars. I figure there's at least ten dollars on him, ain't there, Deputy Long?"

Longarm made a wry face and got to his feet, brushing off his knee as he said, "You'll likely want two bits from him for breakfast, too."

Stover nodded, pleased to see the big lawman was so agreeable, and oblivious of the disgusted looks others were casting his way.

Longarm said, "I'd best see if he had anything in his room," and walked to the doorway, leaving the others to work out the funeral details as they saw fit. He saw that the Mountie was right behind him, but didn't comment on it until the two of them were alone in the dead man's room. As Longarm spread the contents of "Weed's" saddle bags on the bed, the Mountie said, "That was smoothly done, Longarm."

"Oh, it only made sense to have the drop on him before I told him he was under arrest."

"Come now, I've made a few arrests myself. You know you could have taken him alive."

"You don't say?"

"I do say. You tricked him into slapping leather be-

101

cause you had no intention of having to take him in, without the man you came for."

"I heard you Mounties were tolerable good. You likely know this job calls for considering things from all sides before you move. It didn't pleasure me to trick that fool out there into making things simple, but I couldn't leave him running loose."

"I know what you did and why you did it. I know you got rid of the railroad detective rather neatly, too. I think it's time we got something straight between us, Longarm."

"I'm listening."

"My organization's not as old as your Texas Rangers, but we operate in much the same way."

"I know. You always get your man. I read that somewhere. Don't you reckon that's a mite boastful?"

"No, I don't. I have every intention of taking that prisoner, Cotton Younger, before Her Majesty's Bar of Justice, and I'll kill anyone who tries to stop me!"

"You talking about me or them vigilantes all around outside?"

"Both. I've had just about enough of their nonsense and I'm not too happy about the way you've been trying to whittle your opposition down to size. I warn you, if you make any attempt to run *me* out—"

"Hey, look here, he's got a copy of this month's *Cap'n Billy's Whiz-Bang*. It's pretty humorous. You oughta read it sometime. Do wonders for your disposition. Nobody's aiming to run you out, old son. I didn't run the old man or the railroad dick out of Crooked Lance, and I shot that other feller fair and square. What's eating you? You are a real Mountie, ain't you?"

"You want to see my credentials?"

"Nope. My boss told me to expect a Mountie here, and I doubt anyone else would want to wear that red coat." Longarm's eyes narrowed, thoughtfully.

The Mountie asked, "What's wrong? You look like you just thought of something new."

"I did. I'm starting to feel better about that feller I

just shot. There *was* somebody from the Clay County sheriff's office coming out here. That bounty hunter must have waylaid him! Somewhere in the mountains there's at least two lawmen buried!"

The Mountie put a hand in his tunic and took out a leather billfold, saying, "I insist you read my Sergeant's Warrant. You'll note it gives my description in addition to my name."

Longarm scanned it and said, "You're likely Sergeant Foster, right enough."

"William DeVerrier Foster of the Royal Canadian Northwest Mounted Police, to be exact. May I see *your* identification?"

Longarm grinned and took out his own billfold, showing his badge and his official papers to the other. The Mountie nodded and asked, "Have you checked Captain Walthers' credentials?"

"Didn't have to. I asked him a few trick questions since we met. Besides, who but an army man would be after a deserter? You got a point. Maybe you *do* get your man, most times."

"Do I have your assurance you'll not try to get rid of me as you did the others?"

Longarm nodded and said, "You got my word I won't shoot you or try to buy you off with reward money."

He'd already decided there had to be some other way.

Chapter 12

Longarm didn't ask Captain Walthers to show his ID.
He knew the Mountie would, and it was just as well
they didn't get to be friends.

By noon the dead man had been buried, amid considerable whooping and shooting off of cowpoke's guns.
One could get the impression that folks in Crooked
Lance didn't get many occasions for a celebration. Longarm didn't attend the funeral. He was not a friend of
the deceased and it seemed an opportunity to have a
word with the prisoner.

It wasn't. A pair of hard-looking men with rifles
stood by the log jail and when Longarm said he wanted
to talk to Cotton Younger they told him it would be
over their dead bodies.

He considered this for a moment, and decided it
wasn't his best move.

As he walked over to the general store the midget,
Cedric, fell in step at his side, taking three strides to
each of Longarm's as he puffed his big cigar and piped,
"We're gonna have to make our play damned sudden,
Longarm. Cotton Younger don't figure to keep much
longer."

"How'd it get to be *our* play, and what are you talking about, Cedric?"

"There's advantages to being a detective knee-high-
to-a-grasshopper, big man. Us little fellers can get into
places most folks don't consider."

"You been listening to folks from under your wet
rock?"

"That's close enough. Want to know what the talk in town is, now?"

"Maybe. What's making you so friendly, all of a sudden?"

"I don't like you, either. Never have liked you, even before you had your way with my woman, but I don't play this game for likes or don't likes. I'm in it for cash. You want to trade more insults, or do we work together?"

"Depends on what we're talking about, Cedric. Suppose you start with something I don't know."

"They're fixing to lynch Cotton Younger."

"What? That don't make a lick of sense, dammit!"

"You met anybody in this one-horse town with a degree from Harvard yet? I overheard some of Timberline's hands talking about a necktie party. You see, the redhead, Kim Stover, is the brains behind the scheme to build up Crooked Lance with the proceeds of . . . whatever. When I say 'brains,' I ain't saying much, for as me and Mabel see it, the game is as good as up. Ain't nobody here in town fixing to get paid a thing but trouble."

"That's what we've all been telling 'em."

"I know, and everyone but that stubborn widow woman can see it."

"Then why don't Timberline turn the prisoner over and have done with the mess?"

"He can't. He's in love with the redhead and she'd never speak to him again if he double-crossed her like that."

"All right, so how else does he figure to double-cross her?"

"Like I just told you, with a sudden necktie party! He won't be taking part in it, of course. His plan is to be over at the redhead's, trying to steal a kiss or better, when all of a sudden, out of the night—"

"I got you. 'Some of the boys got drunk and riled up about that running iron, Miss Kim, and I'm pure sorry as all hell about the way his neck got all stretched out of shape like that.' "

"That's one thing they're considering. Another is having him get shot trying to escape. Either way, it figures to happen soon."

"They say anything about me and the other lawmen?"

"Sure. They don't figure three big men and a dwarf can stop 'em. I reckon you're the one they're calling a dwarf. Timberline told 'em not to shoot none of us, 'less we try to stop the fun."

Longarm stopped at the store front and leaned against a post as the midget put a tiny boot up on the planks to wait for his next words.

Longarm mused, half-aloud, "The Mountie would fight for sure and go down shooting. Walthers might try, and get hurt . . ."

"You and me know better, right?"

"Against at least fifty armed drunks? You're sure you got it right, though? Timberline's got the odds right, but there ain't much that can be said about his thinking. Hell, he doesn't have to kill the prisoner. They could just let him go with an hour's head start and you, me, the others would be hightailing it out of the valley after him. They'd never see any of us again and Timberline could go back to courting his widow woman. Maybe consoling her on their mutual misfortune."

"I never said he was bright. I only told you what he planned."

"You reckon he might see it, if it was pointed out to him?"

"He might. Then again, knowing his play was uncovered, he might make his move more sudden. There's over fifty men in and around town this very moment."

"I get the picture. When were they planning to murder the poor jasper?"

"Late tonight. The redhead's gone home in a huff, saying the way ever'body's drinking and carrying on over the funeral is disgusting, which I'll allow it is. Timberline figures to ride over to her spread, maybe playing his guitar or something as stupid, just so he's not there when they string the boy up. Later, of course, nobody will remember just who done the stringing, the rest of us will likely ride off and . . ."

"All right, what's your plan, Cedric?"

"We in this together? You'll split us in?"

"Cedric, I'm tempted as hell to lie to you, considering the choices I got, but you're too smart to think I can divide a reward I'm not allowed to accept."

"Hell, who cares about the paper on that pissant, Cotton Younger? It's *Jesse James* that me and Mabel's out to collect on! He knows where the James boys are!"

"You figure I'd let you get it out of him, Apache style?"

"Don't have to. Already made the deal. Like I said, us little folks can get into the damndest nooks and crannies."

"You talked to the prisoner in the jail?"

"Sure. Got under the floor last night and we jawed a while through a knothole. He don't like the idea of getting lynched all that much, so I convinced him his only way out of it was to make a deal. His life in exchange for the present address of Frank or Jesse. He says he don't know where Frank is, but that he knows how to get to Jesse. Half a loaf is better than none, I always say."

"Where'd he say Cousin Jesse was?"

"He didn't. Said he'd tell us once he was clear of Crooked Lance and crazy cowboys with ropes. You think I'd bother to spring the rascal if I knew?"

Longarm took out a cheroot and lit it, running the conversation through his mind again to see where the yarn didn't hold together. He knew the little bounty hunter would lie when it was in his favor, but what he said made sense. Longarm nodded and said, "All right, we get him out right after sundown and make a run for it. You'd better head out early with Mabel and your buckboard. I'll join you at the first pass and we'll hole up somewhere. You'll get your talk with Cotton Younger and then we split up. They'll probably come boiling up out of this valley like hornets when they find him gone, but you and your woman will be riding into Bitter Creek innocent, and I know my way around in the woods at night."

"Was you born that stupid or did a cow step on your head, Longarm?"

"You know a better way?"

"Of course. I got a key to the jailhouse, dammit!"

"You stole Pop Wade's key? How come he ain't missed it yet?"

"Because I never stole it, big brain! I had Mabel jaw with the guards whilst I took a beeswax impression, standing damn near under Pop as he stared down the front of Mabel's dress. I got some tools in my valise, and once I had the impression—"

"I know how you make a duplicate key, dammit. I'll allow it makes it a mite easier, but not much. We still got to get you and your woman out safe while I bang the guards' heads together some."

"Mabel's going to take care of the guards for us."

"Both of 'em at once?"

"Don't be nasty, dammit. Part of *their* play is to keep the drinking and whooping going on all afternoon and long past sundown. Mabel's gonna mosey over, sort of drunk-like, with a bottle. If you meet her and she offers you a drink, don't take it. Mabel's still pissed off at you for the way you spoke to her in Bitter Creek."

"So she gives them knockout drops, we unlock the door and slip the prisoner out quiet, leaving the necktie party to discover things ain't as they seem, long after the four of us are gone. Yep, it's a good plan."

"We'd best split up and meet later, then. Part of our plan is that you and me ain't been all that friendly. I'll give you the high sign after supper and we'll move in around . . . when, nine o'clock?"

"Sounds about right. Summer sun'll be down about

eight. Gives us an hour of dark to spring the prisoner, maybe two, three 'fore they come for him and all hell breaks loose. I'll see you at supper, Cedric. My regards to the missus."

"You fun like that in front of Mabel and it can cost you, Longarm. I'm used to being hoo-rahed. Used to having a woman with round heels, too. But she can be a caution when she's riled at you, and you've riled her enough already, hear?"

Longarm looked down at the little man, catching the hurt in his eyes before he hid it behind his big cigar. Longarm said, "What I said was said without thinking and without double-meaning, Mister Hanks. Whatever you and your woman have between you ain't my business and I'd take it neighborly if we could forget what happened the other night in Bitter Creek. What I done, I done because I was a man and a man takes what's offered. Had I known she was your wife, I wouldn't have. Now that I know she is, I never aim to again."

"Jesus, Longarm, are you *apologizing* to me?"

"I am, if you think you got one coming."

The midget suddenly seemed to choke on his cigar, grinned, and held out a little hand, saying, "By God, *pardner*! Put 'er there!"

Chapter 13

Supper took what seemed a million years, complicated by the terrible cooking of the Stover women and the fact that one of them, at least, was probably planning to crawl into bed with him as soon as she dared. Longarm watched both the mother and daughter for some sign, but neither one met his gaze, and he felt less guilty about what had happened. He'd likely never know which of them it had been, but whichever, she was not only a great lay but damned good at her little game. He wondered how many other times it had happened, and how, if it was the daughter, she kept from getting in a family way. He'd decided she must know about such matters. But, try as he would, he couldn't puzzle out her identity. They both had the same lean figures and onion heads. The one he'd been with had been experienced as hell, but that didn't prove it was the mother. The daughter was no spring chicken, either, and if she'd done it before, she'd had more practice than most spinsters who looked like poor plain sparrows. He hoped she'd know how to take care of herself, though, because anything he'd fathered with either one figured to be one ugly little bastard!

There was little table conversation as, outside, from time to time, a gun went off or some cowhands tore by at a dead run, whooping like Indians. Neither the midget not his wife looked up when Captain Walthers sighed and asked, "How long do you imagine they'll carry on like that? You'd think they'd never had a funeral here before!"

Longarm waited until Cedric excused himself from the table and made as if to go outside to answer a call of nature. Longarm followed at a discreet distance, and on the veranda, Cedric slipped him the key, saying, "Mind you wait for Mabel to get them ass-over-teakettle. I'll move the buckboard out along the trail a mile or so and wait. Mabel gives 'em the bottle and lights out to join me. Give 'em fifteen minutes to pass out before you do anything dumb. You figure on running for it or riding him out?"

"I'll play my tune by ear. Might be riding double, 'less I can steal a mount for Younger."

"All right. You won't see us. We'll be hid. I'll watch the trail and whistle you in. See you . . . when? Nine-fifteen?"

"Give us till nine-thirty before you know I failed. If we don't make it, you and the lady just come back from your ride as if nothing happened. I might need help or I might be dead. I'll expect you to do what you have to, either way."

"I told Mabel you apologized. She says she ain't mad at you no more."

Longarm left the midget and went to his room. He gathered his possessions and threw them out the window to the narrow space between the hotel and the livery shed. Then he locked the door from the inside, climbed out the window, and picked up his belongings before moving quietly to the horses.

His bay nickered a greeting and Longarm put a hand over its muzzle to quiet it. He saddled and bridled the bay and was about to lead it out when something whispering endearments plastered itself against him. He steadied the thin woman in his arms and whispered, "I'm going out for a little ride, honey. Meet me later in my room."

"Just once! Just do it once right now. I want! I need!"

"Honey, the whole damn place is up and about! Have you gone crazy?"

"Yes, crazy for your pretty thing inside me! Please, darling, I have to have it or I'll scream!"

Longarm considered knocking her out, but it didn't seem too gallant and, besides, he couldn't see her tiny jaw to hit it. She was fumbling at his fly, now, whimpering like a bitch in heat. He could feel that she wore nothing under the thin cotton dress. He could tell she was going out of her fool head, too!

Muttering, he led her into a stall and pressed her against the rough boards, letting her fish his half-erect penis from his fly as he loved her up and kissed her to shut her fool mouth. He had to brace his hands against the planks, but she was equal to the occasion, lifting her hem with one hand as she played with him with the other.

He was a tall man and she was short and standing up could be the hard way but she must have done it this way before, too, for she raised one leg, caught him around the waist with amazing skill, and literally lifted herself into position, throwing the other leg around him as he slid into her amazingly positioned hungry moistness.

"Keerist!" He marveled as she settled her lean thighs on his hip bones. She moaned with lust as she gyrated wildly with her tailbone against the rough planks. Longarm moved his feet back, swore when he felt he'd stepped on a horse turd, and started pounding as hard as he dared without knocking down the flimsy stall. He managed to satisfy both of them, for the moment, and as she slid to her knees to talk French, he managed to get her to her unsteady feet and moving in the right direction by soothing, "Later, in my room. We'll do it undressed and I'll lick you to death besides!"

She scampered away in the dark with a knowing chuckle as Longarm got his breath back and wondered how much time he'd lost.

He led the bay out, tethered it at a safe distance, and came back. He worked mostly by feel as he saddled the captain's walking horse with Walthers's own army saddle, bridled it with the first headgear he found, and led it out behind him, soothing the nervous walker with honeyed words. He recovered his own mount and led both over to the creek, where he led them across and tethered them to a willow.

Then he splashed back, crossed the inky darkness of the Stover grounds, and after a long, cautious looksee, scooted across the road. He worked his way through the shadows to the back of the log jail. The chinked corner logs afforded an easy climb to the almost-flat roof. Longarm crept across the roof until he could peer over at the two guards by the front door. Then he settled down to listen.

It took forever before one of the guards asked, "Any sign of him?"

It's too early, Slim. The gal said he'd be coming about nine."

"We're supposed to be knocked out, ain't we? What say we sort of scrootch down?"

"*You* scrootch down, dammit. We got more'n an hour to kill 'fore he comes over from the hotel."

"I wish we had a man inside. That big bastard's faster'n spit on a stove with that .44 of his, and I ain't never gunned nobody before."

"Don't worry, I have. He won't have a chance. I'll just blast him with both barrels of number-nine buck as he bends over to see if I'm sleepin' sound."

Longarm decided he'd heard as much as he needed to. So he gathered his legs under him, dropped off the roof, and materialized before their startled eyes, pistol-whipping the one with the shotgun into unconsciousness as he warned the other, quietly, "You say *shit*, and you're *dead*."

The frightened guard didn't do anything but drop his Henry rifle to the earth without a word. Longarm knew that the key the midget had slipped him was probably worthless, so he said, "Open her up."

"I don't have a key, mister."

"Are you finning with me, boy?"

113

"Honest to Gawd! Pop Wade has the key, not us!"

"Is Younger inside?"

"Yes, but—" And that was all he had to say about it as Longarm knocked him out, slid him down the logs to rest by his partner, and went to work on the door.

One blade of Longarm's jacknife would have gotten him arrested if he'd been searched by a lawman while not carrying a badge. The cheap, rusty lock was no trouble for his pick. He opened the door silently and went in, squinting in the darkness as he called out, quietly, "Younger, you just keep still and don't say a word till I tell you to."

"What's going on?"

"That was *three* words, you son of a bitch. Say one more and I'll feed your heart to the hawks!"

There was no further comment from the improvised cell as Longarm picked the lock. He told the prisoner to come out, locked his wrists behind him with handcuffs, and taking the youth by the elbow, said, "You come this way and make sure it's silent as well as sudden." The prisoner tripped over one of the unconscious guards and gasped, "Who done that?"

"I did. Shut up and stand right there while I roll 'em inside and lock the door. All that idle chatter of yours is making me testy as hell!"

It only took half a minute to shove the guards inside and lock the door a second time. He grabbed Younger's elbow again and led him at a trot across the road, through the Stovers' grounds, and across the creek. He boosted the prisoner up into his own saddle, knowing his own bay would be predictable on the lead. Then he climbed aboard Captain Walthers's walker and led out at a brisk pace as the prisoner yelped, "Jesus! I can't ride like this! There's a big slit in this saddle an' my balls is caught in it!"

"You just hush and do the best you can, boy. My orders are to bring you in dead or alive. You yell one more time and I don't have to tell you which it'll be."

The prisoner fell silent, or tried to, as Longarm followed the trail he'd followed du Val—or Brown—along, by memory. He managed to miss riding through a tree, but the branches whipped both of them in the dark as Longarm set as fast a pace as he dared to in the dark. Once the prisoner announced, apologetically, that he was about to fall off.

Longarm said, "You fall and I'll kill you," and his horsemanship seemed to improve miraculously.

Longarm led his charge to the clearing he remembered and beyond, guiding himself by the stars as he glimpsed them through the overhead branches. They weren't on any trail he knew of. The riders from the valley would know every trail for a good two days' ride from Crooked Lance. They rode through timber and they rode through brush. A couple of times they almost rode over cliffs, but Longarm trusted his mount to see by starlight well enough to avoid obvious suicide, given a gentle hand on the reins and not pressed faster than its night vision could cope with. As they topped a rise high above the valley, Longarm reined in and looked back and down. They were too far away to hear more than an occasional rallying shot, but little lights were buzzing back and forth on the valley floor. Longarm chuckled and said, "They've missed us. But there's no way to even try to read our sign before sunup, so we'll rest the critters here for a minute and be on our way."

The prisoner decided it was safe to speak and asked, "What in thunder is going on?"

"I'm not sure. Couple of folks was setting me up to get killed. Before that, they told me plans were afoot to do the same for you. Could have been true. Could have been another lie. As you see, it don't make no never-mind, now."

"You're the federal man called Longarm, ain't you? Jesus, am I ever glad to see you! You see, it's all a misunderstanding, so you can take these irons off me, now."

"That'll be the day, boy. You're wearing them cuffs till I have you safe in federal custody, which just might take a while. I'll help you when you have to eat or take a leak. You ain't the first man I've rode like this with, Younger."

"God damn it, my name is Jones!"

"Whatever. Like I said, that ain't my job. I was sent to transport you back to Denver, and since both of our critters are still breathing, we'd best be on our way. Hold onto the cantle with your fingers if that McClellan's not your style. Didn't you ride a McClellan when you were with Terry on the Rosebud, a few years back?"

"I don't know what you're talking about. I never deserted from no army!"

"Now, did I say anything about desertion? You stick to any yarn you aim to."

"It ain't no yarn, God damn it! You got the wrong man!"

"Well, if I find out I have, once we get you before a judge in Denver, I'll apologize like a gent to you. Meanwhile, Jones, James, Younger, or whomsoever, that's where you and me are headed, come hell, high water, or a full Sioux uprising!"

Chapter 14

Longarm was tough. Ten times tougher than the good Lord made most men, but his prisoner was only human, and the horses were only horses.

By sunup, he could see he was running all three into the ground and reined to a halt in a tangle of bigleaf maple. He helped his prisoner down and Cotton Younger simply fell to the damp leaves and closed his eyes, falling asleep on his side with his raw, chained wrists behind him. Longarm removed the bits from the animals' pink-foamed mouths after hobbling each with a length of latigo leather. He didn't think either one was in condition to walk away, let alone run, but a front hoof lashed to a hind would discourage them from bolting, should they get their wind back before he was ready to move on.

He'd watered both mounts an hour before dawn at a chance rill of snow-melt, so they were happy to drop their heads and graze the hurt from their muzzles in the sweet-scented orchard grass and wild onion growing in the dappled shade. He unsaddled both, spread the saddle blankets over tree limbs for the wind to dry, then found a patch of sunlight where he placed the saddles bottoms-up. Some said it wasn't good for the sweat-soaked leather, but Longarm had heard that those little bugs Professor Pasteur was writing about over in France, weren't partial to sun baths. He'd risk a cracked saddle skirt against a festered saddle sore any day. He'd started this play by riding out with the two best mounts

117

he knew of in Crooked Lance. He was depending on keeping them that way.

Captain Walthers's tall mount, after eating a few bites of greenery, was already leaning against a tree trunk, head down and eyes closed. The army man hadn't fed it enough oats for its size, most likely. The older army bay he'd borrowed from the remount section he had picked because he looked like a tough one, and he seemed to be living up to Longarm's hopes. He was nearly worn out, but still stuffing his gut like the wise old cuss he was. There was no telling when they'd be taking a break in such good grazery again.

Longarm considered the wild onion and other herbage as he rubbed both mounts down with Captain Walthers's spare cotton drawers from the saddle bags the fool had left attached. Here in the shade it was choice and green, but hardly touched, except for an occasional rabbit-nibble. Longarm saw the healed-over trunk scars where a long-dead elk had rubbed the velvet from his antlers on a good day to fight for love. Once, a grizzly had sharpened his claws on a tree beyond. The sign was fresher. Maybe from early that spring. Longarm patted his mount's rump and said, "Yep, we're on virgin range, oldtimer. Don't know just where in hell it is, but nobody's run cows through here in living memory."

Leaving all three of his charges for the moment, Longarm circled through the shapeless mass of timber, fixing its layout in his mind for possible emergencies. He came to an outcropping of granite, studied it, and decided it would be a waste of time to climb up for a looksee. Even if the top rose above the surrounding treetops, which it didn't, there'd be nothing to see worth mentioning. The land was flattening out as they approached the south-pass country. If a posse from Crooked Lance had found their trail yet, it would be too far back to be visible on gently rolling timberland. Longarm went back to the sleeping prisoner, grabbed him by the heels, and dragged him over to the outcropping, as he half-awoke, complaining, "What the hell?"

"Ain't smart to bed down next to the critters." Longarm explained, adding, "Horses nicker to one another at a distance. I figure that if ours get to calling back and forth with others skulking in on us . . . never mind. If you knew a damn thing about camping in unfriendly country you'd have never got caught by folks who weren't even looking for you."

He placed the prisoner on dry forest duff, strode over to the granite outcropping, and hunkered down with his back against its gray wall, bracing the Winchester across his lap with his knees up, folding his arms across them, and lowering his head for forty winks, Mexican style. He'd almost dozed off when the prisoner called out, "I can't sleep with my hands behind me like this, durn it!"

"You can sleep standing on your head if you're really tired, boy. Now put a sock in it and leave me be. I'm a mite tuckered myself, and by the way, I'm a light sleeper. You move from there in the next half hour or so and you'll be buried a yard from wherever I find you."

"Listen, lawman, you're treating an innocent man cruel and unusual!"

"Shut up. I don't aim to say that twice."

Longarm dozed off. He might just have rested his mind a few minutes. It wasn't important, as long as it worked. In about an hour he lifted his head, saw the prisoner was where he'd last seen him, and felt ready to face the world again.

But he was not an unreasonable taskmaster. Longarm knew others might still be tuckered while he was feeling bright-eyed and bushy-tailed, so he let the prisoner snore as he smoked a cheroot all the way down, chewing on his own thoughts. He had no way of knowing some things, but when in doubt, it paid a man to consider the worst, so he tried to decide just how bad things could possibly me. The idea that the others had simply given up never crossed his mind.

The midget and his woman had sold them out. The

reason could wait for now. Timberline and the Crooked Lance riders would be following, if only because Kim Stover insisted. Certainly the Mountie, and probably Captain Walthers, would be tracking them, too. Either with the posse or riding alone. Whoever was tracking would have picked up the sign at sunup, not that long ago. At best they'd just be over the first rise outside of Crooked Lance, a good eight to ten hours behind him, even riding at a breakneck pace. They would have to ride more slowly than he had, because they'd have to watch the ground for sign. They'd have to scout each rise before they tore over it too; they knew he had guns and could have dug in almost anywhere. Yes, he and the prisoner were in fair shape for a cross-country run. Anyone following would have some trouble on catching up.

Longarm started field stripping and cleaning the Winchester in his lap as he considered what he'd be doing if he was riding with the vigilantes instead of running from them. He decided to appoint the Mountie, Foster, as the most dangerous head of a combined posse, which was the worse thing he could picture tracking him. An experienced lawman wouldn't just follow hoofprint by hoofprint. Sergeant Foster would know he and the prisoner were well-mounted with a good lead. The Mountie would try to figure out where they were headed and ride hard to cut them off.

All right, if he was Sergeant Foster, where would he guess that a U.S. Deputy Marshal and his prisoner would be headed?

Bitter Creek, of course. There was a jail in Bitter Creek to hold Cotton Younger till a train came by. If the Mountie had gone in with the vigilantes and told them that, Timberline's boys, or maybe a third of them, would be riding directly for Bitter Creek, hoping to keep him from boarding the eastbound U.P. with a prisoner he hadn't paid for.

The next best bet? A run for the railroad right-of-way, well clear of Bitter Creek, with hopes of flagging down a locomotive. He'd be set up nicely for an ambush anywhere along the line if he did that. So the Union Pacific was out. Too many unfriendly folks were expecting him to take Cotton Younger in that way.

As if he'd heard Longarm call our his name aloud, the prisoner rolled over and sat up, muttering, "I got to take a leak. You'll have to take these irons off me, Longarm."

Longarm placed the dismantled Winchester and its parts carefully on a clean, flat rock before he got to his feet. He walked over and hauled the prisoner to his feet. Then he unbuttoned the man's pants, pulled them halfway down his thighs, and said, "Leak away. I gotta put my rifle back together."

"Gawd! I can't just go like this! I'll wet my britches!"

"You do as best you can. I don't aim to hold it for you."

The cow thief turned away, red-faced, as Longarm squatted down to reassemble his rifle, whistling softly as he used his pocketknife screw driver.

The prisoner asked, "What if I have to take a crap?"

"I'd say your best bet would be to squat."

"Gawd! With my hands behind me like this?"

"Yep. It ain't the neatest way to travel, but I've learned not to take foolish chances when I'm transporting. You'll get the hang of living with your hands like that, in a day or so."

"You're one mean son of a bitch, you know that?"

"Some folks have said as much. I got my rifle in one piece. You want me to button you back up?"

"I dribbled some on my britches, damn it!"

"That ain't what I asked."

Longarm crooked the rifle through his bent elbow and went back over to pull the prisoner's pants up, buttoning just the top button. "Since there's no ladies present, this'll save us time, when next you get the call of nature. It'll also likely drop your pants around your knees if you get to running without my permission."

"You're mean, pure mean. As soon as I can talk to a lawyer I'm gonna file me a complaint. You got no right to torture me like this."

"You'll never know what torture is, until you try to make a break for it. I got some jerky and biscuit dough in my saddle bags. As long as we're resting the mounts, we may as well eat."

He took the prisoner to another flat rock near the hobbled army mounts, sat him down on it, and rummaged for provisions. He cut a chunk of jerked venison from the slab, wrapped it in soft sourdough, and said, "Open wide. I'll be the mama bird and you'll be the baby bird."

"Jehosaphat! Don't you aim to *cook* it?"

"Nope. Somebody might be sitting on a far ridge, looking for smoke against the skyline. Besides, it'll cook inside you. One thing I admire about sourdough. You just have to get a bite or two down and it sort of swells inside you. Saves a lot of chewing."

He shoved a mouthful into Cotton Younger and took the edge from his own hunger with a portion for himself. After some effort, the prisoner gulped and asked, "Don't I get no coffee? They gave me coffee three times a day in that log jail."

"I'll give you a swallow from the canteens before we mount up again. Tastes better and lasts you longer if you're a mite thirsty when you drink."

He took his Ingersoll out and consulted it for the time. "I'll give the brutes a few more minutes, 'fore I saddle and bridle 'em. I've been meaning to ask: do you reckon they was really fixing to hang you, last night?"

"They never said they was. Pop Wade was sort of a friendly old cuss."

"Somebody told me Timberline was tired of having you on his hands. How'd you get along with him?"

"Not too well. He'd have killed me that first day, if the redheaded lady and Pop hadn't talked him out of it."

"Hmm, that midget's game gets funnier and funnier. Did he really offer you a deal to spring you from the jail in exchange for Jesse James?"

"I told him I'd put him onto Jesse James, but I was only trying to get out of that place. I got no more idea than anyone else where that rascal's hid out."

"Let's see, now. He sends me to get killed. Then, amid the general congratulations, him or Mabel slips you out, they put a barlow knife against your eyelid to gain your undivided attention. It figures. It ain't like they had to transport you out of the valley. They just wanted a few minutes of Apache conversation with you. Once they knew where to pick up Jesse James, you'd be useless baggage to dispose of. Hell, they might even have let you live till the vigilantes found you."

"Damn it, I don't know where Jesse James is hiding!"

"Lucky for you I come along, then. I suspicion you'd have told 'em, whether you knew or not. That Cedric Hanks is a mean little bastard, ain't he?"

"You still think I'm Cotton Younger, don't you?"

"Don't matter what I think. You could be Queen Victoria and I'd still transport you to Denver to stand trial as Cotton Younger."

The owlhoot's expression was sly as he asked, cautiously, "Is cattle rustling a federal charge, Longarm?"

"No. It's a fool thing to say. You rustle up some grub or you rustle apples as a kid. You don't rustle cows, boy. You *steal* 'em! If you ride with a running iron in your saddle bags, it's best to be honest with yourself and call it what it is. Cow theft is a serious matter. Don't shilly-shally with kid names for a dangerous, dead-serious *profession!*"

"If I was to admit I was a rustler—all right, a *cow thief* named Jones, would you believe me?"

"Nope. I ain't in a believing business. You don't know what fibbing is until you've packed a badge six or eight years. You owlhoots only lie to decent folks, so you seldom get the hang of it. In my line, I get lied to every day be experts. I've been lied to by old boys who gunned down their own mothers. I've taken in men who raped their own daughters. I've arrested men for the sodomy-rape of runaway boys, for torturing old misers for their gold, for burning a colored man to death just for the hell of it, and you want to know something? Not one of them sons of bitches ever told me he was guilty!"

"Longarm, I know I've done wrong, now and again, but you've got to believe me, I'm only—"

"A professional thief who's done more than one stretch at hard labor. You think I don't recognize the breed on sight? No man has ever come out of a prison without that whining, self-serving look of injured innocence. So save me the details of your misspent youth. I've heard how you were just a poor little war orphan, trying as best he could to make his way in this cruel, cold world he never made. I know how the Missouri Pacific stole your widowed mother's farm. You've told me about the way they framed you for borrowing that first pony to fetch the doctor to your dying little sister's side. You've told me every time I've run you in."

"That's crazy. You never seen me before!"

"Oh, yes, I have. I've seen you come whining and I've had it out with you in many a dark alley. The other day I killed you in a barber shop. Sometimes you're tall, sometimes you're short, and the features may shift some from time to time. But I always know you when we meet. You always have that innocent, wide-eyed look and that same self-pity in your bullshit. I know you good, old son. Likely better than you know yourself!"

"You sure talk funny, mister."

"I'm a barrel of laughs. You just set while I saddle up the mounts. We're almost to the high prairies near the south pass and we have to ride a full day out in the open. You reckon you know how to sit a McClellan with your hands behind you, now? Or do I have to tie you to the swells?"

"I don't want to be tied on. Listen, wouldn't it make

more sense to wait for dark before we hit open ground?"

"Nope. We have them others coming at us through the trees right now. I figure we can get maybe ten, twelve miles out before they break free of the trees. I'd say they'll be *here* this afternoon. By then we'll be two bitty dots against the low sun. The course I'm setting ain't the one they'll be expecting, but there's no way to hide our trail by daylight. If we make the railroad tracks sometime after dark, they'll cut around the short way, figuring to stop any train I can flag down."

"What's the point of lighting out for the tracks then, if they'll know right off what your plan is?"

"You mean what they'll *think* my plan is, don't you?"

Chapter 15

The moon was high, washing the surrounding grasslands in pale silver as the prisoner sat his mount, watching Longarm's dark outline climb the last few feet to the crossbar of the telegraph pole beside the tracks. He called up, "See anything?"

Longarm called back, "Yeah. Campfire, maybe fifteen miles off. Big fire. Likely a big bunch after us. Leastways, that's what they want me to think. You just hush, now. I got work to do."

Longarm took the small, skeletonized telegraph key he'd had in his kit and rested it on the crossbar as he went to work with his jackknife. He spliced a length of his own thin copper wire to the Western Union line, and spliced in the Union Pacific's operating line, next to it.

He attached a last wire and the key started to buzz like a bee, it's coils confused by conflicting messages on the two lines he'd spliced into. Longarm waited until the operators up and down the transcontinental line stopped sending; they were no doubt confused by the short circuit. Then he put a finger on his own key and tapped out a rapid message in Morse code. He got most of it off before the electromagnet went mad again as some idiot tried to ask what the hell was going on.

Longarm slid down the pole, mounted his own stolen horse, and said, "Let's go." He led them west along the right-of-way. He rode them on the ties and ballast between the rails. The horses found it rough going and stumbled from time to time. As the bay lurched under the prisoner, he protested, "Wouldn't it be easier on the grass all about?" Longarm said, "Yep. Leave more hoofprints, too. Reading sign on railroad ballast is a bitch. That halo forming around the moon promises rain by sunup. *Wet* railroad ballast is even tougher to read."

"What was that message you sent on the telegraph wire?"

"Sent word to my boss I was still breathing and had you tagging along. Told him I wasn't able to transport you by rail and where I was hoping to meet up with such help as he might see fit to send me."

"We're headed for Thayer Junction, right?"

"What makes you think that?"

"Well, hell, we're at least ten miles northwest of Bitter Creek and headed the wrong way. You reckon we'll make Thayer Junction 'fore the rain hits?"

"For a man who says he don't know many train robbers, you've got a right smart railroad map in your head. By the way, I've been meaning to ask: where *did* you figure to run a cow you stole in Crooked Lance? It's a far piece to herd stolen cows alone, ain't it?"

"I keep telling ever'body, I was only passing through! I had no intentions on the redheaded widow's cows."

"But you had a running iron for changing brands. A thing no cow thief with a brain would carry a full day on him if it could be avoided. So tell me, were you just stupid, or did you maybe have one or two sidekicks with you? If there were sidekicks who didn't get caught by the vigilantes it would answer some questions I've been mulling over."

"I was riding alone. If I had any friends worth mention in that durned valley I'd have been long gone before you got there!"

"That sounds reasonable. I sprung you solo. A friend of yours with the hair on his chest to snipe at folks would likely be able to take out Pop Wade, or even the two I whupped some civilization into. That wasn't much

127

of a jail they had you in, Younger. How come you didn't bust out on your own?"

"I studied on it. We're *doing* what stopped me. I figured a couple of ways to bust out, but knew I'd have Timberline and all them others chasing me. Knew if they caught me more'n a mile from the Widow Stover and some of the older folks in Crooked Lance they'd gun me down like a dog. Timberline wanted to kill me when they drug me from the brush that first day."

"He does seem a testy cuss, for a big man. Most big fellers tend to be more easy-going. What do you reckon made him so down on you, aside from that running iron in your possibles?"

"That's easy. He thought I was Cotton Younger, too. Lucky for me he blurted the same out to the widow as she was standing there. When he said I was a wanted owlhoot who deserved a good hanging, she asked was the reward worth mention, and the rest you know."

"Timeberline's been up here in the high country for half a dozen years or more. How'd he figure you to be a member of the James-Younger gang?"

"The vigilance committee has all these durned reward posters stuck up where they meet, out to the widow's barn. That's their lodge hall. Understand they hold a meeting there once a week."

"Sure seems odd to take the vigilante business so serious in a town where a funeral's a rare occasion for an all-day hootenanny. While you was locked up all them weeks did you hear tell how many other owlhoots they've run in?"

"Pop Wade says they ain't had much trouble since the Shoshone Rising a few years back. Shoshone never rode into that particular valley, but that's when they formed the vigilantes. They likely kept it formed 'cause the widow serves coffee and cakes at the meetings and, what the hell, it ain't like they had a opera house."

"Kim Stover's more or less the head of it, eh?"

"Yep, she inherited the chairmanship from her husband when the herd run him down, a year or so ago.

128

Pop Wade's the jailer and keeps the minutes 'cause he was in the army, one time."

"And Timberline's the muscle, along with the hired hands at his and other spreads up and down the valley. You hear talk about him tracking anyone else down since he took the job?"

"No. Like I said, things have been peaceable in Crooked Lance of late. Reckon they're taking this thing so serious 'cause it beats whittling as a way to pass the time. You figure it should be easy to throw them part-time posse men off our trail, huh?"

"They'd have lost us long ago if we only had to worry about cowhands. I'm hoping that Mountie joined up with 'em, along with Captain Walthers and the bounty-hunting Hanks family. Mountie'd be able to follow less sign than we've been leaving."

"Jesus! You reckon this rough ride down these damn tracks will throw him off?"

"Slow him, some. Hang on, we're getting off to one side. I see a headlamp coming up the grade."

Longarm led his mounted prisoner away from the track at a jogging trot until they were well away from the right-of-way. Then, as the sound of a chuffing locomotive climbed toward them on the far side of a cut, he reined them to a halt and said, "Rest easy a minute. Soon as the eastbound passes I'll unroll my slicker and a poncho for you. I can smell the rain, following that train at a mile of so down the tracks."

"We're right out in the open, here!"

"That's all right. The cabin crew's watching the head-lamp beam down the tracks ahead of 'em. Folks inside can't see out worth mention through the glass lit from inside. Didn't your cousin Jesse ever tell you that?"

Before the prisoner could protest his innocence again the noisy Baldwin six-wheeler charged out of the cut and passed them in a haze of wet smoke and stirred-up ballast dust. Longarm waited until the two red lamps of the rear platform were fading away to the east before he put Captain Walthers's poncho over the prisoner and started struggling into the evil-smelling stickiness of his own tightly rolled, oilcloth slicker. He smoothed it down over his legs, covering himself from the shoulders to ankles, but didn't snap the fasteners below a single one at the collar. He'd almost been killed, once, trying to draw his gun inside a wet slicker he'd been fool enough to button down the front.

In the distance, the locomotive sounded its whistle. Longarm nodded and said, "They've stopped the train to search for us. Means one of 'em flashed a badge or such at the engineer. Means at least five minutes for 'em to make certain we didn't flag her down for a ride. I'd say the searching's going on about six or eight miles from here. Must be the Mountie leading."

He heard a soft tap on his hat brim and smiled thinly, saying, "Here comes the rain. Hang on."

He led off, south-southwest, away from the track and up a gentle grade in the growing darkness of the rain-drowned moonlight. The prisoner called out, "Where in thunder do you think you're going? The railroad hugs the south edge of the gap through the Great Divide!"

"We're on the west side of the divide, now. All this rain coming down is headed into the Pacific, save what gets stuck in the Great Basin 'twixt here and the Sierra Nevadas."

"Jehosaphat, are we bound for California?"

"Nope, Green River country, once we cross some higher ground."

"Have you gone plumb out of your head? There's no way to get from here to the headwaters of the Green, and if there was, there's nothing there! The Green River's birthed in wild canyon lands unfit for man or beast!"

"You been there, Younger?"

"No, but I heard about it. It's the wildest, roughest, most tore-up stretch of the Rocky Mountains!"

"Not quite. We got to ride over *that* part before we *get* to Green River country."

130

Chapter 16

Longarm took advantage of the remaining darkness to cover most of the gently rolling Aspen Range between the U.P. tracks and the mighty ramparts of the Green River Divide. Morning caught them winding up a trail fetlock-deep in running rainwater. They were above the hardwoods, now, and rode through gloomy corridors of sombre, dripping spruce. Longarm took a deep breath, and while the smell of the rain-washed timber was pleasant, the air was a mite thin for breathing. He knew he was good for a run up Pike's Peak to even thinner air, but he had to consider the horses. He led slowly on the upgrades and resisted the temptation to trot when the trail, from time to time, ran downhill a few yards.

Even covered with waterproof canvas and oilcloth, they were both damp and chilled to the bone by now. Somewhere above them the sun was trying to break through, but the sky was a fuzzy gray blanket of wet, dripping wool. Off through clearings in the timber, silver veils of rain whipped back and forth in the morning breezes like the cobwebs of a haunted pagan temple. From time to time one of the mountain gods roared majestically in the sky and another spruce died in a blinding lightning flash. More than once that morning lightning whip-cracked down too closely for comfort, but Longarm took little notice of things he couldn't do anything about. Folks who were afraid of lightning had no business riding in the high country. Electrical storms went with the territory.

Somewhere in the dripping tanglewood they crossed the Utah line.

There was no sign-post, no natural feature. Someone back in Washington had drawn a line with a ruler on the map. Half of the jumbled peaks and ridges had never been properly surveyed by a white man. The way the Rockies had been thrown together here made little sense to the Indians, who said Lord Grizzly and the Great Spirit had wrestled in the Days of Creation and left the Shining Mountains as their trampled footprints in the torn-up earth of their Great Buffalo Grounds.

Longarm reined in near a giant potato of lichen-covered granite that leaned toward the trail, and helped the prisoner down, saying, "We got to spell the mounts on foot for a while. I'm going to build a fire and dry our bones a mite."

"Could I have these cuffs in front of me for a change? My shoulder sockets are sore as hell."

"I'll study on it. Just stand against the rock and dry off some while I find something dry enough to light."

He did think about the prisoner's discomfort as he peeled damp bark from spruce branches and dug dry punk from under the soaked forest duff at the base of the rock. Unless the prisoner was a superb actor, he was neither bright nor given to sudden courage. He'd let them hold him for nearly a month in a ramshackle log jail guarded by old Pop and unskilled cowboy jail guards. Longarm took a spare cartridge, pulled the slug with his teeth, and sprinkled loose powder into the dry punk between his whittled frizz-stick kindling and struck a match to it. There was a warm, smoky *whoosh* and Longarm put his face near the ground to blow into the smoldering beginnings before he leaned back, squatting on his boot heels almost atop the little Indian hand-warmer and suggested, "Put your hands in front of you, if you want."

"Don't you have to unlock these blamed cuffs, first?"

" 'Course not. Ain't you ever worn irons before?"

"Not often enough to know how to unlock 'em with no key."

"Hell, scrootch down on your heels till your hands are on the ground. Then just haul your ass and feet over the chain between your wrists. That'll leave your hands in front of you when you stand up."

The prisoner looked puzzled, but slid down the rock, fumbling about under the poncho and grunting as he got his knees up against his chin and struggled. Then he suddenly grinned and said, "I done it! My hands is in front of me! Why'd you have me chained like this so long when you must have knowed all the time a man could work his hands to a more comforting place?"

"Wanted to see how educated you were. You got a lot to learn if you intend to follow your chosen trade serious."

The prisoner moved closer to the fire, putting his numb, linked hands out from under the poncho to warm them as he grinned and asked, "Are you starting to believe I ain't one of the James-Younger gang?"

"Don't matter what I believe. My job's to take you in. Save the tales for the judge."

"Wouldn't you let me go if I could get you to believe my real name's Jones?"

"Nope. They never sent me to find out who you were. Like I said, you could be named Victoria Regina and I'd still deliver you to Denver, Lord willing that we ever get there."

"You're a hard man, Longarm."

"Hell, you don't know what hard can get to or you'd know better than to wander about with a running iron and a name like Jones. I know a dozen deputies who would have gunned you by now just 'cause it's easier and safer to transport a dead man. The papers on you said dead or alive, as I remember."

"Jesus, meeting up with you has given me second thoughts on stealing cows for a living. When they find out I'm not Cotton Younger and cut me loose, I reckon I'll go back to washing dishes!"

Longarm didn't answer. The boy was a born thief, whether he was Cotton Younger or some other reprobate. There was maybe one chance in a hundred that he was telling the truth and that this had all been a fool's errand. The odds of the prisoner living to a ripe old age hadn't changed worth mentioning. If they didn't hang him this year for being Cotton Younger, they'd hang him sooner or later anyway. He was a shifty-eyed and probably vicious thief, no matter how it turned out in Denver.

The prisoner glanced up and said, "Smoke's rising over the top of this rock shelter. You reckon anyone can see it?"

"Not unless they're close enough to smell it. The whole sky is filled with drifting gray."

"How much of a lead do you reckon we have, Longarm?"

"Can't say. We took the two best mounts I knew of and they're bound to be held back by the slowest pony in the posse, 'less they like to ride after an armed man all strung out. I suspicion we're a good fifteen miles or more out front. We'd be farther if somebody wasn't leading who knows his business."

"Yeah. They'd have had to be cat-eyed and hound-nosed to follow us along the railroad tracks like they done."

"Hell, they didn't follow us by reading sign. They followed us by *knowing*. I'd say they sent a party in to Bitter Creek and another down the track, covering all bets. They got more riders than they need, so they ain't riding bunched together. They'll be split into half a dozen patrols, sweeping everywhere we'd be likely to head."

"Jesus, how you figure to shake 'em, then?"

"Don't. Not all of 'em. No matter which fork we take, at least half of 'em will be following us up the right one. Ought to whittle 'em down some if we keep offering choices."

134

"I see what you mean. How many men you reckon you can hold off if any of 'em catch up?"

"Not one, if he's better than me. Any number if they don't know how to fight. I doubt if they'll dare split up into parties of less than a dozen. I'm hoping the Mountie won't make me shoot him. Man could get in trouble with the State Department, shooting guests."

"He'll as likely be riding off with someone in the wrong direction as on our trail, won't he?"

"Nope. The only ones likely to follow the right trail are the *good* trackers."

He threw another faggot on the fire, watching it steam dry enough to burn as he mused, half to himself, "The cooler heads among the party will likely stay attached to Sergeant Foster. So if push comes to shove we'll be up against Timberline, the Hankses, maybe even Captain Walthers. He's likely riled about me stealing his walker and would know the Mountie knows his business."

"If we get cornered, you could give me a gun and I'd be proud to side you, Longarm."

"Not hardly. I never sprung you from that jail to shoot U.S. or Canadian peace officers. Don't like getting shot all that much myself."

"Hell, you don't think I'd be dumb enough to try to gun *you*, do you?"

"You'll never get the chance from me, so we'll most likely never know."

"Listen, you can't let 'em take me, handcuffed like this! You'd have to give me a chance for my life!"

"Son, you had that chance, before you took to stealing from folks."

"Gawd! You mean you'd let 'em kill me, if it comes down to you or me?"

"If it comes down to you or me? That's a fool question. I'd boil you in oil to save myself a hangnail, but don't fret about it. We're both a long way from caught up with."

It didn't stop raining. They rode out of the storm that afternoon by getting above the clouds. The slanting rays of the sun warmed and dried them as they rode over the frost-shattered rocks where stunted junipers grew like contorted green gnomes on either side. Cushion flowers peeked at them between boulders, not daring to raise a twig high enough for the cruel, thin winds to bite them off. Surprised, invisible ground squirrels chattered at them from either side of the trail, which now was little more than a meandering flatness between patches of treacherous scree or dusty snow patches. The air was still, and drier than a mummy's arm pit, but only warm where the sun shone through it. Each juniper's shadow they rode through held the chill of the void between the planets. They passed a last wind-crippled little tree and knew they'd reached the timberline. It wasn't a real line painted over the shattered scree, it was simply that after you got high enough on a mountain, nothing grew tall enough to matter.

Longarm led them to a saddle between higher, snow-covered peaks to the east and west, and at the summit of the pass, reined in for a moment.

There was nothing to see back the way they'd ridden but the carpet of pink-tinged clouds, spread clear to the far horizon with an occasional peak rising like an island above the storm below them.

The prisoner asked, "See anybody?"

Longarm snorted, "We'd be in a hell of a fix if I did. Let's ride."

The other side of the pass was a mirror image of the one they'd just ridden up. The prisoner looked down into the carpet of cloud spread out ahead of them and groaned, "Hell, I was just getting comfortable."

"We ain't riding for comfort. We're riding for your life, and Denver. How long you figure to live once we get there ain't my worry."

"How far do you reckon Denver is, Longarm?"

"About four hundred miles, as the crow flies. We ain't riding crows, so it's likely a mite farther."

"Four hundred miles across the top of the world with half of it chasing us? Jehosaphat, I wish I was back in that fool jail!"

"No, you don't. They would have buried you by now. By the way, you made a deal with that midget to save yourself from a necktie party. You mind telling me what it was?"

"I told you. He said he'd get me out if I'd tell him where Jesse James was hiding."

"I remember. Whereabouts did you say that was?"

"Hell, *I* don't know! I'd'a said most anything to get my ass out of there!"

"Well, your ass is out. What did you aim to tell Cedric Hanks?"

"I told you. He said he'd get me out if I'd tell him some yarn."

"Spin her my way, then. I listen as good as anyone."

"Oh, hell, I dunno. I'd'a likely told him the stuff as is going around the barrooms. You ask any two men where the James boys went after that big shootout in Minnesota and you get three answers."

"Which one do you reckon makes most sense?"

"You heard about them lighting out to Mexico?"

"Sure, and I don't like it much. The James boys has gotten by all these years by hiding out amid friends and kinfolks they grew up with.

"They have to be somewhere in or damn near Missouri. Surprise me if they was even far from Kansas City. Clay County's been pretty well searched over, but they'll be somewhere in the Missouri River drainage when we catch up with 'em. That fool raid they made up into Minnesota likely taught 'em the value of hiding out with folks they can trust to keep a secret."

"I did hear one story about Saint Joe. Where is that from Kansas City?"

"Up the river a few hours by steamboat. I heard it, too. Sheriff of Buchanan County wires that nobody's held up anybody in or about Saint Joe."

"Well, I hear tell Jesse and Frank is trying to g(

straight. You see, Cole Younger was the real brains behind the gang, and with him in prison—"

"You just lost me, boy. Why do you fellers always spin that same old yarn about being led astray by wicked companions? Goddam James boys has been robbing and killing folks since before they knew why boys and gals were different. If you'd told that midget that Jesse James is reformed after fifteen years of shooting at everybody but his mother, he'd have laughed before he killed you. Though, come to think of it, the Hankses were figuring to kill you anyway."

The light began to fade again as they rode down into the clouds beyond the pass. The top of the storm was only cold and damp, but they were back in rain before they rode under man-sized timber again. The prisoner asked. "When are we fixing to make camp?" and Longarm shot back, "We made it, over on the other side."

"You aim to just keep riding, into the night as she falls?"

"Nope. We'll rest the critters, along about midnight. If it's still raining, we'll build a fire. If it ain't, we won't."

"Gawd, you're fixing to kill me *and* the horses the way you're pushing us!"

"Ain't worried about you. The critters and me know how hard we can push."

"Listen, you said by now we don't have more'n a third or so of the bunch from Crooked Lance trailing us."

"Maybe less. Day or so on a cold, wet trail can take the first flush off the enthusiasm. More'n one will have given up by now, I suspicion."

"We've passed a dozen good places to make a stand. I mean, that Winchester of yours might discourage anybody."

"You want me to bushwhack fellow peace officers?"

"Why not? They're out to kill us, ain't they?"

"That's their worry. It wouldn't be neighborly of me to blow holes in anybody wearing a badge. And I don't

138

want to hurt any of them fool cowhands either, if it can be helped."

"Longarm, these fool horses ain't about to carry us no four hundred miles in country like this!"

"I know. It gets even rougher where we're headed."

Chapter 17

The Green River is born from countless streams in the Uinta Range, a crossgrained spur of the Rockies, rubbing its spine against the sky near where Wyoming, Utah and Colorado come together on the map. As Longarm had thought before, those lines were put there on the map by government men who'd never seen the country and wouldn't have liked it much if they had.

The Green makes a big bend into Colorado in its upper reaches, then turns toward the junction with the brawling Colorado River near the southern border of Utah. To get there, the Green runs through canyonlands unfit for most Indians to consider as a home. The Denver & Rio Grande's western division crossed the Green halfway to Arizona's Navajo lands at a small settlement called, naturally, Green River. The lack of imagination implied by the name was the simple result of not having to name any other towns to the north or south in Longarm's day.

They didn't follow the river when they reached it. For one thing, the cliffs came right down to the boiling rapids along many a stretch. For another, Longarm knew the men trailing him might expect him to try this. So he led his prisoner the shorter way, across the big bend. The shorter way was not any easier; the route took them through a maze of canyons where the floors were choked with brush and the steep, ugly slopes of eroded shale smelled like hot road tar where the sun beat down on it.

They'd been riding for three full days by now and

Longarm figured they were nearly a hundred miles from Crooked Lance. Anyone who was still trailing them wanted pretty badly to have the prisoner back.

It was a hot and dusty afternoon when they hauled over another pass, and looking back, spied dust in the saddle of a shale ridge they'd crossed several hours before.

Longarm tugged the lead and muttered, "That Mountie's damn good," as he started them down the far side. Captain Walthers's big walker had proven a disappointment to him on the trail. The army man had chosen it for show and comfort, not for serious riding over rough country, and while the bay he'd gotten from the remount section was still holding up, the walker under him was heaving badly and walking with its head down.

The prisoner called out, "I might have seen a dot of red back there. That'd be the Mountie's jacket, right?"

"Yeah. I saw it, too. Watch yourself, and if that bay starts to slide out from under you, try to fall on the high side. This shale is treacherous as hell."

"Smells awful, too! What in thunder is it?"

"Oil shale. Whole country's made out of it. Gets slippery when the heat boils the oil out of the rock."

As if to prove his point, the walker he was riding suddenly shot out from under him and forward, down the slope. Longarm cursed, tried to steady his mount with the reins, and seeing that it was no use, rolled out of the saddle as the screaming horse slid halfway down the mountain.

Longarm landed on one hip and shoulder, rolled to his feet, and bounced a few yards on his heels, before he caught a juniper bush and came to a standing stop. He looked quickly back and saw that the bay had stopped safely with the prisoner still aboard. He yelled, "Stay put!" and started down the slope of sharp, slick shale in the dusty wake of his fallen mount.

The walker was trying to struggle to its feet at the bottom of the rise, screaming in dumb terror and pain. Longarm could see it hadn't broken any bones. It had

141

simply gutted itself on the sharp rocks after sliding a full two hundred yards down the trail!

He drew his .44 as he approached the dreadfully injured gelding with soothing words. The animal got halfway to its feet, its forelegs out in front of it and its rump high, as its bloody intestines writhed over the cruel, sunbaked surface. Then Longarm fired, twice, when he saw the first round hadn't completely shattered the poor brute's brain.

Swearing blackly, he stepped over to the quivering carcass and got his Winchester and other possessions free, glad it was the captain's saddle he didn't have to mess with cleaning. He put the rifle and supplies on a rock and walked up to where the prisoner watched with a silly grin on his face.

Longarm said, "It ain't funny. Guess who gets to walk?"

"Hell, I don't aim to stay up here like this with the ground under hoof greased so funny!"

Longarm helped him down and led both him and the bay to where he'd piled the other things. As he lashed everything worth carrying to the surviving mount's saddle, the prisoner asked, "You figure we got enough of a lead on them other fellers, with one pony betwixt us?"

"No. Riding double or walking, we ain't got till sunset before they make rifle range on us."

"You don't mean to leave me, do you?"

"Not hardly. Just keep walking."

"Listen, Longarm, if you was to turn me loose afoot I'd be willing to take my chances. I could cover my boot prints, I reckon, if you just rode on, leaving 'em a few horseshoe marks and a turd or two on the trail."

"Didn't carry you all this way to lose you, Younger. You see that half-bowl in the cliffs across the creek we're headed down to?"

"Sure. It looks to be a blind alley, though. A rifleman could doubtless make a good stand in there, but the walls behind him would be sheer."

"I know. We'll dig in there, behind such rocks as

we'll have time to fort up in front of us. 'Bout the time they make it to the dead horse, I'll spook 'em with a few rifle rounds and they'll fan out ever' which way, diving for cover. By then it'll be getting dark."

"What's to stop 'em from working around behind us, up on the rim rocks?"

"You want to climb a shale oil cliff in the dark? They won't have us circled tight before, oh, a couple of hours after sunup."

He led the handcuffed man across the ankle-deep creek and up the talus slope beyond to the amphitheater some ancient disaster had carved from the cliff face. He sat the prisoner down beside the tired bay he'd tethered to a bush and proceeded to pile slabs of shale between them and the valley they faced. The dead walker was a chestnut blob across the way. It was just at the range Longarm was sure he could handle. Any man who said he knew where a bullet was going once it got past three hundred yards, was a liar.

The prisoner said, "If you'd take these cuffs off, I could help."

"You want to help, take the horse up-slope as far as you can and tie him to something, then come back."

"Won't he be exposed up there?"

"Sure. Out of range, too. They'll spot him, but so what? They'll know we're here. Might save me a round if they grow cautious before I have to waste good lead just funning."

"Won't they know, once you miss a couple of times, that you don't mean to kill nobody?"

"Don't aim to miss by all that much, and if it comes down to real hard feelings, I've been known to draw blood, in my time."

The prisoner led the bay away, and by the time he returned, Longarm had erected a breast-high wall of slabs.

He said, "Look around for some sticks, dry grass, and such. You can work as well with your hands together."

143

"There ain't enough dry weeds and cheat-grass here for a real fire, Longarm. The thing you had in mind was a fire, wasn't it?"

"Get moving. I got some shifting to do, here on this breastwork."

"I'm moving, I'm moving, but you are pure loco! What in thunder do we want with a fire, not saying we could build one?"

Longarm didn't answer. He was a fair hand at dry-wall construction and figured his improvisation would stand up to anything but a four-pound cannon ball, and he knew they wouldn't be bringing along heavy artillery.

He saw the prisoner was doing a shiftless job at gathering dry tinder, so he went to work himself, gathering an armful of bone-dry weeds and cheat-grass stems. He threw it in a pile a few yards back from his stone wall.

The prisoner added his own smaller offering and Longarm started putting chips of shale on the tinder, with smaller fragments first and some fair-sized slabs topping off the cairn.

The prisoner watched bemusedly, as Longarm struck a match and set the dry weeds alight. As the acrid blue smoke of burning cheat curled up through the rocks he said, "I can see you're trying to cook them rocks. What I can't figure out is why."

Then a thicker smoke, coiling like an oily serpent, slithered up and through the shale slabs to catch a vagrant tendril of breeze and float skyward like a blob of ink against the blue of the sky.

Longarm said, "Oil shale burns, sort of. Learned it from a friendly Ute, last time I passed this way."

"That's for damn sure! Look at it catch! Burns with a damn black smoke, though. You says there's Utes in this neck of the woods?"

"Utes, if we're lucky, Shoshone if we ain't."

"You figure they'll see this smoke signal and come running?"

"They'll more'n likely come creeping, wondering who's here in their hunting grounds. Not many white

144

men have ever been this way and Indians are curious cusses."

"Won't the white boys trailing us see the smoke, too?"

"If they've got eyes they've seen it by now. They won't know if it's us or some Shoshones fixing to lift their hair."

"Hot damn! It may just turn 'em back, don't you reckon?"

"Not hardly. Men willing to chase a man with my rep and a Winchester don't scare so easy. If they read this smoke as Indian signals, it might slow 'em to a cautious move-in, though. I'm hoping they won't be here too long before sundown. If they climb up behind us in good light, we're in one hell of a fix."

"What's to stop 'em doing it tomorrow just after sunup?"

"Tomorrow is another day, and like I keep saying, you eat the apple a bite at a time."

"Yeah, I figure you got maybe twelve to fifteen hours before your apple's all et, too! Man up there on the rim above us could save ammo and likely kill us just by chucking down some rocks! You reckon you could pick a man off against that skyline up there?"

"Doubt it. It's about a quarter-mile straight up. Things look closer than they really are in this clear air of the high country."

"But he'd have no trouble shooting down, would he?"

"Not hardly. Likely miss his first few shots, but we'll have no cover, and like you said, a fistful of rock could do us in, thrown down from that height."

"Gawd, you're pretty cheerful about it all, considering!"

"Well, losing that horse threw me off my feed for a few minutes back there, but we're in pretty fair shape again."

"The hell you say! Can't you see the fix they got us in, Longarm?"

"Yep. They'll likely figure it the same way and move in slow and careful, like I want 'em to. Hate to have to hurt anybody who don't deserve a hurt, this close to the end of our game."

"Longarm, I am purely missing something or you are out of your fool head! We are boxed in here with our backs to a quarter-mile-high cliff! You got a rifle and a pistol to hold off Gawd knows what-all in the way of white folks, and likely a tribe or two of Injuns!"

"Yep. Nearest Utes are about a ten-hour ride away. Boys from Crooked Lance should get here sooner."

"Then what in tarnation are you grinning about? You look like a mean old weasel some dumb farmer just put to work guarding his hen house for the night!"

"I'll allow some chicken-thieving tricks have crossed my mine since we lost that horse back there. I was worried we might have thrown 'em off our trail, too, till I spied that Canadian's fool red coat on the far horizon. You reckon they wear them red tunics to make a good target or to impress the Cree, up Canada way?"

"Back up. What was that about not trying to throw 'em off our trail? Are you saying you could have lost 'em in the mountains?"

"Hell, can a jaybird suck robin's eggs? I'll allow that Sergeant Foster's a fair tracker, but I've been tracked by Apache in my time, and lost 'em good."

"In other words, you've been playing ring-around-the-rosie with them Crooked Lance vigilantes all this time?"

"Sure. Hadn't you figured as much? Hell, a pissant like *you* could have lost 'em by now! We've been over some rough ground in the last few days, boy. You mind when we crossed that ten-mile stretch of bare granite yesterday? Had to drop some spent cartridges along the way, pretending we'd been shooting birds for provisions. They know I pack .44-40 ammo, so . . ."

"But *why*, Gawd damn it? I thought your mission was to bring me in to Denver safe and sound!"

"I aim to. But I'm a peace officer, too. Can't see my

146

way to leave folks disturbing the peace and carrying on like wild men on federal range land, can I?"

"You mean you aim to arrest somebody riding with that posse of vigilantes?"

"Nope. If things go as I've planned, I aim to arrest the whole damn kit and caboodle!"

Chapter 18

It was getting late when Longarm spied the red tunic of Sergeant Foster on the skyline, far up the other wall of the valley. The Mountie had others with him. One rider was too tall in the saddle to be anyone but Timberline. Another distant figure had to be the midget, Cedric Hanks. Longarm looked for anyone riding sidesaddle, but the little detective had apparently left Mabel behind. He counted a good dozen-and-a-half heads up there and the sunlight flashing on glass told him Foster was sweeping the valley floor with field glasses. He'd probably seen the dead horse down on the far side of the creek. He had to have seen the big black mushroom of oil smoke still rising behind them.

Longarm turned to the prisoner at his side and said, "Lie down behind this barricade and stay put. I'll be too busy to keep more'n a corner of my eye on you and I get testy if folks interfere when I'm working."

"Longarm, we are boxed in here like mice in a cracker barrel with the cat peering over the top!"

"Just do as you're told and hush. They're moving down, sort of slow. I'll tell you what's going on, so's to rest your mind. Don't you raise your fool head, though. I only aim to have my own to worry about!"

"What are they doing now, then?"

"What you'd expect. There's only one trail down from the top, so they're riding down in file, and slow. Likely having as much trouble with that shale as we did . . . yep, pony just slipped some, but its rider

148

steadied it nicely. Looks like that redheaded Kim Stover. She sure sits a horse pretty."

"Jehosaphat! Ever'body from Crooked Lance is coming to pay us a call with guns, and all you can talk about is how pretty that redhead is!"

"Hell, she *is* pretty, ain't she? I'd say Pop Wade must be laying for us with some of the others in Bitter Creek. Don't see Slim Wilson. He'd have led another bunch along the tracks west of Thayer Junction, most likely. The big hoo-rahs are sticking with the Mountie. All except Captain Walthers. He's with one of the other scouting parties. That's good. I was wondering what he'd say about me gutting his walker."

Longarm removed his Stetson and placed it on a rock atop his wall, peering through a loophole he'd left below the highest course of shale slabs. He moved the muzzle of his Winchester into position and levered a round into the chamber as the band of riders across the way reined in and began to dismount, just upslope from the dead horse. He nodded and said, "Good thinking. They see this wall in front of the smoke and have the range figured. Yep, I see some of 'em's fanning out, working the rocks for cover."

"Longarm, we don't stand a chance here!"

"Sure we do. They daren't come much closer. They'll stay on the other side of the creek for now."

The Mountie, Foster, approached on foot until he was well within range at the edge of the stream. He took off his hat and waved it, calling out, "I see you, Longarm! You've made a big mistake, Yank!"

Longarm didn't answer.

"You can see that it's eighteen to one! You want to parley or have you gone completely mad?"

Longarm called back, "What's your deal, Foster?"

"Don't be an idiot! You know I'm taking Cotton Younger back to Canada!"

"Do tell? Speaking of idiots, I just saw one wearing a red coat! You really think the others will let you ride north with him, Foster?"

"Yes. We've made our own compromise. The people of Crooked Lance are only interested in the reward for Jesse James. They say the prisoner is mine, once we get a few facts out of him!"

"Sure he is. Why don't you just move back out of range for a spell?"

"We've got you trapped in there, Longarm!"

Longarm didn't answer. Foster wasn't saying anything interesting and it was a far piece to holler.

A rifle suddenly squibbed from among the rocks across the way and Longarm's hat flew off the wall as Foster spun on his heel and ran for cover, shouting, "Stop that, you damned fool!"

Longarm considered speeding him on his way with a round of his own, but it didn't look like the Mountie could run much faster. The shot they'd put through the crown of his hat had sounded like a Henry deer-load, not a .30-30. Longarm marked the rock its smoke was drifting away from and intended to remember it. Timberline and the girl were behind that other big boulder to the left of it. Likely one of the hands had gotten silly. The midget, Hanks, was behind that low slab, and was almost certainly too slick to be taken in by the old hat trick.

Someone else fired from behind another rock, so Longarm bounced a slug off it to teach him some manners, moving to another loophole with his gun since the one he'd fired from proceeded to eat lead. Longarm counted and marked each of the smoke puffs as they fired at the place he'd just been. A woman's voice was screaming at them to stop firing, but the prisoner at his side was spooked too badly to listen. He was suddenly up and running—running in a blind panic up the slope toward the sheer cliff of the amphitheater. Longarm yelled, "Hang it all! Get *back* here, you fool!" But it was too late. The handcuffed prisoner staggered, fell to his hands and knees, and rolled over. Then he was up again and running back to Longarm, eyes wide and mouth hanging open, in a rattle of small arms fire!

Something hit the prisoner hard enough to stagger him, but he kept coming and in another few seconds was stretched out behind the wall, sobbing and carrying on like a cat whose tail had been stomped.

Longarm snorted, "Jesus H. Christ! Of all the fool stunts! Where'd they hit you?"

"All over! I've been killed!"

The gunfire died away as cooler heads prevailed across the way. The big lawman crawled over to the prisoner and rolled him onto his back. He whistled thoughtfully and sighed, "Damn it, you *did* get hit, boy! The one in your shoulder ain't worth mention. But the one in your side don't look so good. You feel like throwing up?"

"I just want to be someplace else! *Any*place else! I'm too young to die!"

"You just hold on and lie still, then. You ain't bleeding too bad. I'll stuff some wadding in the wound and wrap it tight for you."

"Gawd, I'm so thirsty, all of a sudden! Can I have a drink of canteen water?"

Longarm had been afraid he'd say that. He shook his head and said, "You're gut-shot, you poor, dumb son of a bitch! What ever made you do a fool thing like that?"

"I was scared! I'm still scared! You reckon I'm fixing to die?"

"Not for a few hours."

"You said you was fixing to bandage me. Ain't you aiming to?"

"No. Best to let the gas escape as it forms. You just lie there quiet. That fool Mountie over yonder's waving his hanky at me and I'd like to see what he wants."

Longarm called out, "That's close enough, Foster!" and the Mountie halted, holding a white kerchief in his hand as he called back, "That wasn't my idea, Longarm. Did they kill him?"

"Nope. But you're starting to piss me off. Why don't you all settle down and make some coffee or something? You know you daren't rush me before dark and

151

somebody figures to get hurt with all this wild shooting."

"Longarm, it's not my job to have a bloodbath here. Why can't you listen to reason?"

"Hell, I'm about as reasonable as anyone for a hundred country miles. You'd best ride home to Canada before they turn on you, Foster. You ain't taking my prisoner, now that I have him. Not without killing a U.S. Deputy Marshal for your durned old queen!"

"Damn it! That's what I'm trying to prevent! This gunplay's not my idea, Longarm, but your only chance is to hand the prisoner over."

"You're not only pissing me off, you're starting to bore the shit out of me! It's tedious talking in circles and we've all had our say. So ride on out, or join in and be damned to you!"

The Canadian lawman walked back to the boulder that Timberline and the girl were behind. The wounded prisoner gasped, "What's going on?"

"Beats me. They'll likely jaw about it for a spell. How are you feeling?"

"Terrible. It don't look like I'm gonna make it to Denver, does it?"

Longarm didn't answer.

"It's funny, but I ain't as scared now, as I was. You reckon it's on account of I'm dying?"

"Maybe. Most men are more scared of it when it's coming than when it actually arrives. You might make it, though. I've seen men hit worse and they've pulled through."

"They say a man knows when he's sinking, but I can't tell. It's funny, but I'd rest easier if I knew for sure, one way or the other."

"Yep, I know what you mean. You got anything you'd like to get off your chest while there's still time, old son?"

"You mean, like a deathbed confession?"

"Must be some comfort to such, since we get so many of 'em."

152

The wounded man thought a while, breathing oddly. Then he licked his lips and said, "You might as well know, then. My name ain't Jones and I ain't from Cripple Creek."

"I figured as much. You're Cotton Younger, right?"

"No, my name is Raymond Tinker and I hail from Omaha, Nebraska."

"You ain't dying, boy. You're still shitting me!"

"It's the truth. I told ever'body my name was Jones 'cause I done some bad things in Nebraska."

"That where you started stealing cows?"

"Nope. Learnt to change brands about a year ago. What I done in Omaha was to cut a man."

"Cut him good?"

"Killed the old son of a bitch! He had it coming, too."

"Maybe. What was his name?"

"Leroy Tinker. The mean old bastard whupped me once too often."

"You say his name was Tinker? Was he any kin to yourself?"

"Yep, my father. I told him I was too big to take a licking, but he never listened. Just kept comin' at me with that switch and that silly grin of his. He was still grinning when I put a barlow knife in his guts."

Longarm took another look through the loophole. The sun was low. If anyone had considered moving up or down the valley to scale the cliffs around them, the light would fail them before they got halfway to the top. He glanced at his smudge fire of oil shale. It was still sending up thick clouds of inky smoke. No need to put more shale on it. It'd burn past sundown.

The youth calling himself Raymond Tinker groaned and said, "You must be thinking I'm one ornery cuss, huh?"

"That's between you and the State of Nebraska. Patricide ain't a federal offense."

"You don't believe me. You think I made it up to get out of being Cotton Younger!"

"The thought crossed my mind. We'll settle it in Denver."

"You know I won't live long enough to get there, don't you?"

"Don't hardly matter. Either way, I aim to take you there."

"How—how you transport a dead man, Longarm? I know it's a dumb thing to worry about, considering, but I'd sort of like to know."

"Well, if you want to die on me, I can't stop you. It's cool up here in the high country, so you'll likely keep a few days before you get rank."

"Ain't there no way to keep me from stinking after I go? I smelled a dead man, once. I'd hate to think of myself smelling like that."

"It don't figure to bother you. I was at Shiloh, and the dead were rotting under summer rains. None of 'em sat up to apologize for the way they smelled, so they likely didn't care."

"That ain't very funny, Longarm."

"Never said it was. Shiloh was no joking matter. If I can't pack you in ice, some way, I'll just remember you said it wasn't your own idea. You got any other old murder charges you'd like to unload, Raymond?"

"Nope. Never killed nobody but my father. Is changing brands a federal matter?"

"Not unless it's a cavalry horse's brand. You're turning out to be a big disappointment to me, old son."

"I know, but it just come to me that I'm getting you killed for no good reason. I mean, after I die, you can hand me over to them others and just ride out, right?"

"Wrong. For one thing, you ain't dead yet. For another, you're my prisoner, not theirs. You and them don't seem to get my point, no matter how many times I say it. I was sent to Crooked Lance to bring you in. That's my intention. Dead, alive, Younger, Jones, Tinker, or whomsoever, you can give your soul to Jesus but your ass belongs to me!"

Chapter 19

Sundown came without an attack from across the way. To make sure nobody had foolish nighttime notions, as soon as it was completely dark, Longarm sneaked out and built another fire-stack of oil shale well to the front of his breastwork, working silently in the dark. He pulled the slug from a cartridge with his teeth and laid a trail of gun powder toward the breastwork. It took him four cartridges to make it back to cover.

He struck a match and set the powder trail alight, rolling aside with a chuckle. Someone fired at the match flare as he'd expected.

The powder carried his flame to the shale pile and in a little while the space out in front of him was illuminated in smudgy-orange oil light. It left the slope across the creek black as a bitch, but he hadn't been able to see anything that far, anyway, and anybody creeping in was asking for a bullet between the glow of his or her eyes. Longarm was of the opinion that anyone that foolish didn't deserve to go on breathing.

The prisoner coughed and asked, "What's going on?"

"Nothing. They'll likely wait us out till sunup before they make the next move."

"Be a good chance for you to make a break, wouldn't it?"

"Not hardly. Only way out of here is forward, into at least a dozen and a half guns."

"You couldn't scale the cliffs back there?"

"Not with you. And if I did, where would I go?"

"Longarm, I thought my Pa was stubborn, but you

155

got him beat by a mile. Don't you know they'll be shooting down on you an hour or less after sunup?"

"Take 'em longer than that. Be nine or ten before they can work up the cliffs behind me."

"Then we'll both be dead, huh? I feel all empty-like below the belt line, now. I doubt I'll last 'til sunup."

"Why don't you try? I'll never speak to you again if you up and die on me, boy."

The dying man laughed bitterly and said, "You've been joking, but joking softer since I got hit. What's the matter, do you feel sorry for me now?"

"Never was mad at you. Just doing my job."

"You never cussed me out for killing my own father. I've been ashamed to tell anybody, even the friends I rode with."

"You rode into Crooked Lance with friends, Raymond?"

"No. I never lied about that part. I've been alone since my partner got caught up near the Great Northern line. I was working my way south to meet some other rustlers . . . all right, cow thieves, in Bitter Creek. You was right about that running iron being foolish, but I never expected to get caught with it."

"Most folks don't. Tell me about your friends in Bitter Creek. Does one of 'em pack a .30-30 rifle?"

"Don't suspicion so. I can't tell you their names. It's against our code."

"The rifle's all I care about. You reckon them other cow thieves waiting to rescue you in Bitter Creek would be serious enough to gun some folks? Say a Missouri sheriff's deputy or a U.S. Deputy Marshal?"

"Hell, they likely took off like big-ass birds when I got caught. Don't you reckon?"

"Maybe. That's part of the cow thief's code, too. I want you to think before you lie to me about this, boy. I won't press you about who these friends of yours was if you'll tell me one thing true. Was any one of 'em from Missouri?"

"No. I ain't giving anything away by telling you one

was from Nebraska like me. The other was a Mormon boy from Salt Lake City."

"Hmm, if I buy that, neither would have reason to pick off folks who knew their way around Clay County. You'd best rest a mite. I don't like the way you're breathing."

Longarm sat silently in the dark, digesting what the dying youth had told him. He assumed that most of what his prisoner had told him might be true. But *some-one* had gunned two lawmen from Missouri and at least one man who knew the James boys on sight.

It couldn't be Frank or Jesse James. He'd managed to get at least a glimpse of everyone in or about Crooked Lance and the James boys were not only better at holdups than acting, but were known to Longarm at a glance. He'd studied the photographs of both men more than once.

The prisoner gasped, "Longarm, do you reckon there's really a place like hell?"

"Don't know. Never planned on going there if I could help it."

"If there's a hell, it's likely where I'm headed, for I was birthed mean and grew up ugly. The good book says it's wrong for a boy to love his mama, don't it?"

"Hell, you're supposed to love your mama."

"All the way? I mean, like sort of fooling with her?"

"Are you telling me that's what you and your pa had words about?"

"Hell, no, he never caught us. Ma and me was careful. We only done it when he was off hunting or something."

"But you did commit incest, huh?"

"I don't know what we committed, but I purely screwed her ever' chance I got. She showed me how when I was about thirteen. Said I was hung better'n Pa. You reckon I'll have to answer for that, where I'm headed?"

"Don't know. What you want is a preaching man, old son. I don't write the laws. I just see that they're obeyed."

157

"Well, couldn't you *pretend* to be a preaching man, damn it? I mean, I'd take it kindly if you'd say a prayer over me or something. It don't seem fitting for a man to just lie here dying like this without somebody says somethin' from the good book."

Longarm searched his memory, harking back to a West Virginia farmhouse where gentle, care-worn hands had tucked him in at night. He shrugged and began, "The Lord is my shepherd, I shall not want . . ."

By the time he'd finished, the invisible form at his knees had stopped breathing. Longarm felt the side of his prisoner's throat for a pulse and there didn't seem to be one. He sniffed and muttered, "Never thought I'd miss a poor little pissant like you, but you left me with a long, lonesome night ahead of me."

But the night did pass, and in the dim, gray light of dawn nothing moved across the way, though once, when the breeze shifted, Longarm thought he smelled coffee brewing.

It reminded him he had to keep up his own strength, so he gnawed jerked venison, washed down with flat canteen water, as he watched for movement across the creek.

If they tried to talk some more it meant more precious time. If they didn't, it meant more than one of them was working around behind him. How long would it take to work to the top of a strange cliff a quarter of a mile high? It was anybody's guess.

The sun was painting the opposing clifftops pink when Foster showed himself once more. He called out, "Longarm?"

"We're still here, as you likely figured. What do you want?"

"Timberline and some of the others are working up to the rim rocks above you. You haven't a chance of holding out till noon!"

"I can try. What's your play, pilgrim?"

"I've been talking to Kim Stover and some of the

158

cooler heads. If you give up now, we can probably work out a compromise. Frankly, this thing's getting uglier than we intended."

"I'll stand pat for now, thanks."

"Longarm, they're going to kill you. Even if they don't shoot to kill from up there, you're taking foolish chances. We can't control things from down here. Once men get to shooting . . ."

"I know. Why don't you ride out with the gal before you both get in deeper? I can promise you one thing, Mountie. You won't make it back to Canada with a dead U.S. Deputy to answer for!"

"I can see that, damn it! That's why I'm willing to compromise! If you'll come back to civilization with me now, I'll abide by a legal ruling in Cheyenne about the prisoner. If they say he's mine, I take him. If they give him to you, I give up. Agreed?"

"Hell, no! I got the jasper and possession is nine-tenths of the law. I don't need no territorial judge to say who he belongs to. The prisoner belongs to *me*!"

"Longarm, you're acting like a fool!"

"That makes two of us, doesn't it?"

Kim Stover called over to Longarm, "Please be reasonable, Deputy Long. I don't want my friends to get in trouble!"

"They're already in trouble, ma'am! This ain't coffee and cake and let's-pretend-we're-vigilantes! You folks wanted the fun without considering the stakes. I'll tell you what I'll do, though. You and any others who've had enough of this game can ride out peaceable, and I won't press charges."

"What are you talking about! You're in no position to press charges! We're trying to save your life, you big idiot!"

"Well, I thank you for the kind thoughts, ma'am, but I'll save my own life as best I can."

Foster yelled, "I'm moving Mrs. Stover out of range, Longarm. You're obviously crazy as a loon and the shooting will be starting any minute now!"

159

Longarm watched them go back to their boulder, then rolled over on one elbow to gaze up at the cliffs above him. The prisoner's face was pale and cold, now, and the eyes were filmed with dust. Longarm pressed the lids closed, but they popped open again, so he went back to watching the skyline.

His eyes narrowed when, a good ten minutes later, a human head appeared as a tiny dot up above. Another, then another appeared beside it. Longarm suddenly grinned and waved. One of the figures staring down at him waved back. Longarm went to the still-smoldering shale-oil smudge fire, and keeping his head down, used his saddle blanket to break the rising column of smoke into long and short puffs. The next time he looked up, the dots on the rim rock had vanished.

He crawled back to the breastwork, tied his kerchief to the barrel of his Winchester, and waved it back and forth above the wall until Foster hailed him, calling out, "Do you surrender?"

"No, but you're about to. Tell the folks around you not to get spooked in the next few minutes. Some friends of mine are moving in behind you and some old boys shoot first and ask questions later when they see Indians. Tell 'em the ones coming in are Utes. They won't kill nobody, 'less some damn fool starts shooting!"

"What in the devil are you talking about? It's my understanding the Utes are not on the warpath!"

" 'Course they ain't. They're on the Ouray Reservation, about a ten-hour ride from here, when they ain't investigating smoke on the horizon. The Ouray Utes are wards of the U.S. Government, so I thought I ought to send for 'em. Some of 'em don't speak our lingo, so make sure nobody acts unfriendly as they come in to disarm you."

"Disarm us? You can't be serious!"

"Oh, but I am, and so are they. I just sort of deputized the whole damn tribe. You said eighteen-to-one was hard odds? Well, I figure I now have you out-

160

gunned about ten- or twelve-to-one. So don't act foolish."

"My God, you'd set savage Indians against your own race?"

"Yep. Had to. Only way I could do what I aimed to be doing."

"What's that, get away from us with my prisoner?"

"Hell, I could have done that days ago. The reason I led you all down here was to put you under arrest."

"Arrest? You can't arrest *me*!"

"If you'll look up the slope behind you, you'll see that I've just done it."

The Mountie turned to stare open-mouthed at the long line of armed Indians on the skyline and the others coming down the trail on painted ponies. He saw white men getting up from behind rocks, now, holding their hands out away from their gunbelts as they tried to look innocent. A pair of Ute braves had Timberline on foot between their ponies and to avoid any last-minute misunderstandings, Longarm got up from behind his little fort and walked over to them, waving his Stetson.

An older moon-faced Indian on a stocky pinto rode it into the creek and waited there, beaming broadly as Longarm approached. He said, in English, "It has been a good hunt. Just like the old days when we fought the Sioux and Blackfoot in the high meadows to the north. What is my brother from the Great White Father doing here? Do you want us to kill these people? They do not seem to be your friends."

"My blood brother, Hungry Calf, is hasty. Is the agent over on your reservation still my old friend, Caldwell?"

"Yes. He is a good man. He does not cheat us as the one you arrested that time did. We did not bring him. Agent Caldwell is good, but he says foolish things when we ride out for a bit of fun."

"I'd like to have all these people taken to the reservation, Hungry Calf. I'm arresting them in the name of the Great White Father."

"Good. We will take them to Agent Caldwell, and if he gives us his permission, we will hang them all for you."

"Tell the other *Ho* not to harm them in any way. Most of them are not bad people."

"Ah, but some of these *saltu* have broken the white father's law. Can we hang them?"

"You won't have to. You *Ho* have herds of longhorns, now. You know how a hand cuts the critters he wants from a rounded-up herd?"

"Of course. Herding longhorns is less fun than hunting, but we are now fine cowboys, if what Agent Caldwell says is true. We shall drive them all in together, then my brother can cut the bad ones out for the branding. It should be interesting to watch. I have never herded white people before."

Chapter 20

It took Longarm and his Ute allies most of the day to get the outraged whites over to the Ouray Reservation, to the east. One of the Indians was kind enough to pack the dead prisoner in, wrapped in a tarp across a pony. When they rode into the unpainted frame buildings at the government town called White Sticks, as the sun went down, a tall man in a rusty black suit came out with a puzzled smile.

Longarm rode up to him and smiled back, saying, "Got a dead man with me, Mister Caldwell. Can I store him in your icehouse for a few days?"

"God, no, but I'll bury him under ice and sawdust in a shed till you want him back. Who are all these other folks, Longarm? What have you and my Indians been up to?"

"I'm citing them for helping me make some arrests. They're be bringing in some others before morning. I deputized some of Hungry Calf's young men to round up the others headed this way by now." Foster rode over to protest, "See here! I am on Her Majesty's business under an agreement with the State Department!"

Longarm said, "He don't work for the State Department, Sergeant. You're on land controlled by the Department of the Interior and they don't *like* State all that much. Ride back and take charge of the others, if you're all so anxious to help. Tell 'em to make camp and sort of stay put, for now, while I make arrangements with my friends. You do have your own grub, don't you? These *Ho* friends of mine don't have all that much to give away."

Interested despite his outrage, Foster asked, "Why do you call them *Ho*? This is the *Ute* reservation, isn't it?"

"Sure it is. Ute is what others call 'em. They call themselves *Ho* 'cause it means *folks,* in their own lingo. They call you *saltu* meaning *strangers,* for reasons you can likely figure out. So don't mess up and nobody will get hurt."

Caldwell said, "Longarm is delicate about Indian niceties. He calls Apaches by their own name of Na-dene. Calls a Sioux a Dakota."

"All but the western Sioux," Longarm corrected. "They say *La*-ko-tah."

The Mountie sniffed and said, "All very interesting, I'm sure. Do you have a telegraph connection here, Agent Caldwell?"

"Sure. Wired into Western Union."

"May I use it to notify Her Majesty's Government I've been abducted by Ute Indians?"

Caldwell glanced at Longarm, who nodded and said, "Why not? He's a guest."

Longarm saw that the Mountie wasn't going to explain things to the others, so as Foster and Caldwell went inside the headquarters building to send the message, Longarm ambled over to the large group of whites around the Indian campfire they'd helped themselves to. Longarm saw that his Ho friends had given them back their sidearms, as he'd told them to, and had hidden their horses someplace as he had instructed.

Timberline had been squatting on his heels next to Kim Stover, who sat crosslegged on a saddle blanket near the small fire. The tall foreman smiled thinly and said, "I'd better never see you anywhere off this reservation, Longarm. You've pushed me from obliging a lady to *personal!*"

Longarm figured Timberline was just showing off for the redhead, so he ignored him and announced for all to hear, "I'm holding the bunch of you overnight on what

164

you might call self-recog. The Indians won't pester you 'less you try to reclaim a horse."

The midget, Cedric Hanks, piped up from across the fire, "You've no right to hold us here! We're white folks, not Utes! Your writ don't apply to us here! The Bureau of Indian Affairs has nothing to say about the comings and goings of such as we."

"You may be right, Hanks. When that Mountie's through, I'll wire my office for a ruling. Meanwhile, you'd all best figure on a night's rest here in White Sticks. I'll see, later, about some entertainment. Hungry Calf likes to put on shows for company. By the way, I got some Ho out looking for your wife and the others. We'll sort it out once all the interested parties are together."

"You say they have a telegraph line here? I'd like to send some wires."

"You don't get to. Reservation wire's for government business only. The Mountie rates its use because he's a real peace officer with a government. Private detectives are just pests. As for the rest of you, since some of you put all that effort into keeping the Western Union line to Crooked Lance out of order, you got no reason to send messages into a busted line."

Kim Stover asked, "Do you have any idea who among us might have cut the wire to Crooked Lance, Deputy Long?"

"Got lots of ideas. But I'm trying to work out proof that would hold up in court. There's more'n one reason to cut an outlying cow town off from communications. Friends of the prisoner one of you shot might have wanted things quiet while they made a private play to spring him. Then again, the eastern meat packers might not want folks with a hard-scrabble herd in rough range to be abreast of the latest beef quotations back East. I'll save you asking by telling you. When I left Denver, range stock was selling for twenty-nine dollars a head at trackside."

The girl smiled for a change, and said, "Oh, that *is* a good price! We had no idea the price of beef was up!"

"I figured as much. We're going into a boom on beef after the bad times we've been having. They've been having bad crops and politics over in the old countries. Queen Victoria and Mister Bismarck are buying all the tinned beef they can get for their armies. France is bouncing back from the whupping the Prussians gave 'em a few years back and is carving slices out of Africa with an army that has to be fed. I'd say the hungry days are over for you cow folks."

Timberline's voice was almost friendly as he finished counting on his fingers and observed, "Jesus! Figuring all our herds consolidated, we got near fifty thousand dollars worth of beef up in our valley!"

"I know. You'll be able to build your schoolhouse without obstructin' justice and such. As long as we're on the subject, that prisoner of yours . . ." Then Longarm caught himself and decided he'd said enough, if not too much, for now.

He was saved further conversation by the arrival of Hungry Calf at the fire. On foot, the chief looked much shorter than he had while astride a pony, for the Ho were built like their Eskimo cousins in the northlands they'd wandered down from before Columbus took that wrong turn to India. Hungry Calf's arms and legs were a bit shorter than most white mens'. Yet his head and torso were bigger than Longarm's. Given legs in European proportion to his body, he'd have been as tall as Timberline instead of being a head shorter than Longarm. It was just as well he was friendly. A hand-to-hand set-to with the bearlike Hungry Calf would be one hard row to hoe.

The Indian said, "The people are happy to have something new to talk about. The maidens would like to have a fertility dance to entertain our guests."

Longarm nodded and said, "That's right neighborly of my brother's people. You tell 'em it's all right. Then come back. I'd like a few more words with my Ho brother."

As the Indian waddled off in the darkness Longarm turned back to the crowd of mostly-young male cowhands and said, soberly, "I want you all to listen up. The Indians are trying to be neighborly, and some of them young squaws can be handsome-looking to a healthy man, so I'd best warn you, Indians on a reservation are wards of the state and you're not allowed to trifle with 'em."

One of the Crooked Lance riders snorted, "That'll be the day! This whole durned camp smells like burning cow— excuse me, Miss Kim."

"Burning cow pats is what you're smelling, sure enough. I don't want anyone here to get close enough to smelling any squaws to consider himself an expert on the subject. If the Indian agent catches you at it, it's a federal charge. If the squaw's old man does, it can get more serious. So you let 'em flirt and shimmy all they want, and keep your seats till the entertainment's over, hear?"

As he started to leave, Kim Stover asked, "Is this . . . fertility rite liable to be . . . improper?"

"You mean for a white lady to watch? No, ma'am. You'll likely find it sort of dull, considering the message."

He excused himself and walked a few yards toward the clustered outlines of the agency. Hungry Calf materialized to say, "The one in the red coat is standing around the ponies. Can my young men kill him?"

"No. Just have them watch him, without hindering him in any way. I want to know whatever he does, but he's allowed to do it."

"What if he steals ponies? Can we kill him then?"

"No. The Great White Father will pay you for anything he steals from my Ho brothers."

"Hah! I think my brother is baiting some kind of trap! Can Agent Caldwell tell you the message he sent on the singing wire!"

"He doesn't have to. I know."

"Longarm has strong medicine. He knows everything. We know this to be true. When that other agent was cheating my people, none of us suspected it, for the man was cunning. Longarm's medicine unmasked his trickery, even after his written words on paper fooled the other agents of the Great White Father. The red coat is a fool. We shall watch him, cat-eyed, through the night, until he does what Longarm knows he will."

Longarm thanked his informant and went over to the agency, where he found Caldwell seated at a table with his vapidly pretty white wife. As Longarm remembered, her name was Portia.

Portia Caldwell remembered him, too. She literally hauled him inside and sat him in her vacated chair, across from her husband, and began to putter with her cast-iron stove, chatting like a magpie about fixing him something to go with his coffee.

Longarm grinned across the table at his host and said, "I'll settle for maybe a slice of that apple cobbler you're famous for, ma'am. What I came to ask about was the disposition of the remains I had packed in."

Caldwell grimaced and said, "I might have known you'd want to talk about it at the table. Is it true the dead man was kin to Jesse James and wanted in Canada on a very ugly charge I'd as soon not repeat in front of my wife?"

"You read the sounds of the Mountie's key as he was sending, huh? Who'd he wire, Washington or Fort MacLeod?"

"Both. He said he'd gotten his man, whatever that means."

"It's Mountie talk. You got the—you know—properly guarded?"

"Couple of Utes are keeping an eye on the shed it's stored in. You don't expect anyone to try and steal a—preserved evidence?"

Portia Caldwell shoved a big bowl of apple cobbler in front of Longarm, saying, "For heaven's sake, I know there's a corpse in the smokehouse! I'm an army brat, not a shrinking violet. I saw my first body when my mother took me to visit my Daddy, three days after Gettysburg!"

Caldwell grimaced again and said, "She says the worst smell was when they burned the dead horses. Ain't she something?"

"You're lucky to have the right women for your job. The Shoshone try to steal any of your charges' ponies, lately?"

"No, we're having trouble with a few Apache bands to the south, as always, but I'd say the day of real Indian Wars is over, wouldn't you?"

"Maybe. I filed a report from a 'breed informant a few months ago. If I was you, I'd keep an eye peeled for a wandering medicine man called Wava-something-or-other. They say he's a Paiute dream-singer who has a new religion."

"Paiute? Nobody's ever had much trouble from that tribe. They maybe shot up a few wagon trains back in '49, but, hell, every young buck did that in them days just for the hell of it. Most of the fighting tribes despise the Paiute."

"Well, this one young jasper I've heard of bears watching, just the same. He ain't trying to stir up his own people. He wanders about, even riding trains, selling medicine shirts."

"Medicine shirts? What kind of medicine?"

"Bulletproof. Not bulletproof *iron* shirts. Regular old buckskin shirts with strong medicine signs painted on 'em. I ain't certain if this young Paiute dream-singer's a con man or sincere, but, like I said, we're keeping an eye on him."

Portia Caldwell asked, "If you know who he is, why can't you just arrest him, Longarm?"

"On what charge, ma'am? If there was a law against religious notions I'd have to start with arresting Christian missionaries, which just might not be such a bad idea, considering some I've met."

"But this Paiute's selling crazy charmed shirts he says can stop a bullet!"

"Well, who's to say they can't, as long as no Indian does anything to get his fool self shot at? The danger as I see it ain't in *wearing* a lucky shirt. It's in wearing it on the warpath."

Caldwell shook his head and said, "My Ute are a pragmatic people. Besides, who'd buy medicine made by another tribe?"

"The Pine Ridge Dakota for openers. This Paiute priest, prophet, or whatever has been selling his shirts mail-order."

"Oh, the damned Sioux can't be serious about it. They've been whipped too many times. And besides, why should they think the magic of another tribe would be any good to them?"

"Don't know. I ain't a Dakota. Sitting Bull has said much the same about the crosses and bibles the Catholic mission at Pine Ridge has been distributing."

"That's not the same. Christianity is not an Indian superstition."

"You're right. It's what us whites call good medicine."

"Longarm, if you intend to start another religious argument—"

"I don't. I'm outnumbered two-to-one, hereabouts. I've passed on my information. You BIA folks can do what you've a mind to with it."

"I thank you for it, and I'll keep an eye peeled for those crazy bulletproof medicine shirts, but I'm certain we've seen the last of Indian uprisings in this century."

"Maybe. 'Bout thirty, forty years ago another white man collected some information on another kind of Indian. He was an Englishman named Burton, but he was sensible, anyway. He told Queen Victoria's Indian agents about some odd talk he'd picked up from some heathen informants. They told him they knew better. British India had seen the last of Indian risings, too.

Couple of years later the Sepoy Mutiny busted wide open and a couple of thousand whites got killed."

He excused himself and got up from the table to let them ponder his words of cheer as he left. Outside, the night was filled with the monotonous beat of a dog-skin drum as Longarm sauntered back to where he'd left his "guests."

A circle of Ho women were around the fire, arms locked, as they shuffled four steps to the left, followed by four steps to the right. Longarm hunkered down by the widow Stover's blanket and observed, "I told you there wasn't all that big a shucks to it, ma'am."

"How long do they keep that up?" she asked.

"Till they get as tired of it as we already are, I reckon. I've seen it go on all night."

"Is that all there is to it? Neither the beat nor the dance step varies. If you could call dragging your feet like that dancing."

"Indians set great store by repeating things, ma'am. The number four is sacred to the spirits. They think everything either should or does happen in fours."

"Where'd they get such a fool superstition?"

"Don't know. Where'd *we* get the notion of the Trinity and everything happening in threes?"

"I'm not a Roman Catholic, either. You said this was a fertility rite. I expected something . . . well, more pagan."

"Oh, they're pagan enough. But Indians don't act dirty about what comes natural. That drum beat's calculated to heat things up, if you'll listen to it sharp."

"What is there to listen to? That fool medicine man just keeps whacking it over and over, bump, bump, bump."

"You missed a beat. He hits it four good licks and starts over. The normal human heart beats just a mite slower than that drum. After a time, though, everybody listening sort of gets their own hearts going with that drum. Hearts beating faster heats the blood and, uh, other things. The fertility part just comes natural, later, in the lodges."

"You mean we're likely to see an all-night Indian orgy?"

"Nope. You won't see or hear a thing. They don't show off about such matters."

"Well, if it's all the same to you, I'm bored as well as tired and I'd like to get some sleep."

"I figured as much. If you'll allow me, I'll take you over to the agent's house and they'll bed you in a spare room."

"Oh? That's right thoughtful of you and your friends. I was afraid I'd have to spend another night on the ground in my blankets."

"No need to, ma'am. If you ask her, Portia Caldwell might work out a bath for you, too. Let me help you up."

He rose, hauling Kim to her feet, and took her by an elbow to guide her toward the agency.

Timberline suddenly appeared in front of them to demand, "Just what do you think you're up to, damn it?"

"Don't think nothing. I'm carrying this lady over to the agency to put her to bed."

The big ramrod swung, saying something about Longarm's mother that he couldn't have possibly been informed about. Longarm ducked the roundhouse and danced backward, drawing his .44 as he sighed and said, "Now that's enough, old son."

"Damn it, if you was any kind of man at all you'd fight me fair."

"If I fought you with fists I'd be more fool than any other kind of man worth mention. You're too big for me and I'm too fast on the draw for you, so I suspicion we ain't able to have a fair fight, either way."

Kim Stover got between them and soothed, "Don't be silly, Timberline. He was only taking me over to stay with the married couple at the house."

"Oh? I thought—"

Longarm knew what he'd thought, but a man was

172

wasting time to jaw with a fool. So he said, "We'd best get over to Portia Caldwell, ma'am. I got other fish to fry, this night."

Timberline tagged along, muttering under his breath, but he didn't do or say anything until they had all reached the porch of the agency. Kim Stover turned to him and said, "You'd best stay out here, Timberline."

"I mean to see you're safe, little lady."

"Safe? I'm under arrest, thanks to going along with this foolishness. If you're talking about this other man trifling with me, nobody knows better'n you I can hold my own on any front porch."

"I ain't leaving you alone with him."

Longarm said, "Yes you are. I'll go along with some showoff for the diversion of a lady, but she's just asked you to git, so you'd best do it."

Timberline didn't move away, but he stopped following as Longarm escorted the redhead up the steps. As he was about to knock, she put a hand on his sleeve and said, "One moment, sir. You didn't disagree when I just said I was under arrest!"

"Ain't polite to correct a lady, ma'am."

"May I ask what I'm under arrest for, now that you have your prisoner and the rest of us are left out in the cold?"

"You ain't half as cold as my prisoner is on that bed of ice, ma'am."

"I'm right sorry he got killed, but you know I never fired a shot at anyone!"

"Somebody did. Hit him twice, too. I ain't charging you with killing him, ma'am. Let's say you're a material witness."

"Dang it, *I* don't know who's bullets hit that boy! Half the men with me were shooting at Cotton Younger!"

"I know. Obstruction of justice and killing a federal prisoner under a peace officer's protection could be taken seriously, but I'd be willing to overlook past misunderstandings, if that was all that happened."

173

"You mean you're still investigating the missing law men and the killing of Sailor Brown?"

"Don't you reckon I ought to?"

"Of course, but none of us knows anything about any of that!"

"There I go, correcting ladies again, but you're wrong, ma'am. Somebody either with you or headed this way knows more'n they're letting on."

"That may well be, but I don't see why you're holding me or the other innocent folks."

"Funny, Hungry Calf did, and he ain't been herding cows as long as you. What we're having here is a tally and cut, ma'am. My Indian deputies are still rounding up the herd. I suspicion some will come in willingly, on their own. By this time tomorrow I hope to be done marking and branding."

"And then my innocent friends and me will be riding out?"

"Maybe. Depends on who gets arrested. I'd best knock now. I've other chores to tend to."

As he knocked, the redhead demanded, "Are you accusing *me* of . . . something?"

The door opened. Longarm introduced the two women, and before he had to answer more questions, left them to work things out.

Timberline was still waiting, and this time, he had his old hogleg out and pointing. Longarm said, "Oh, put that fool thing away, kid. No gals are watching."

"God damn you! I ain't scared of you!"

"That makes us even. You'd best get back to the dance. The squaws'll be passing drinks and tobacco in a while. They ain't supposed to have no liquor, but you'll likely get some passable corn squeezings."

Timberline kept the pistol trained on Longarm as the lawman walked right past him. Timberline called out, "Stand still, God damn it! I ain't done with you!"

Longarm kept walking. Timberline followed, blustering, "Turn around, God damn it! I can't shoot no man in the back!"

174

Not looking back, Longarm said, "Not here, you can't. Quit showing off without no audience, Timberline. We both know you're stuck on a reservation filled with friends of mine. You got no horse. You got no nerve to go with your brag. You keep pestering me and you'll have no gun. I'm coming to the conclusion you ain't grown up enough to wear sidearms, the way you keep carrying on."

Timberline holstered his gun, muttering, "One day we'll meet where you ain't holding all the winning cards, Longarm."

Longarm didn't bother to answer. He went near, but not all the way, to the fire, and took up a position where he could watch, standing back from the glow and the shifting shadows. He didn't watch the dancers. Once you watched the first eight steps of most Indian dances you'd seen about all that was about to happen. He watched the vigilantes and the little bounty hunter, Hanks, long enough to see that they didn't seem to be up to anything interesting, either. Foster wasn't near the fire. Across the way, Timberline had hunkered down by some of his sidekicks, scowling fiercely.

A soft female voice at his side asked, "Has Longarm a place to sleep this night?"

Longarm turned to smile down at a pretty, moon-faced girl of perhaps eighteen summers. Like other Ho women she wore a shapeless, ankle-length Mother Hubbard of cotton, decorated with quillwork around the collar. Longarm said, "Evening, Dances-Humming. Is my brother, your husband, well?"

"This person is no longer the woman of Many Ponies."

"Oh? Something happen to him?"

"Yes, he got older. This person is not a woman for a man who'd gotten old and fat and lazy. Many Ponies was sent home to his mother's lodge."

Longarm nodded soberly. He knew the marriage laws of the Ho well enough not to have to ask foolish ques-

175

tions. Some whites might say they were sort of casual about such things. He considered them practical.

On the other hand, while the man he knew as Many Ponies might be getting fat, he was big for a Ho and inclined to brood. The girl called Dances-Humming, while very pretty, had learned English from the last agent, the one arrested for mistreating the Indians. If there was one woman to be trusted less than a Larimer Street play-pretty, it was a squaw who spoke perfect English.

He said, "How come you ain't dancing with the other gals?"

"This person is tired of the old customs. They mean so little when our men grow fat and drunk on the Great White Father's allowance."

"Some healthy young cowboys, over by the fire?"

"This person has seen them. None of them look interesting. The last time you were here, this person was younger and you laughed at her childish ways. Since then, this person has learned how white women make love. Would you like to see how Dances-Humming can kiss?"

"Like to. Can't. It's against the law."

"The Great White Father's law, not ours. Come, we can talk about it in my lodge."

Longarm was about to refuse, but a sudden suspicion made him reconsider. Dances-Humming giggled and took his hand, tugging him after her through the dim light. He allowed himself to be led, muttering, "Sometimes there's nothing a gent can do but lay down and take his beating like a man."

Dances-Humming's lodge was not a tent. Like most of her people on the reservation, she'd been given a frame cabin neatly placed along the gravel street leading to the agency. The BIA furnished whitewash, with the understanding that the Indians would paint their cabins. They never did so, not because they were shiftless, but because they thought it was silly to paint pine when the sun soon bleached it to a nice shade of silver-gray that never needed repainting.

Dances-Humming led him inside and lit a candle stub, bathing the interior in warm, soft light. The cabin was furnished with surplus army camp furnishings. The walls were hung with painted deerskins and flat gathering baskets woven long ago. Dances-Humming seldom worked at the old skills. Reservation life was turning her and her people into something no longer Indian, but not yet white. Prostitution had been unknown when the various bands of Ho had roamed from the Rockies to the Sierras in a prouder time.

Dances-Humming sat on a bunk, atop the new-looking Hudson Bay blanket. She patted the creamy wool at her side and said, "Sit down. This person's guest looks puzzled."

"I reckon I am. Last time I was here you said something about a knife in my lights and liver."

"This person was angry. You arrested a man who had been good to her and they made her marry an old man. But that was long ago, when this person was a foolish child."

She suddenly drew her legs up under her and was kneeling in the center of the bunk. She pulled the loose Mother Hubbard off over her head and threw it aside. She laughed, stark naked, and asked, "Has not this person grown into a real woman?"

Longarm said, "That's for damn sure!" as he stared down at her firm, brown breasts in the candlelight. Then he sniffed and said, "My medicine don't allow me to pay a woman, Dances-Humming."

"Did this person ask for presents? What do you take her for, a whore?"

Longarm did, but he didn't say so. He said, "If Agent Caldwell caught us, he'd report me to the BIA."

"No, he wouldn't. He owes his job to you. Besides, how is he to know?"

"Well, you might just tell him."

"Why would this person do that?"

177

"Maybe to get a white man who riled you in trouble. You did say you'd *fix* me, last time around."

Dances-Humming cupped her breasts in her hands and thrust the nipples out at him teasingly, asking, "Is this the way you're afraid this person will fix you?" Her voice took on a bitter shade as she added, "You are a white man with a badge. Do you think they'd take this person's word against yours?"

He saw that there were tears in her sloe eyes and sat beside her, soothing, "Let's not blubber about it, honey. You're just taking me by surprise, is all. I mean, I didn't know we were friends."

"You men are all alike when it comes to a woman's mind! Don't you know that a woman is a cat? Don't you know why a woman, or a cat, spits most at those who ignore her?"

"Ignoring you would be a chore, considering."

"Good. Let's kiss and make up, then, shall we?"

Without waiting for an answer, Dances-Humming was all over him, bare bottom in his lap as she rubbed everything else against him while planting a wet, open-mouthed kiss full on his lips. She had his back to the wall now and was fumbling at his buttons, complaining with her mouth on his, "You white men wear so many clothes! Don't they get in the way at times like these?"

"They sure as hell do!" Longarm said, pushing her clear enough to start undressing himself, as he added, "Snuff that candle. You ain't got curtains on the windows!"

She laughed and leaped from the bunk, a tawny vision of desire as she bent to put the light out. By the time she crawled up on the bunk beside him, Longarm had gotten rid of most of his duds. The first thing he'd removed was his gunbelt, and he'd shoved it between the bunk and the wall, the grips of the .44 handy.

She wrestled playfully with him as he finished undressing and they were both laughing when, at last, their nude bodies melted together.

Dances-Humming was hotter than a two-dollar pistol

178

and moved it like a saloon door on payday, but there was something wrong. Longarm had been with enough women to know when they were taking pleasure as well as giving it. The little squaw made love like a professional, and since that way's calculated to pleasure a man, Longarm enjoyed it.

After a time, as they rested with him still inside her, he ran his hand down between their moist warm torsos to tickle her wetness. She stopped him, asking, "What is the matter, didn't you enjoy it?"

"You know I did, honey. I'm trying to make you come."

"Why? This person didn't ask it."

"Well, hell, it's common courtesy! Don't you *want* to come, honey?"

"I already did, before. You can just do as you wish. This person does not mind. She is tired."

Longhorn frowned, wondering why she was lying. She'd acted like she was going crazy, a minute ago, but he'd been with too many others to be fooled. She, while she wasn't getting paid like a whore, she was doing it like a whore. He'd wondered where she'd gotten that new blanket.

He said, "Well, if you're tired, you're tired. I'll just be on my way, soon as I can find where I threw my boots."

She stiffened and said, "You can't leave now! It's too early!"

"Maybe nine o'clock, maybe ten. I thank you for the hospitality, but I can see I ain't wanted, so—"

"Don't go! I'll let you play with me! I'll do anything, anything you want!"

"Uh-uh. Your Indian powwow stuff is slipping, too. I'd better get it on down the road, honey."

He swung his bare legs over the edge and sat up, bending over to reach for his socks. Dances-Humming reached for the holstered .44 against the wall, drew it, and placed the muzzle against the back of Longarm's head as she pulled the trigger.

179

The gun clicked twice before he'd reached around and taken it from her, saying, "First thing they ever told me was not to leave a loaded gun where a whore could get at it, Dances-Humming. I took the liberty of unloading it before leaving it there to bait you."

She tried to back away as far as possible, but she only got as far as the corner. She sat there, knees drawn up, and trembling as she gasped, "I don't want to die!"

"Well, not many folks do. Did the man who put you up to this say how you were to get away with killing me, or are you just dumb?"

"I didn't think! I had to—I *have* to keep you here, no matter what!"

"Well, blowing my brains out my nose was a piss-poor idea, honey. You weren't gonna sing that same old song about the wicked white man trying to rape an Indian lady defending her honor, were you?"

"I don't know! There wasn't time to think!"

"You'd better *learn* to think, girl! If I'd been as dumb as you, we'd both be in a pickle. I'd be dead and you'd be explaining things to Hungry Calf and the other chiefs. I'll allow an Indian Agent will believe most anything, but you'd last less than five minutes when the elders got to asking what happened."

She buried her face in her hands and began to bawl like a baby.

Longarm reached out and put an arm around her, soothing, "Oh, hush, no harm's been done."

"Are you going to tell on me?"

"Don't reckon I need to, now. You do see how another wicked white man led you astray, don't you? I swear, Dances-Humming, you do get led astray more'n any Ho gal I've met. You sure you didn't have an Apache grandmother? No, that don't figure. Apache blood would have left you smarter. You see, honey, if folks can't be smart, they have to be good. Dumb and wicked is a fearsome combination."

"If you won't beat me, I'll tell you who paid me to keep you here all night."

"I don't aim to beat you, and I know who paid you. As long as he never paid you to kill me, what the hell."

"What are you going to do when you leave here? Are you sure you'll be able to kill him? He said he would be very cross with me if I let you out, tonight."

"Well, I'll tell you what we'd best do. Since I'm supposed to spend the night here, I'd just as soon. You did say you didn't want me to tell Hungry Calf and the others, didn't you?"

"Don't tell them! I'll do anything."

"I know. I'm going to have to tie you up. Not that I don't trust you, you understand, but I'd never in this world be able to fall asleep with you running about maybe looking for knives and such."

"I wouldn't try again to hurt you. This person is afraid."

"That makes two of us. I'll tie you gentle, but I'll tie you fast. You want to do anything, first?"

She started to protest, but she knew he meant it, so as Longarm rummaged through her things for a rope she pulled a chamber pot from under the bed and relieved herself. From the long, hissing sound, he knew she was badly frightened.

He found a length of cotton clothesline, tested it with a few snaps, and decided it would do. He brought the coil to the bunk and sat down, fishing in his pants for his jackknife. Dances-Humming rose to her feet and stood before him, resigned to his will.

Longarm cut the rope into four sections and got up, pulling the top blanket from the bunk. He threw it out in the middle of the floor and patted the quilted surface as he said, "Climb aboard and pick out a comfortable position; you'll be in it for some time."

"I sleep best on my stomach."

"There you go, then. Face down, hands above your head. I'll give you a little slack, but I'll hear you if you get to jerking it, and I'll whup your bare ass for it."

The treacherous little squaw lay across the mattress on her belly and Longarm lashed a wrist to each head-post of the bunk while she sniffled and protested. He tied her ankles to the posts at the foot of the bunk, leaving her some slack to shift a bit. Then he sat down with his back to her and started pulling on his socks. She asked. "Why are you getting dressed?"

"To keep from freezing before morning, of course. I'll throw the blanket over you, directly. Then I'll hunker down in a corner in my duds, facing the door."

"It's so early. Even Many Ponies used to make love to me more than once a night."

"Honey, you are full of shit as well as frigid. You won't get out of them ropes by stirring up the love potion pot. I'll allow it figures to be a tedious cold night, but what the hell."

"Won't you do it one more time? Now that this person has less fear, she remembers how nice you felt inside of her. She was too worried to let herself go, before. This time will be different."

"Oh, hell, I got my socks on and you're hogtied just right, and face down to boot!"

"I can raise myself high enough. See?"

He saw indeed, as the moonlight now lancing through one window shone on the firm, plump hemispheres of her tawny buttocks. He ran his free hand over her flesh, soothingly, and sighed, "Don't know as it's right to do it to a gal tied up with ropes. Read someplace about this French feller who liked to do it that way, and the book said he was touched in the head."

"Untie me, then."

"In a pig's eye! You don't want to get humped. You only want to have them ropes off you!"

"That's not this person's reason. Feel the way she's gushing with her need!"

He explored the crevice between her writhing buttocks and warm brown thighs with his fingers, noting, "You're drooling like a woman in love and that's a fact."

"Do it! For some reason this person is excited by the ropes!"

Longarm got up and climbed aboard the bunk, resting his weight on all fours as he positioned his knees up and to either side of her hips. It was awkward in this position, but as Dances-Humming felt his erection in the wet crevice between them, she moved herself into line and took advantage of the slack bondage to engulf him with a hungry sigh.

"Oh, it feels so . . . *interesting* this way!" she giggled, as Longarm, getting the hang of it, began to rock back and forward on his knees. It was well for him that he was a practiced horseman with well-developed riding muscles; even so, his thighs began to cramp by the time it was too late to stop. The Indian girl began to gyrate wildly as she literally screwed herself on and almost off, biting her lip as she groaned delighted words in her own language, for Dances-Humming was not a white man's love-toy now. She reverted to her birthright as a natural, hot-blooded girl who a missionary, in his ignorance, might describe as "primitive."

This time she didn't fake an orgasm. She had one, then another and another as the man who'd mastered her pounded and pounded her from the rear. Longarm gasped, "Oh, Jesus H. Christ!" and let her rip. It felt funny as hell to come with both legs fixing to bust.

He was tempted to untie her and make a night of it, now that they'd become better acquainted, but he knew he'd need his strength, come sunup, and he still didn't trust her far enough to spit.

He climbed off and got dressed, throwing the Hudson Bay blanket over the crooning, sex-drugged little squaw.

He bent and kissed her on the ear. Then he went to a corner and slid down to squat Mexican-style with his holster pulled around between his thighs. He reloaded the .44. Then he crossed his arms over his raised knees and lowered his head to them, trying to think if he'd left any loose ends.

He couldn't think of any. His saddle and possibles were stored in the Agency, along with Kim Stover. If any of the others got in trouble with squaws or corn squeezings it wasn't his duty to worry about it. Agent Caldwell and the tribal council were getting paid to keep things down to a roar, hereabouts.

It was already getting chilly, as the thin air of the high country surrendered its stored sunlight to the stars. He knew he'd have a frozen ass by daybreak, but he'd been cold before, and he aimed to rise early and to be wide awake as soon as he did so.

He might have dreamed. He must have dreamed, for he was thinking about how cold it was out here on the picket line tonight with the enemy just across the river and no picket fires allowed this close to the front by order of the general when, somewhere, a rooster crowed, and he sat up, blinking the cobwebs from his brain and shivering in the icy dawn.

He sat still for a moment, gazing across the little cabin at the girl on the bunk. She was watching him from under the edge of the blanket, her sloe eyes unreada' le. Longarm nodded and said, " 'Morning."

"This person has been trying to understand you. Even for a white man, you act crazy."

"It was your idea to do it that way. I'm damned if I can see what that French feller got out of it. Can't change position worth a damn."

"This person wasn't talking about that. It was very exciting to be taken as a captive. Now the tales of the old women make more sense. What makes no sense at all is the way you acted after you made this person tell you the truth."

"Would you rather I'd have spanked you?"

"No. Many Ponies tried to beat me, once. I sent him home to his mother's lodge. I thought you'd go after the man who paid me to betray you."

"And miss all the fun we had? Along with being dumb, you lack the imagination of your people, Dances-Humming. The Ho are famous hunting and fighting folks. The Dakota call 'em their favorite enemies; it's hard as anything to outwit the Ute band of the Ho."

184

He got up, stretching and moving his holster over to his left hip as he came over and removed the blanket to untie her. Dances-Humming rolled over and writhed invitingly on her back, asking, "Would you like to do it the old-fashioned way, this time?"

"I'd like to. Can't. Got too many chores to tend to. I'll be leaving now, with some parting words of advice. If you repeat 'em to the BIA I'll have to call you a liar, but you ain't making it as an Indian, gal. If I was you, I'd move down to Salt Lake and take up the trade near the U.P. station. You're a pretty little thing, and you could make your fortune off railroad roustabouts and whisky drummers looking for what you're so good at. You stay here on the reservation, selling half-ass treachery along with what you're good at, and some night one of the decent folks hereabouts will surely cut your throat."

He left as she was still protesting her inborn goodness.

Outside, the air had a bite to it, but tasted crisp and clean. The girl's cabin, like most Indian dwellings, was unventilated and smoke-scented, for folks living close to nature with few warm clothes valued warmth more than their tears, and Indains could put up with more smoke than you'd think was good for their eyes.

As he walked toward the agency, he wondered if Caldwell would notice the squaw-smell clinging to his unwashed hide. He probably wouldn't The whole little town smelled Indian. It wasn't a bad smell, just different. White towns smelled of coal smoke, unwashed wool, and horse shit. Indian villages smelled of burning dung, greased rawhide, and the dry, corn-husk odor of Indian sweat. By now, Caldwell and his woman smelled that way themselves.

As he approached the agency, a young Ho fell in beside him and said, "I am called Spotted Bear. Hungry Calf had me watching the dead man in the smokehouse."

"I know, brother. How long ago did the man in the red coat steal the body?"

"Many hours ago. He took his own and one of our ponies, too. He rode out just after midnight, but his sign is easy to read. When shall we go after him?"

"We're not going to train him, brother. I'll see that the owner of the stolen pony gets paid double. You and your friends did well."

The Indian smiled at the compliment. "We did as you asked, but we don't understand it. Wasn't it your plan to let the red coat do a bad thing so you could kill him?"

"No. He was not a bad man. Just a fool pest I wanted to get rid of. I knew he wouldn't leave without the dead man as a present for his she-chief, so I let him steal the body."

"Does the crazy red coat's she-chief eat human flesh?"

"No. She wants the dead man's, uh, scalp. She thinks he did a bad thing to one of her people."

"Oh. What did the dead man do to the red coat's tribe?"

"Nothing. But he don't know that. He's likely huggin' himself right now for being so all-fired foxy. We can forget about him. He's a good woodsman, and since he thinks we're tracking him, he'll make sure nobody sees him again till he gets where he's going. Did anybody else try to get away during the night?"

"No. All the white men are sleeping in their blankets by the fire. Some of them had firewater and got drunk. The reservation police are watching them, but your orders were not to interfere, just watch, is this not so?"

"You are a good and clever warrior, Spotted Bear. I'll leave you now. I don't want the other white men to know we're close."

As the Indian dropped back, Longarm went on up to the agency. He smelled ham and eggs, so he knew the Caldwells were early risers, like their charges.

Someone had been watching from a window, because

186

the door opened as he came up the steps and Caldwell said, "We've been looking for you. Sent a Ute out to fetch you when the wire came, but he said he didn't know where you were."

"I sleep private. What wire are we talking about?"

Caldwell handed him a piece of yellow paper, explaining, "This came in right after the Mountie telegraphed his own report. Your own outfit was likely listening in."

Longarm held the telegram up to the light and read:

TO: DEPUTY LONG OURAY RESERVATION STOP #ONE WHAT ARE YOU DOING IN UTAH TERRITORY STOP #TWO WHAT HAPPENED TO KINCAID STOP #THREE DO YOU NEED ASSISTANCE STOP.

Longarm chuckled and folded the telegram away, following the agent inside. He nodded to the two women seated at the breakfast table and when Portia Caldwell invited him to some ham and eggs, he said, "In a minute, ma'am. I have to send a message to my chief. If he doesn't find one waiting for him at his office, he'll be hard on the help."

Caldwell took him into an office where a sending set sat under a rack of wet-cell batteries. Longarm sat down at the table and began to tap out his reply, routing it through the Bureau of Indian Affairs to the Justice Department and thence to the Denver office. With the salutations out of the way, he sent:

ANSWER TO #ONE MY JOB STOP ANSWER TO #TWO LIKELY DEAD STOP ANSWER TO #THREE NO STOP SIGNED LONG."

Agent Caldwell, who'd sent some Morse in his time, had listened in. He said, "If that don't confuse your boss, it pure confuses me! Would you mind letting me in on just what the hell you're up to, old son?"

"Cutting and branding, like I said. Just got rid of that feller from Canada, and by the way, you can use your smokehouse again. Sergeant Foster rode off with the body."

"You let the Northwest Mounted steal a U.S. federal fugitive?"

"No. I let him think he did. That owlhoot was just a poor shiftless thief who never did anything Uncle Sam's interested in. Got at least a couple of birds with one shot, too. By slickering the Mountie into vanishing off into the blue with the evidence, I can forget who might have to answer to Utah for killing him. I'd be obliged if we kept all this between us, though. Might be a few birds left to that shot I just mentioned."

"What was that about Kincaid?"

"He's another deputy, turned up missing. I'm looking for the one that bushwhacked him on his way to Crooked Lance. Been snooping around for Mexican heels and a .30-30 deer rifle amongst the folks I bought over here yesterday evening. Ain't found anybody that fits, yet. But we'll have more company, soon. Let's see about them ham and eggs. I've worked up a real appetite, likely from the mountain air."

Chapter 21

A band of mounted Indians brought in Mabel Hanks and the six riders from Crooked Lance who'd been with her when she tried to cut Longarm and his prisoner off at Bitter Creek. They'd given up there, and followed sign as far as the scene of Tinker's death before being jumped and captured by Longarm's Indian allies.

Mabel rode in dusty but trying to look elegant, sitting sidesaddle under her feathered hat, which the Indians admired immensely. Her little husband came over as Longarm helped Mabel dismount, stealing a feel of the holstered, mansized S&W she wore around her corseted waist. Cedric Hanks said, "You shouldn't have let 'em take you, damn it!"

"Oh, shut up! What were we supposed to do, make a stand in a dry canyon against all these Injuns? What's going on hereabouts? It looks like you-all had a firefight where these jaspers surrounded us."

Cedric shrugged and said, "They surrounded us, too. This lawman's pretty slick, but he lost his prisoner. Damned if I can figure what he wants with the rest of us."

Mabel glanced at Longarm and asked, "Is that right? Did the prisoner get away after all the work we did?"

"Didn't get away, ma'am. He's on his way to Canada, dead. That Mountie rode off with the body."

"And you're still standing here? What's the matter with you? He can't be more'n a few miles off. Why ain't you chasing him?"

"Got bigger fish to fry. Besides, I've transported

189

dead ones before. Gets tedious to smell after a day or so on the trail. I figure packing a rotting cadaver all the way to Canada is punishment enough for being more stubborn than smart. You and these boys hungry? The agent sent some husked dry corn over from the stores and the Indians will sell you jerked beef and coffee. For folks as aimed to track me and mine from hell to breakfast, you didn't store much grub in your possibles."

"We thought you was making for Bitter Creek, like you said."

"I figured you might. Where's Captain Walthers? Following the tracks across the Great Salt Desert?"

"How should I know? The army man peeled off along the way. He rode off talking dark about a telegram to the War Department."

"That's good. Why don't you set a spell and make yourselves to home? I'll be over at the agency if you need anything. Anything important, that is. I don't split firewood and the Indians will show you where to get water, answer the call o' nature, or whatever."

He walked away, leaving the newcomers to jaw about their position with those already gathered, worried and restless, around the campfire.

As he crunched across the gravel, Hanks fell in at his side, protesting, "Not so fast, dammit. You got no right to hold Mabel and me. We ain't done nothing. Hell, the other night, I thought you and me was fixing to spring Cotton Younger together!"

"So did I, till I got a better grasp on the situation. You were right about Mabel being riled with me, but what the hell, she had her reasons."

"I don't know what you're talking about. Did Cotton Younger say anything to you 'fore he passed away? You must know it wasn't my idea to shoot him before he told us where the James Boys was hiding!"

"He died sort of sudden." Longarm lied.

"Jesus, didn't you get anything out of him? How come you let that Sergeant Foster steal him? Wasn't your orders to bring him in dead or alive?"

"Yep, but I just explained all that. They'll likely rawhide me some for losing the body, but not as hard as they would have for gunning a guest of the U.S. State Department, and Foster was a serious cuss. Besides, what can you really do to a dead owlhoot? He can't talk and hanging him without a fair trial seems a mite uncivilized. I reckon they could hold a trial, if the jury had clothespins on their noses and the judge didn't ask how he pleaded, but as you can see, it'd be a waste of time and the taxpayer's money."

"You're funning me, Longarm. I'll bet you got it out of him. I'll bet you know where Jesse James is hiding! I know you marshals from old. You wouldn't take that Mountie pulling the wool over your eyes unless you was on to something bigger than old Cotton Younger!"

"Well, you just go back to your woman and study on it. I've had my say about the missing cadaver and this conversation's over."

He left the bewildered little man standing there and continued to the mission. The sun had topped high noon and he found the Caldwells and Kim Stover out back, seated in the shade behind the kitchen shed as the harsh, cloudless light made up for the cold night before by baking the dusty earth hot enough to fry eggs on.

Agent Caldwell started to ask more questions, but his wife, Portia, looked knowingly at Kim and said something about making the rounds of the village, adding something about sick Indian kids.

Caldwell muttered, "I don't remember any of the Utes being sick," but he let her lead him off after she'd tugged firmly on his sleeve a time or two.

Kim Stover smiled wanly and said, "She's quite the little matchmaker, ain't she?"

Longarm sat on the kitchen steps near her camp chair in the shade and said, "She's got a lot of time on her hands, out here with no other white women to talk to."

"She was advising me on the subject. I reckon we sort of told the stories of our lives to one another, between supper and breakfast. She doesn't think I ought to marry up with Timberline."

"I never advise on going to war or getting married, but the gal who gets Timberline ain't getting much in the way of gentle. He rides good, though. Must know his trade, to be working as ramrod for a big outfit. Maybe he's out to marry you for your cows."

"I know what he's after, and it ain't my cows. Ben and me didn't have much of a herd when he died. It's thanks to Timberline my herd's increased by a third since then. I know you don't like him, but he's been very kind, in his own rough way."

"Well, maybe he don't like my looks. How'd he add to the size of your herd? Not meaning to pry."

"He didn't steal them for me, if that's what you're getting at. Timberline's been honest and hard-working, for his own outfit and all the others in Crooked Lance. He's the trail boss and tally man when we drive the consolidated herd to market because the others respect him. More than once, when the buyers have tried to beat us down on the railside prices, Timberline warned us to hold firm. Working for an eastern syndicate, he always knew the going and fair price."

"That figures. His bosses back East would wire him the quotations on the Chicago Board. That's one of the things I've been meaning to get straight in my head, ma'am. You folks needed that telegraph wire. When did it first start giving you trouble?"

She thought and said, "Just after we caught that cow thief, Cotton Younger. We wired Cheyenne we had him and they wired back not to hang him but to hold him till somebody came to pick him up. Right after that the line went dead. Some men working for Western Union fixed it once, but it went out within the week. Timberline and some of the others rode up into the passes to look at it. They said it looked like the whole line needed to be rebuilt."

"Were any of those other lawmen in Crooked Lance while the line was up that one time? More important, did any of them send a message from your father-in-law's store?"

"I wouldn't know. I don't speak to him or to his two awful women. My ex-mother-in-law said bad things about me that weren't true. Her snippy daughter backed her."

"Do tell? What did they say against you?"

"Oh, the usual small-town gossip about a woman living alone. My sister-in-law's a poor old maid who likely doesn't know what grown folks do in the dark. Her mother can't know much better. All her man thinks about is money. You notice they only have one child, and she was born long enough ago to be getting long in the tooth now. Poor things are spiteful 'cause they never get no . . . you know."

"Ummm, well, they did seem sort of lonesome, now that you mention it. They gossiped about you and Timberline, huh?"

"Oh, that's to be expected, even though he's never trifled with me. What they suspicioned was even more vicious!"

"You mean they had more'n Timberline about your dooryard?"

"They as much as accused him of Ben's death. When he was killed in a stampede they passed remarks about how Timberline had never liked Ben as much as he seemed to like me."

"That's a hard thing to say about a man. Anybody go along with it?"

" 'Course not. You may as well know I took it serious enough to study on it, too. I questioned all the hands who were on the drive with my late husband. Talked to hands who weren't fond of Timberline as well as his own Rocking H riders. Them two old biddies should be ashamed of themselves!"

"Just what happened to your man, if you don't mind talking about it?"

"It was a pure accident, or, more rightly, Ben was a pure fool. They were driving in rough country when the herd was caught by a thunderstorm. A lightning flash spooked the herd and they started to stampede. My husband rode out wide to head 'em off and turn the leaders. Riding in fallen timber at a dead run. They say Timberline shouted a warning to him. Called him back and told him not to try, but to let 'em run, since the running was poor and there was a ridge ahead that would stop 'em."

"That sounds like common cow sense, ma'am. What happened then?"

"Ben's pony tripped over a log and went down. The herd ran over him and the pony, stomping both flat as pancakes. Later, my in-laws allowed it was Timberline's fault. They said he'd put Ben on the point, knowing it was dangerous."

"Well, somebody has to ride the point, though some trail bosses tend to pick unmarried men for it."

"Ben knew cows as well as anyone. Nobody got him killed. He got himself killed trying to prove he was the best cowboy in the valley."

She looked away as she added, bitterly, "He had to prove he was good for *something,* I reckon."

Longarm sat silently, mulling over what she'd told him. He had to admit the boss bully of Crooked Lance hadn't done much more wrong than any other trail boss would have, and even if he'd had a hankering for another man's wife, Timberline didn't look like a man who could scare up thunder and lightning with a wave of his hat.

Longarm's groin tingled slightly as he mulled over her words about the Stover women. The one in his room had moved her tail from side to side like a fish. In the livery stable, had it been the same one? It was hard to tell. Nobody does it the same way standing up. Had he laid the mother, the daughter, or *both* of 'em? And did he really want to know?

Kim Stover was asking, "When are you going to let us ride out? I asked the Caldwells, and while they're friendly enough, I couldn't get a straight answer from either one."

"That's 'cause they don't know, ma'am. They're likely as puzzled about it as yourself."

"Don't *you* know?"

"Well, sure. Ain't ready to say, just yet."

"Portia Caldwell said you were given to sly ways, but I think you've passed sly and ridden into ridiculous! You've lost Cotton Younger. You know everything we do. What are you waiting for now?"

"The full cast assembled, ma'am. By now, Captain Walthers has intercepted the wires sent from here and will know where we are. He should be riding in directly, madder than a wet hen and likely leading a troop of cavalry."

"Good Lord! Are you waiting for the whole world to ride onto this reservation?"

"No, ma'am, just all my suspects. If you're getting bored, I'd be proud to take you for a ride in the hills or something."

"I'll pass on the something. Every time Timberline takes me for a ride we wind up wrestling."

"I don't wrestle with gals, ma'am. My offer was meant neighborly."

"I'll still pass on it. Timberline's enough to handle. You've got a very sneaky habit of saying one thing and meaning another!"

Chapter 22

Captain Walthers rode in from the west late that afternoon. The Indians had not rounded him up. It would not have been a well-advised move, for the captain rode in full uniform at the head of two troops of U.S. Cavalry under fluttering red and white guidons.

Longarm was waiting for him on the front porch of the agency, along with Caldwell and some of the others, including Kim, the Hankses, and Timberline.

Captain Walthers rode directly up and stared down grimly without dismounting. "I have two questions and a squadron to back them up, Longarm. Where is my horse, and where is my prisoner?"

"Both dead. Your walker slipped and gutted himself on sharp shale, so I had to shoot him. My office will pay damages, of course."

"We'll settle that later. What's this about my prisoner, Cotton Younger, wanted for desertion in time of war?"

"The man I lit out with is dead and gone, whether you wanted him or not."

"What do you mean, gone? Where's his goddamned body? Sorry, ladies."

"He was killed by one of these vigilantes. I don't know which one. That Canadian peace officer, Foster, made off with the remains last night. He's likely got a good start on you by now."

"He stole a man wanted by the War Department? Which way did he ride out?"

"Headed for Canada, most likely. You'd be wasting

196

your time trying to catch him, Captain. He's a hell of a tracker and has a day or more of lead on you. I doubt I could find him myself, now."

"I'll see about that. I'm charging you with horse theft, Deputy."

"Why make more of a fool of yourself? I said we'd pay for the critter and my defense at any trial would be that I requisitioned the nearest mount at hand to save a man from a lynch mob. As a peace officer, I have the right to do such things as the need arises."

"Why didn't you ask me to help you, then?"

"You'd only have got in my way. As it was, I had a hell of a time making it here before these others caught up."

The army man turned to the Indian agent and asked, "Aren't you the law, hereabouts?"

"I sure am, soldier."

"I demand you arrest that man for obstructing me in my duties!"

Caldwell's face was calm as he answered, "I demand you flap your wings and lay an egg, too, but I don't suppose you have to if you don't really want to."

"You don't intend to let a few past misunderstandings between the army and the Bureau of Indian Affairs obstruct justice, do you?"

"I sure do, soldier. Once upon a time, when I had some Navajo all set to ride back peaceable, some hot-headed second lieutenant charged in with his troop and— Never mind, some of our men have acted like idiots, too, in the past. Suffice to say, I don't reckon your office and mine owe one another favors."

"I see. You intend to side with the Justice Department in this jurisdictional dispute."

"No, I intend to side with Longarm. He's a friend of mine. I never met *you* before."

Captain Walthers turned in his saddle to address a burly, middle-aged noncom, saying, "Sergeant! Arrest that man!"

The sergeant looked thoughtful and replied, "Begging the Captain's pardon, but we're on Indian land."

"God damn it, Sergeant, are you afraid of Indians?"

"Ute Indians? Yessir, and Fort Douglas might just like to know our plans before the Captain starts an Indian war without their say-so."

"I am surrounded by maniacs!" the captain protested to anyone who wanted his opinion. Then he scowled down at Caldwell and demanded, "Would you sic your tame Utes on us if we just took this sassy deputy off with us?"

Caldwell shrugged and said, "I don't know how *tame* they might be if you tried to arrest their blood-brother, soldier. It's my duty to try and keep them off the warpath and if they got unruly, I'd have to chide them for . . . whatever. You'll notice I've told my wife to stay inside until this is settled. I've told these other folks to take cover, but nobody listens to me around here. Not even the Indians, when they get riled up about things."

The sergeant leaned toward the captain to murmur, "Sir, some Utes are covering us from those houses on our left flank. Just saw some movement off to the right."

"Damn it, the War Department's going to get a full report on this entire matter!"

Caldwell asked mildly, "Would you like to send a telegram on my agency wire, Captain? It'll be dark soon. You and your men are welcome to spend the night on my reservation."

Walthers hesitated as Longarm cast an anxious glance at the sky. The damned sun *was* getting low again. That was the trouble with soldiers. They moved like greenhorns riding snails.

He suddenly brightened and asked, "Hey, Captain? As long as you and your troopers will be riding back to Fort Douglas in the morning, what do you say to helping me transport some prisoners to the Salt Lake railroad depot? From there I'll make connections over the divide and down to Denver, and—"

"What prisoners are you talking about? Are you holding that army deserter after all?"

"No, the one we were all fighting over in Crooked Lance is dead and gone. I'm figuring on arresting the killer of Deputy Kincaid, once I tie up a few loose ends so—"

"You ask the *army* to help you, after the way you've thwarted me at ever turn?"

"Well, it would be neighborly, and we are working for the same government, ain't we?"

"How would you like to flap your wings and lay an egg, Longarm?"

"I thought it was funnier the first time I heard it. Does that mean you won't help me?"

"I'd join the Mexican army first! As soon as my men and their mounts are rested I'm going back to Fort Douglas to file an official complaint, and you—you can go to the devil!"

"I'll tell Marshal Vail you were asking about him. You're leaving me in a bit of a bind, though. Can't deputize these Indians to transport prisoners off the reservation. Yep, it figures to be a chore."

For the first time since riding in, Captain Walthers looked pleased as he asked, "You don't say? My heart bleeds for you, Longarm, but I just can't reach you. I hope you sink, you—never mind. Ladies present."

The captain wheeled and rode off to find a campsite for the night as his troopers followed, some of them grinning and one corporal tipping his hat to the ladies as he swung past.

Kim Stover asked, "What was that about you making some arrests?"

Longarm looked around, as if worried about being overheard before he confided, "I'm going to have to ask a favor, ma'am. Timberline?"

"I'm listening, but I don't feel up to doing favors, either."

"Just listen before you go off half-cocked. It's a long, hard ride back to Crooked Lance, the way we've all

199

come. On the other hand, it's an easy downhill ride from here to Salt Lake City."

"What in thunder do I want to go to Salt Lake City for?"

"A ride, of course. Free ride on the railroad back to Bitter Creek, from where you'll be only a spit an' a holler from Crooked Lance. Wouldn't you like to save Miss Kim here, and the others, a long hard ride for home?"

"Maybe, but what's the tricky part?"

"I aim to deputize you as a U.S. Deputy's deputy. You'll get a dollar a day, vittles, and a free ride almost home in exchange for doing nothing much."

Kim Stover's eyes widened as she smiled hopefully.

Cedric Hanks said, "Hell, why not deputize *me*? He's only a cowboy, big as he may be! Me and Mabel are professionals!"

"I thought abut it," Longarm soothed, "but my boss ain't partial to private detectives since he had a set-to with Allan Pinkerton's Secret Service, during the war. As for your wife, I've never heard of a female working for the government."

Timberline's suspicion had faded to anticipation as he asked, "Would I get to wear a badge?"

"Not on temporary duty. As a peace officer, I'm empowered to deputize posses and such, but I won't need more'n one hand to help me herd my suspects in."

Mabel Hanks asked, "Who on earth are you talking about, Longarm? Who are you fixing to arrest?"

"Ain't sure yet," Longarm lied. "We'll work it out come morning, after the troopers and that pesky captain leave."

Longarm didn't spend the night with Dances-Humming. For one thing, he couldn't trust her. For another, he wasn't sure he should take his clothes off. He spent the night in the agency, in a spare room next to Kim Stover's. As he lay across the bed, fully dressed, he could hear the redhead moving about on the other side of the thin wall. Once he heard her using the chamber pot. It shouldn't have made him think of what it did, but the redhead had a nice shape and it was hard not to picture what he caught himself seeing clearly in his mind.

He knew his boast had been spread around by now. Timberline had strutted off like a rooster, feeling important, most likely. Hungry Calf's young men were watching to see if anyone tried to make a break for it. They had instructions not to try and stop him—or her. The killer—or killers—of Deputy Kincaid and that Missouri lawman were dangerous as hell, but wouldn't get far, once they made their play.

He could hear the bedsprings under the woman in the next room. She seemed to be tossing and turning as if she found it hard to fall asleep, too. Longarm lay there, puffing his cheroot and blowing smoke rings at the ceiling as he thought about Kim Stover, mostly to keep awake.

There was a soft tap on his door. Longarm frowned and rolled quietly to his feet. He slid over to the door and asked, "Yeah?"

A man's voice said, "It's Captain Walthers. I'd like a word with you."

Longarm muttered, "Shit," and opened the door.

The army man didn't come in. He said, "Some of those hands were talking to my troopers by the fire. What's going on here, now?"

"You mean Timberline helping me transport a prisoner or two? You already said you wouldn't do it."

"I don't owe you spit, but I'll admit I'm curious. Do you really have anything nailed down, or are you trying to bluff someone into making a break for it?"

"I owe you an apology. You ain't as dumb as you seem. I didn't think it was possible, anyway."

"I figured you were bluffing. Unless your suspect's awfully dumb, he'll figure it out as well. There's hardly a chance of getting away from here. Anybody can see that. You let the Mountie get away with our prisoner because you weren't expecting it. By now, you'll have your Utes watching every route out of the reservation, won't you?"

More to pass the time than in any hope of learning anything, Longarm said, "Maybe the one, or ones, I'm after ain't as smart as you and me."

"It's not my mission, but I've put a few things together. Your friend, Kincaid, had worked in Missouri, as had the other missing lawman and the old man who apparently came to help Cotton Younger. That means your man is from Missouri, probably well-known there. He had to kill the three of them because they might have recognized him on sight."

"You aiming to help me, or are we just jawing?"

"Unless you can nail a prisoner with a military charge, I have no authority to help you. Cotton Younger was the only possible member of the James-Younger gang wanted on an army warrant, and thanks to you, his corpse is halfway to Canada by now!"

"You do go by the book, don't you? It's no wonder Cotton Younger deserted your old army. It's gotten chickenshit as hell since I was in the service. 'Course, in those days we were fighting, not lookin' up rules and regulations. It's been nice talking to you, Captain."

He closed the door softly in Walthers's face. While he wanted to annoy the captain, he didn't intend to disturb the lady next door.

He chuckled as he heard the angry boot-heels stamping off. If he couldn't use the infernal soldiers, at least he might get rid of 'em by rawhiding their leader every chance he got.

He sat on the bed and pondered whether to get some sleep or not. The Indians would awaken him if anything important happened. He knew he might have a hard day ahead of him, too.

A tiny beam of light caught his eye. He saw that it came from a chink in the pine panelling between the rooms. He shrugged. She was likely under the covers, anyway. He lay back and tried to doze, but sleep refused to come. He muttered, "What the hell, curious is curious."

He got up and tiptoed to the wall, putting an eye to the peephole. He was almost too late. Kim Stover had just turned from the dressing table and was headed back for the bed, stark naked. Longarm held his breath as she crossed the room and snuffed the light before getting under the quilts. Then he went back to his own bed, grinning.

He'd been right as rain. She was red-haired all over.

The army column rode out just after breakfast, taking their own sweet time, as always.

Hungry Calf found Longarm eating beans by the pony line and said, "Nobody left last night. What does my brother think this means?"

"Means I was wrong, or that I'm up against somebody smarter than I figured. Are your young men watching the soldiers?"

"Of course. It is fun to scout them from the rimrock. Just like the old days. Both you and Agent Caldwell said it would be a bad thing to attack them. Could we just frighten them a little?"

"No. I just want to know when they're clean off the reservation and out of my hair. I'd like to have that snoopy captain at least half a day's ride away from me before I make my next move."

"We will do it, but the way you white men do things is very boring. Do you always take so much time to take an enemy at a disadvantage?"

"Some of us do. Lucky for us, your folks never got the hang of it."

"If you know who you're after, why don't you just kill him?"

"Like you said, our ways are boring. I have to be able to prove my suspicions in a court of law. Sometimes, when a bad white man is very clever, he refuses to fight. He just says he didn't do it. Then I have to get twelve other white men to see if he lies."

"Can't you choose these twelve from among your friends?"

"Not supposed to. How long a ride is it to Salt Lake City, maybe with some kicking and fussing along the way?"

"Two days, as white men ride. Maybe three, with trouble. The big town you speak of is sixty, maybe seventy of your miles."

"Good roads?"

"Yes. Wide wagon trace. Plenty water. Easy riding. Just far. Didn't you ride that way, the last time you were here after bad white men?"

"No, took the hard way home. That's how I knew about that holdout in the oil shale country. With all the folks and the fooling about, I'll figure on a seventy-two hour ride. It's gonna be a tricky bitch, but I'll manage."

Hungry Calf wandered off and Longarm spent the morning trying not to go out of his head from inaction. By noon, more than one of the people in White Sticks had pestered him for an idea of when he intended, for God's sake, to *do* something.

A little past noon he wandered over to the crowd around the cold campfire. His scouts had told him the army troops were long gone, and he saw that Kim Stover had joined her Crooked Lance friends, along with the Hankses and Timberline.

He moved into position, took a deep breath, and let half of it out as he said flatly, "Cedric Hanks and Mabel Hanks, you are under arrest. Anything you say may be used as evidence against you."

Everyone looked more than startled, but the midget leaped to his feet as if he were about to have a running fit. Mabel started to reach under her duster as Longarm's .44 came out. "Don't do it, Mabel. I'd hate to gun a lady."

Cedric gasped, "Longarm, have you been drinking, or were you always crazy? You are reaching for straws! We ain't done a thing you can fine us ten dollars for!"

The others were on their feet now, moving to either side as the little detective danced in front of Longarm, protesting his innocence.

Longarm said, "Deputy Timberline, disarm them prisoners."

The big ramrod grinned and started to do so. "Hot damn! But what are we arresting 'em for, pardner?"

"The murder of Deputy Kincaid is enough to hang 'em. We'll get the details of the other killings out of 'em in the Salt Lake City jail!"

Cedric Hanks pointed a pudgy finger at his wife and blurted, "It was her that took that shot at you in Bitter Creek, God damn it! But we were only trying to scare you!"

Mabel gasped and said, "It was his idea! I only wanted to be friendly, remember?"

"I remember it fondly, Mabel. You wore them same high heels when you smoked up the law office in Bitter Creek that night. A .30-30 is a light as well as an accurate weapon, too. I'll allow you made good time, beating me back to the hotel like that. Then you and Cedric made up that fool story about someone running down the hall when I caught him trying to sneak in for another try at me."

"Longarm, you know I had my head against that panel while you were—"

"Watch it. There are ladies present and you're talking about your wife."

"Hang it, I couldn't have overheard what I overheard unless—"

"You had your head next to my keyhole. Where did you folks bury Kincaid and the other lawman, Hanks?"

"Bury? We never laid eyes on either. We was in Bitter Creek till after you reached Crooked Lance. Hell, we met you on the train, halfway to Cheyenne!"

"So what? It's a short run and the trains run both ways from Bitter Creek. You were laying for me. Just like you laid for them others sent for Cotton Younger!"

"Hell, there was a whole mess of you sent! You think we'd have been dumb enough to try and stop you all?"

"No, just the smart ones. You used me to do what you aimed to do all along. I'll allow you got me to spring your friend from the Crooked Lance jail. Or if that wasn't it, you were trying to get one more lawman out of the way. We'll settle the details when we carry you before the judge."

"Longarm, you don't have a thing on us but hard feelings for some past misunderstandings. Hell, you don't even have no *bodies* to show that judge!"

Longarm chuckled and said, "Sure I do. I got both of yours. You mind your manners, and I'll try to deliver 'em both alive!"

Chapter 23

"I feel sorry for the poor thing," Kim Stover said as she sat by Longarm on a log, a day's ride from Ouray Reservation.

They'd made camp for the night at a natural clearing near a running brook of purring snow-melt from the Wasatch Mountains. The hands had built a roaring white man's fire of fallen, wind-cured timber, and the Hankses were across from Longarm and Kim Stover. The midget's left hand was handcuffed to his partner's right, for the female of the species in this instance was likely deadlier than the male.

Longarm chewed his unlit cheroot as he studied his new prisoners across the way. Then he shrugged and said, "Nobody asked her to marry up with the little varmint, ma'am."

"Oh, I'm not feeling sorry for her! It's the poor little midget she's obviously led into a life of crime."

"Nobody gets led into a life of crime, ma'am. Though most everyone I meet in my line of work seems to think so. Folks like to shift the guilt to others, but it won't wash. The man who murdered Lincoln had a brother who's still a fine, decent man. An actor on the New York stage. I'd say his baby brother led himself astray. Most folks do."

"I can see your job might make you cynical."

"No might about it, ma'am. It purely does!"

"Just the same, I'd say that woman was the cause of it all. She's hard as nails and twice as cold. She's been spitting at you with her eyes all day."

"She's likely riled at me for arresting her and the midget."

"There's more to it than that. A woman understands about these things. I can tell what's passed between the two of you!"

"Oh?"

"Yes. She obviously feels scorned by you. Tell me, did she flirt with you, when first you met?"

"Well, sort of."

"There you go. And being a man who'd be too much of a gentleman to take the likes of her seriously, you likely laughed at her pathetic attempts to turn your head."

"Now that you mention it, I did have a chuckle or two at her expense."

"She's been flirting with Timberline and some of the others. I told him what she was and he said I was probably right. You don't reckon she'd be able to seduce any of our party, do you?"

"Not with her husband handcuffed to her and the key in my pocket."

"I know most of the boys pretty well, but some of 'em are young and foolish, and she's not bad-looking, in her cheap, hard way. You're probably well-advised to keep them chained together. She'd do anything to get away."

"I'd say you were right on the money, ma'am. But we got Timberline and over two dozen others guarding 'em. So I reckon they'll be with us as we ride into Salt Lake City."

"Which one do you reckon will hang for the murders, the trollop over there or her poor little husband?"

"Don't know. Maybe both of 'em, if they get convicted. They're both sticking tight as ticks to their innocence."

"You think the woman did the shooting, don't you? It took me a few minutes to figure out what you meant about that .30-30 rifle. Won't you need that as evidence?"

"I could use it, but I made a dumb move back in Crooked Lance when I jawed about it in front of everybody. I suspicion the rifle's as well hid as the bodies, by now. They both packed S&W .38s till Timberline took 'em away."

"He's so easy to please. I do think Timberline's starting to like you, Longarm."

"Well, most boys like to feel important in front of a pretty gal. He's never really gone for me, serious. Them few brags and swings were sort of like walking a picket fence. Not that I blame him, all things considered."

"I thank you for the compliment."

"Just stating the facts as I see 'em, ma'am."

"Stop flirting. You know it flusters me. There's something else I've been wondering about."

"What's that, ma'am?"

"If there is one thing I've learned you're not, it's a fool, Longarm. You played a foxy grandpa on that Mountie, didn't you?"

"Did Portia Caldwell give away anything about government business while the two of you jawed about me?"

"She didn't have to. I figured out why you were so calm and collected when Sergeant Foster rode off like a thief in the night with the body of that man we'd been holding. He wasn't Cotton Younger at all, was he?"

Longarm laughed and said, "You weren't behind the kitchen door when the brains got passed out, Miss Kim. I told you all in Crooked Lance you were wasting a lot of time by holding out on everybody over that fool reward. If you'd sent him on to Cheyenne right off, we'd have all known it sooner."

"But the Mountie still thinks he's packing the real Cotton Younger off to Canada? Oh, my, that's rich!"

"Might be getting ripe, too. I wonder if he'll smoke him, salt him, or just hang tight and tough it through. Hell of a long ways, considering it's summer."

"You waited until Captain Walthers came and left,

satisfied that another man had his deserter. You are the sly one, but why did you do that?"

"Why? Had to. Had to whittle it down to where I was the only lawman left. These jurisdictional matters can be a real pain, as you may have noticed when you were still in the game."

"I'm sorry now, that we were so dumb about it all. I know we'd have been tricked out of the reward some way, even if we had been holding the real Cotton Younger. Would you mind telling me who we *were* holding, all that time?"

"He was almost who he said he was. His real name was Tinker, 'less his dying confession was another lie. Doesn't seem likely, though, considering some of the other things he confessed to. There was no reward on him. So despite our past misunderstandings, you'll have to settle for the rising beef market."

"I feel like such a fool! Imagine, holding an innocent boy and almost seeing him hung improper!"

"Don't be too hard on yourself, ma'am. I don't go along with improper hangings. but it turned out all right in the end. As for him being innocent, he wasn't Cotton Younger, but he wasn't all that innocent, either. Your friends were right to grab him as a cow thief, 'cause that's what he was. He wasn't out for your particular cows, but he wasn't packing that running iron for fun. either."

"Some of the boys are worried about the fact that one of them shot him before we got, well, more friendly-like. I told them you'd said you'd forget about it when we all rode into Salt Lake City. Can I take it I told 'em true?"

"Well, I never forget much, but I overlook a few things. My report will say he got shot trying to escape, which is close enough to the way it happened. No way on earth we'll ever know just whose round finished him, and most of you were shooting at him, as I remember it."

"You're very understanding. I'm truly sorry if I

210

seemed snippy when first we met. But one thing puzzles me. When you first rode into Crooked Lance, you said you weren't going back without Cotton Younger."

"I know what I said, and I meant it. But as you see, it wasn't Cotton Younger you were holding. It ain't my fault I can't make good my brag. The man we were all fighting over answered Cotton Younger's description, but he was somebody else. Meanwhile, half a loaf is better than none, and I *am* taking in the killer of Deputy Kincaid. So it'll most likely pay for my time and trouble."

"Longarm, who do you think you're bullshitting?"

"I beg your *pardon*, ma'am?"

"Come on, I've gotten to know you, and you are not the wide-eyed country bumpkin you pretend to be! You have no intention of going back to Denver without Cotton Younger, have you?"

Longarm laughed and said, "That's true enough, if I can lay my hands on the cuss, but who do you suggest I pick to fit my warrant?"

"I don't know how I know this. Maybe it's because there's something sort of smug crawling around in them innocent eyes when you don't think I'm looking. But I think you're too satisfied about a job well done. I think you know where Cotton Younger is!"

Longarm's mouth went dry as he forced himself to meet her level, questioning gaze, but his voice was calm as he shrugged and said, "You have a lively imagination, ma'am. I told you the man we all thought was Cotton Younger, wasn't. That don't leave us with anyone who answers to his description, does it?"

"I thought maybe you had your eye on one of the hands from Crooked Lance."

"Do tell? What makes you say that?"

"The midget and the woman likely gunned those other lawmen, like you said. If they were sent out to free the man they thought was Cotton Younger, that makes sense. The other man, the man who was a mem-

211

ber of the James-Younger gang could have only been killed by the *real* Cotton Younger!"

"Keep talking."

"Don't you see? The Hankses are private detectives who'd do anything for a dollar. That old man pretending to be a Canadian would have been valuable to them as an ally. Why would they have gunned him?"

"Beats me. Why would Cotton Younger have done it, if Cotton Younger wasn't the man in your jail?"

"That's simple. The real outlaw's been hiding out in Crooked Lance all this time. You know we're way off the beaten track, and ordinarily, no one would ever look for anyone there. Then a man answering to his description got picked up by us vigilantes and you know the rest. All hell broke loose. Old Chambrun-what's-his-name came busting in to free his kinsman, learned we had the wrong man, and started to light out. That's when the real Cotton Younger might have killed him, to shut him up for good. The Mountie saw through the fake Canadian accent. No telling how many ways a reckless old outlaw could have been caught, later, knowing the whereabouts of a wanted man who aims to lay low in Crooked Lance for keeps!"

Unfortunately, she was hitting damned close to home, considering she hadn't heard the dying Sailor Brown's last, wondering protest about being gunned unexpectedly.

Longarm chuckled and said, "You'd have made a great detective yourself, Miss Kim. But you're forgetting something. Nobody hereabouts fits Cotton Younger's description. Timberline's too big and the midget is a mite short. I don't know exactly what color hair you and that other gal might have started out with, but even if it should be cotton-blonde, the feller I'm after is man." He didn't think he should tell her how he knew that both she and Mabel Hanks were definitely female, so he added, "I've looked all the others over, more'n once. There ain't one in a whole score of riders that

212

would fit the wanted posters for Cotton Younger, real or otherwise."

"Half the men in Crooked Lance aren't here."

"I know. If there's anything to your suspicions, I might look the entire population of Crooked Lance over with a hand lens, some day. But I aim to carry my prisoners in as I catch 'em, not as I'd like 'em to fit wishful thinking."

"Then, in other words, you're saying I'm just running off at the mouth!"

"Well, I do see some points you've raised that will have to be answered. If ever we get that odd-matched pair to talk. To tell the truth, I don't *know* just what they were up to."

"You don't? Then why did you arrest them?"

"I told everybody at the time. For the murder of Deputy Kincaid. You eat the apple a bite at a time, ma'am. It ain't my job to get all the details out of 'em."

"But you said you didn't know what they were up to!"

"I meant I didn't know *why*. They might have been out to set the prisoner free. They might have been after the reward, just like they said. It don't matter all that much. You heard 'em admit they took a shot at me in Bitter Creek. That's against the law, no matter how you slice it. Just why they did it and who they're working for will come out in the wash. Since the midget is the brains, and she's the brawn, he'll no doubt tell a few tales on her to save his neck, before it's all over."

"Brrr, they are a pair, ain't they? What was that he said about having his head to some plywood, listening to you talk to somebody in Bitter Creek?"

"Oh, I don't remember just who I was talking to, ma'am. After his wife took a few shots at me I caught him listening, is all."

"Oh, I got the impression he was listening in on you and that slut of his. I'm trying to remember just what it was he said."

213

"Well, don't you worry your pretty head about it, Miss Kim."

This redhead was too quick-witted to be let out without a leash! A muzzle wouldn't hurt, either! How many of the others had she been to with her infernal speculations?

She suddenly blurted out, "Oh, I remember. He said he was listening when you and that hussy were . . ."

"What, ma'am?"

"You told him to hush, 'cause there were ladies present. Meaning me, I take it, since I'd hardly call Mabel Hanks a lady."

"I thought he was fixing to cuss. He was pretty riled when I arrested him."

"Longarm, were you and that awful woman—? Oh, I can't believe it!"

"That makes two of us. You do have a lively mind, and a mite dirty, meaning no disrespect. The woman is his wife, Miss Kim. Allowing for her being no better than you think she is, what you're suggesting is mighty wild, if you ask me!"

"I'm sorry, but it did cross my mind. She's not bad-looking, and you are a man, after all."

"Heaven forbid I'd be *that* kind of man, Miss Kim! Do I look like the sort of gent who'd trifle with a woman with her husband listening, watching, or whatever?"

She laughed a sort of earthy laugh and said, "As a matter of fact, you do. But I can't see you loving up a gal who'd just shot at you, with her husband next door, listening, or not. Nobody would do a thing like that but a very stupid man, which I'll allow you ain't."

"There you go. I knew you'd drop them awful notions, soon as you reconsidered 'em a mite!"

Chapter 24

Somewhere, somebody was hollering fit to bust, so Longarm woke up. He rolled, fully dressed, from under his canvas tarp and sprang to his feet, Winchester in hand and headed over toward the smoldering embers of the fire, in the direction of the confusion.

He found Timberline kneeling over Mabel Hanks, shaking her like a terrier shakes a rat as he thundered, "Gawd damn it, lady! I don't aim to ask nice one more time!"

Longarm saw the open handcuff dangling from the one still locked to Mabel's right wrist and said, "Let her be, Timberline. Even when she's talking she don't tell the truth worth mention."

He shoved a pine knot into the embers and waited, squatting on his heels, until it was ablaze. Meanwhile, everyone in camp converged around Timberline and his smirking captive. As Longarm got to his feet with the torch held out to one side, Kim Stover asked, "What happened? Where's the midget?"

"Damned if I know. My own fault. I locked that bracelet as tight as she'd go, but he has a wrist like an eight-year-old's and we hardly arrest enough that young to mention."

He fished the key from his pants and handed it to her. "When Timberline gets through shaking her teeth loose, get him off her and cuff her to a sapling till I get back."

"Are you going after him in the dark?"

"I don't aim to wait till sunup."

215

He found a tiny heel mark in the forest duff and started away from the clearing. A couple of the hands fell in beside him, anxious to help.

He said, "Go back and check to see if he lit out with anybody's weapon. I have enough to worry about, tracking him, without having to keep you fellers from getting shot."

"How do you know he has a gun, Longarm?"

"I don't. But I never track, trusting to a man's good nature. Put out them embers and keep together. He ain't got a mount. He may decide he needs one and you likely know by now, he's a slippery little imp!"

He left them to debate the matter and started ahead, making out a scuff-mark here and a heelprint there, until he came to the bank of the stream.

"Wading in water so's not to leave tracks, huh? Poor little bastard. Don't you know how cold it gets up here at night?"

He assumed his quarry would come out on the far side. Nine out of ten did. A distant, steady roar, far up the slope, told him there was a waterfall within a mile. Taking into account the size of the strides Cedric took, a mile in icy snow-melt seemed about right. Longarm shoved the sharp end of the pine knot in the mud beside the stream, leaving it glowing there as a distraction visible for a good distance. Then, swinging wide, he ran up the slope through the trees. He ran until his lungs hurt, and ran some more, making no more noise than he could help in his soft-soled boots over spongy, fallen fir needles.

He was out of breath by the time he reached the waterfall, and anyone making better time would have to have longer legs. The midget's only chance was that he'd been gone longer than Longarm figured.

He hadn't. After Longarm had squatted near the lip of the falls for about five minutes, he heard a splash downstream and the crunch of a wet boulder turning under foot. He waited until a barely-visible movement caught his eye across the falls. Then he said conversationally, " 'Evening, Mister Hanks. Going someplace?"

The darkness exploded in a flashing roar of brilliant orange. Longarm knew, as something smashed, hard, into the wood above his head, that the little bounty hunter had stolen someone's saddle rifle.

He fired back, rolling away from where he'd just been, as another shot flared across the stream, followed by the patter of little running feet.

Longarm ran across the slippery lip of the falls, calling out, "Hold on, old son! You're turning this into serious business!"

His quarry fired again, aiming at the sound of Longarm's voice. The shot went wild, of course, since Longarm knew enough to crab sideways after sounding off. He fired back, not really expecting to hit a savvy gunfighter in the dark by aiming at the flashes. He noticed that the little man had fired and crabbed to his right both times as a broken twig betrayed his next run. He kept running uphill, too. It figured. A man that size hadn't seen army training or he'd know more about dismounted combat in the dark. The first thing you learned from old soldiers was that most men crab to the right and instinctively run uphill when they're lost in the dark.

Longarm got behind a tree and called out, "Cedric, I'm pure tired of chasing you! You drop that thing and come back here!"

A bullet thudded into the trunk. The ornery little cuss was shooting to kill. So Longarm let out a long coyote-wail and gasped, "Gawd! I'm hit! Somebody help me! I'm hit in my fool leg!"

Then he moved quietly off to one side and waited.

Something crunched in the dark. What seemed like ten years later, Longarm heard another sound, closer. The little cuss was *serious*!

Longarm decided to end it.

He fired blindly in the direction of the last sound, moving to his left as he levered the Winchester and watched the bright wink of the other's rifle. Then Longarm fired, not at the flash, but to its left as he was racing. He heard a thump and the sound of a metal object sliding downhill over roots and pine needles, followed by some thrashing noises and a low, terrible curse.

Then it became very quiet.

Longarm counted, "One, Mississippi, two Mississippi . . ." to a hundred. Then he moved in, knowing that not one man in a thousand plays possum through a hundred Mississippis.

He heard harsh breathing, which was either somebody dying or damned fine acting. So he circled uphill and approached quietly from the far side.

In the almost-total darkness Cedric Hanks was only an inkblot against a blackboard. Longarm moved in, squatted, and put his Winchester's muzzle against the blur before he said, quietly. "I'm fixing to strike a light. One twitch and this thing goes off."

"You've done me, you big bastard!" the midget groaned.

Longarm held the match well out to the side, anyway, as he thumbnailed its head aflame. Then he whistled and said, "Smack in the chest. You're right, mister. You're dead."

"You big bully! I never had a chance."

"Sure, you did. You could have stayed put. What made you make such a fool play, Hanks? Your best bet would have been to face the charge in court. As your wife, Mabel, didn't have to bear witness against you, and vice versa."

"That bitch woulda sold me to save her own twitching ass! Why'd you put that light out? I can't see a thing."

"Nothing to look at," Longarm soothed, holding the lighted match closer to the little man's glazing eyes. He said, "Mister Hanks, you are done for and that's a fact. Before you go, would you like to give me Mabel's ass?"

"You already had it, you son of a bitch! Everybody's had her. She was always sayin' mean things about my size. How tall I am, I mean."

"She's a tartar, all right. Did she gun Kincaid, or was it you?"

"I don't know who she might have gunned in her time. You know who broke her in? Her own stepdaddy. Ain't that a bitch?"

"Yeah, but let's stick to serious crimes. When did you learn the man in Crooked Lance wasn't the real Cotton Younger?"

"Don't josh me, dammit. You know he was Cotton Younger."

"Let's try it another way. Who sent you out here? Who were you working for?"

"I told you, dammit, we was working it on our own, for the reward!"

"Then why did you and Mabel try to get rid of me?"

"It was her idea. She said she'd seen you once before, when one of the other gals in this . . . place she worked, pointed you out. She knew you were fixing to steal our chance at the reward. Shit, you know the rest."

"After she missed me on the streets of Bitter Creek, you worked out that old badger game to take me in bed, huh?"

"Sure. If you ask me, she enjoyed the screwing part best. I was to creep in and do you after she'd wore you out. I told her you looked like a hard man to wear out that way, but she said she'd give it her best."

"All right, how'd you do Kincaid? Fall in with him on the trail and maybe finish him off as he was dozing restful in her arms?"

"I told you, I never seen this damn Kincaid!"

"What about that lawman from Missouri?"

Cedric Hanks didn't answer.

He couldn't.

Longarm closed the dead man's eyes and got to his feet, heading down the slope. The little man would have been a messy load to carry. The cowhand who'd been careless about leaving firearms about could fetch him when he came to pick up his rifle.

Longarm made plenty of noise and called out, "It's

me, coming in!" as he approached the campsite. As others crowded around, asking all sorts of questions, he called out, "Let's get some light on the subject. It's all over."

Someone kicked ashes off the banked coals and threw some sticks of kindling on. They blazed up. Longarm looked at Mabel Hanks, kneeling by an aspen sapling with her wrist chained to it, and said, "I'm sorry, ma'am. Your man is dead. Before he passed on, he named you as the murderer of Deputy Kincaid. He died before I could find out about the others, but—"

Then Mabel Hanks was screaming like a banshee and fighting her handcuffs like a chained grizzly as she glared at him insanely, calling him a mother-loving son-of-a-whore for openers.

The she really started talking dirty.

Longarm saw Kim Stover staring at the raging woman, openmouthed, and suggested, "You'd best go off and stop your ears, ma'am. I suspicion she's a mite overwrought."

"For God's sake, she should be! You just said you killed her husband!"

"Yes, ma'am. He was trying to kill me, too. I was a mite better at it."

Longarm had studied women, but the longer he'd been at it the harder it was to figure them out. After having called Mabel all sorts of things, Kim Stover went over to comfort her, as the more recent widow shouted, "He was twice the man you were, you son of a bitch!"

Timberline sidled up alongside Longarm, asking softly, "What was that about her killing them fellers?"

"Let's put it this way: what he said to me was sort of fuzzy, but what I'll remember to the judge might put her away for a spell."

"Hot damn! You aim to railroad her, right?"

"Now, that's putting it unfriendly, Timberline. Let's say I'm worn out tying up all the loose ends of this case and, what the hell, I know for sure she shot at me. I'll allow it ain't neat, but at least it's enough to satisfy a grand jury and let me get on to something more worthy of my time. I don't really care if they convict her or not. I just want to be rid of this whole infernal mess!"

"You reckon any of us will get called as witnesses?"

"Why? Did any of you see her gun Kincaid or anyone else?"

"Hell, nobody but that old tattooed man ever *got* to Crooked Lance!"

"There you go. We'll just deliver the gal to the Justice Department and let them worry about her."

"You still need me as a deputy? I mean, what the hell, one old gal don't seem to rate all this guarding, if you ask me."

Longarm shrugged and said, "We'll be in Salt Lake City by tomorrow afternoon, deputized or singing Dixie. It would be a favor if you were with me when I took her to the federal courthouse. I'll likely need a witness, transporting a female prisoner as I just did."

"A witness? Federal courthouse? You just said you wouldn't need us in court. I wish you'd make up your mind."

Longarm laughed and explained, "Not as a witness against her. As a witness for me, just while I sign her in. You've heard the mouth on her, and half the women a lawman beings in sing that same old tune of rape."

Timberline's eyes widened. Then he grinned lewdly, and exclaimed, "Hot damn! I never thought of that! A man *would* get some golden opportunities in your line of work, wouldn't he?"

"People suspicion as much. A lawman with a lick of sense won't trifle with female prisoners, though. Usually, I like to bring 'em in with at least one deputy, making it two words against one. You won't have to sign statements or anything. They'll record you as my deputy and, of course, you'll get a check from the Justice Department that you can cash in Bitter Creek when you and the others get off there."

"Well, we're all headed to Salt Lake City, anyways. What's this thing about recording me?"

"You'll be in our files as a sometime law man. It won't interfere with your job at the Rocking H. We just like to keep a record on who's for or against us."

"Hell, that sounds good. Can I go on calling myself Deputy Malone?"

"Well, it wouldn't be official, once I drop you off the payroll, but I doubt if you'd get arrested for it. Malone's your last name, huh?"

"Yeah, but you can call me Timberline like everybody else. They been joshing me so long with that fool name I've gotten used to it."

One of the hands came over with a worried look and said, "I can't find my saddle rifle. Anybody see a Henry .44-40?"

Longarm said, "Didn't see it, but I know where it is. Get a tarp or a waterproof groundcloth and some latigos or twine. Got another package up the slope I'd be obliged if you'd wrap for me, seein' you're wearing leather chaps. My wool britches are soiled enough as it is."

Timberline followed Longarm and the cowhand up the slope to where their torchlight revealed the missing rifle ten yards from the toadlike body of the midget. Cedric Hanks had been ugly in life. Glaring up at them in death he looked like something that should have been carved on the parapets of Notre Dame. Timberline grimaced and said, "Funny, he looks so ugly for such a tiny thing. Didn't it bother you, Longarm? Picking on somebody so much littler than you?"

"Why should it? Never bothers *you*, does it?"

"Hey, I thought we'd made up!"

"Couldn't resist getting in a lick for fun. As to who was picking on who, the midget had the advantage, as well as the choice to make it a serious fight."

"Advantage? Poor little turd didn't come up to your bellybutton!"

"Making me the bigger target. As you can see, we

were both throwing .44-40 balls at one another, so if anything, I had to aim better, since there was so much less to hit. He likely became a gun-slick in the first place when he noticed that while God created Man, Sam Colt and other gunsmiths made them equal."

Timberline watched the cowboy roll the little corpse up in the groundcloth as he shuddered and said, "My head tells me you're likely right. But I'm glad it wasn't me that killed him. Looks like Windy's wrapping up a baby!"

"Let's get back with him. It's too late to think of bedding down, 'cause the sun's creeping up on us. We'll get an early start. We can eat right away and break camp by first light."

He turned and walked toward the campfire winking up at him through the trees, feeling more morose about the killing than he'd really let on to the men behind him. It didn't bother him that the man he'd killed had been so small. It bothered him that he'd had to kill at all. He'd trained himself not to show the sick feeling these affairs left in his stomach. He'd steeled himself to eat his next few meals mechanically, tasteless as they might be. He knew why so many men in his line of work wound up with bleeding ulcers, or like poor Jim Hickock, got to be ugly drunks toward the end.

He wasn't given to probing the dark shadows of his own mind, but he knew one night he'd dream about that ugly little gargoyle, as he had again and again, about the others he'd had to kill. It wasn't as if he felt guilty. He couldn't remember shooting anyone who hadn't deserved it. At least, not since the war. As a matter of fact, he wasn't sure *why* he should feel so drained after a gun fight—and disappointed.

Maybe it was just the waste. People lived such a short while at best. Man was born with a death's-head less than an inch below the soft skin of his face. By the time he was old enough to talk, he knew the graveyard waited just up the road ahead. What was it that made some men *rush* the process so?

He remembered that first one in the dawn mists of Shiloh, shouting fit to bust as he charged through the spring greenery into another boy's gunsights. He remembered the kick of the old Springfield against his shoulder as the world dissolved in gray-blue smoke for a long, breathless moment and how, as the smoke cleared, that other boy had been lying under a budding cherry tree with a surprised look on his face, and how the cherry blossom petals had fluttered down like gentle, pink snowflakes as the body stopped twitching. The first man he'd killed had been fourteen or so. A farm boy, from the looks of his dead hands as they lay, half open, near the stock of his musket in the cherry blossoms. It was later, when the kitchen crew brought the evening grub up to the line, that he'd noticed the ball of fuzzy, gray nothingness in his gut. He hadn't been able to eat a thing. By the second evening of the battle, he'd been hungry as a bitch wolf and pinned behind a stone wall without so much as a plug of tobacco to chew on. He'd learned, by the time they marched him beyond Shiloh Church through the sniper-haunted forests, not to let his feelings show.

But he still wondered sometimes, late at night, who that other boy had been, and why he'd been in such an all-fired hurry to end the life he'd hardly started.

Chapter 25

"The City of the Saints" lay at the base of the Wasatch Range, staring out across the desert to the west. Salt Lake City had grown some since Longarm had been there a few short years before. The outlying houses now extended into the foothills and the party had to ride for more than an hour through the town before they could get to the part they were headed for.

Little kids came out of the somber Mormon houses along the gravel road to stare at the big party riding in. Some of the kids threw sassy words or poorly aimed horse turds at them before scooting behind a picket fence. Longarm didn't know whether they were just being kids, or whether the Mormons were still telling them bedtime stories about how cruel the outside world could be. As long as they didn't improve their aim or throw something solid, it wasn't worth worrying about.

Timberline was leading the mount Mabel Hanks, handcuffed to the saddle horn, was sitting. Mabel had simmered down to a sullen silence, with a *just-you-wait!* look in her smoldering eyes.

Longarm found himself riding alongside Kim Stover, who seemed sort of quiet herself, since breaking camp. Longarm thought he knew what was bothering her, so he didn't say anything. They were riding in at an easy walk, for they were too far from the center of town to lope the rest of the way in and Longarm had warned his Wyoming companions not to make sudden motions in sight of the sometimes-truculent Mormon folk they were paying a call on.

After perhaps five minutes of silence, the redhead said with a disgusted tone in her voice. "I'd as soon you'd ride with someone else, Deputy Long."

"Oh? Well, you can drop back if you've a mind too, Miss Kim. I'm up here near the head of the column 'cause I know the way to Main Street and will likely be dismounting, first, at the Federal Building."

"If it's all the same to you, I mean to head direct to the depot."

"I never try to change a lady's mind, but I did offer you and yours a free ride up to Bitter Creek. I figure it'll take an hour or so to do the paperwork on my prisoner. Then I'll be free to see about getting all these hands and horses fixed with transportation."

"You're not taking that woman back to Denver?"

"Nope. They never sent me to get her. I'll let the Salt Lake office do the honors. Maybe ride back to Denver in one of them fancy Pullman cars. Be nice to stretch out between clean sheets for a change and I'm overdue for a good night's rest."

"I should think you'd enjoy another night with Mabel Hanks. But I suppose you've tired of her, eh? You men are all alike."

Longarm rode in silence for a time before he sighed, observing, "I might have known you gals would have your heads together on the only subject womenfolk never get tired of jawing about."

"Don't look so innocent. She told me—everything."

"She did? Well, why are you keeping it a secret? Where did she say she buried Kincaid and that other feller from Missouri?"

"Damn it, she didn't talk about any murders. She told me about you and her, in Bitter Creek."

"Well, I know I can hang the sniping in Bitter Creek on her. I was hoping she'd let her hair down to another woman on the details of her life of crime."

"Don't pussyfoot with me, you animal! She says you had your way with her in—in a fold-up bed. She said

226

that's why her poor little husband tried to kill you. He was defending her honor."

Longarm fished a cheroot from his vest pocket and lit it without comment.

After a time, Kim asked, "Well?"

"Well what, ma'am?"

"Aren't you going to deny it?"

"You reckon you'd believe me, if I did?"

"Of course not. Her description was, well, vivid."

"Funny, ain't it? Ten aldermen of the church could swear a man was tuning the organ of a Sunday, and if one woman told his wife he'd been at a parlor house instead—"

"Then you do deny it!"

"Ain't sure. Maybe I'd better study on it before I say one thing or 't'other. I don't aim to have you think I'm all that wicked. On the other hand, I wouldn't want you to put me down as a sissy."

Despite herself, the redhead laughed. Then she recovered and said, "I don't think she could have made that up about you folding her up in the wall when her husband busted in on you."

"By golly, that's a good touch I'd *never* have come up with! Next time the boys are bragging in the pool hall, I'll see if I can get them to buy such an interesting yarn."

He puffed some smoke ahead of him, and addressing an invisible audience, pontificated, "That story about the one-legged gal in Dodge was right interesting, Tex. But did I ever tell you about the time in Bitter Creek I made mad gypsy love to this gal married to a midget?"

"It does sound sort of wild. Are you suggesting she told me a lie? Why would any woman lie about such a thing?"

"Don't know. Why do men swap stories about Mexican spitfires and hotblooded landladies? Old Mabel's likely practicing up for when we carry her before the federal district judge, up ahead. Wait'll she gets to where you helped hold her down while Timberline and

227

all them other riders behind us took turns with me at—whatsoever."

"Oh! Do women play such tricks on you when you arrest them?"

"Not *all*. Only three out of four. Some ladies who shoot folks are sort of modest."

"She *is* a murderess and the wife of a gun-slick, isn't she? I hadn't considered that angle."

"I know. Most folks are more partial to dirty stories."

"Look, I'm sorry if I've wronged you, but damn it, she made it sound so *real*!"

"Do tell? Who'd she say was better at it, me or the midget?"

This time her laughter was less forced. She recovered and grinned, "I daren't repeat what she told me. As a woman who's been married, I'm not sure all the . . . details were possible."

Longarm didn't answer.

After a while, Kim said, "Yes, I see it all now. She's been trying to drive a wedge between us. I'd forgotten she was facing the rope. Tell me, do you think they'll really hang her?"

"If she's found guilty."

"Brrr. It seems so . . . so awful to think of a *woman* hanging."

"Ain't much fun for anybody. Mary Surratt was a woman, and they hung her for conspiring to kill Abe Lincoln. Some folks figured she was innocent, too."

"Oh, my what an awful thought! Doesn't it bother you to think of innocent people getting hung?"

"A mite. But since I've never hung nobody, it ain't my worry."

"I can't believe you have no pity for her. Even after what she did."

"I feel pity for everybody, ma'am. Mostly, I feel pity for the victims more'n I do the killers. Deputy Kincaid and likely that other feller had families. They'd likely expect me to do the right thing."

"An eye for an eye and a tooth for a tooth, eh? Isn't there something else about *mercy* in the good book?"

"Sure there is. I've read things written by philosophers. They say two wrongs don't make a right. They say the death penalty don't really stop the killings out our way. They *say* all sorts of things. But when it's their own son or daughter, husband or wife who's the victim, you'd be surprised how fast they get back to that old 'eye for an eye!' "

"Someday, we may be more civilized."

"Maybe. Meanwhile, we don't hang folks because they've killed someone. We hang 'em in order that someone else won't get killed. I've read what Emerson and them have to say about reform. Maybe some killers *can* be reformed. I don't know what makes a man or woman a killer. But I do know one thing. Not one killer has ever done it again, after a good hanging!"

It was a long time before she broke the silence once more to say, "I think I understand you better, Longarm. I'm afraid I had some cruel thoughts about you. I thought maybe you were bringing Mabel Hanks in for those killings just to, you know, wipe the slate. I can see you're a proud man, and a man sent on a mission that fell apart when it turned out we'd captured the wrong man. I thought, just maybe, you were out to nail just anyone, in lieu of Cotton Younger."

"Not quite, ma'am. Don't think I could get anyone to buy Mabel Hanks as Cotton Younger. She ain't built right."

Chapter 26

The Federal Building was near the Mormon Temple
grounds on the tree-shaded Main Street of Salt Lake
City. A crowd of curious onlookers gathered as the big
party of strange riders stopped in front of the baroque
outpost of far-off Washington.

Longarm dismounted and told some of the hands to
keep the crowd back as he and Timberline helped the
handcuffed woman down from her horse. A worried-
looking bailiff came out to watch as they led Mabel
Hanks, sputtering and cursing, up the stone steps.

Longarm noticed Kim Stover tagging along as his
side and muttered, "You'd best wait out here, ma'am."

"I've ridden too long a way to miss the ending, Longarm. I promise not to say anything or get in the way."

He saw there was no sense in trying to stop her, so he
dropped it. He nodded to the bailiff and said, "I'm Deputy Long. Denver office. You likely got the wire I sent
from Ouray Reservation about this suspect. Where do
you want her?"

"Judge Hawkins ain't arrived yet, Deputy. We'd best
get her to his chambers and I'll send over to his house
for him. Ought to be just finishing breakfast by now."

Longarm followed the uniformed man inside, along
with Timberline, Kim, and Mabel Hanks, who kept
swearing at them.

They went up a flight of marble steps with iron rail-
ings to the second floor, where the bailiff ushered them

into a deserted courtroom and then into the judge's smaller, private chambers beyond.

When he had left them alone there, Kim asked, "What happens now?"

Longarm said, "We wait. Waiting is the worst part of this job."

Timberline asked, "Do we have to sit through a trial, like?"

Longarm said, "No, just a preliminary hearing before the judge. He'll set her bail and a date for the trial. She'll likely spend a month or more waiting 'fore it gets serious."

Kim asked, "Won't you have to attend the trial, Longarm?"

"Sure. They'll send me back from Denver when it starts. But like I said, we're getting to the slow part. By the time it's all wrapped up you two will be up in Crooked Lance, fighting the buyers over the price of beef. Sometimes I wish I'd stayed a cowboy."

Mabel Hanks suddenly spat, "I'll never swing for it, God damn your eyes! This is a raw pure railroad job you're pulling on me, Longarm!"

"Oh, I don't know. I disremember if you said Cedric killed Kincaid."

"You know he didn't. The poor little mutt wouldn't hurt a fly, you big bully!"

"Let's save it for the judge. It's tedious to remind you over and over about them .44-40 slugs he was throwing my way in his innocence."

As if he'd been announced, Judge W.R. Hawkins came in wearing everyday duds and a frown. He was dabbing at some egg-stains on the front of his vest as he sat behind his imposing desk and asked, "What's all this about, Deputy Long?"

Longarm saw that the others had all found places to perch, so he lowered himself to a chair arm and asked, "Don't we rate a proper hearing with some bailiffs and all, Judge? Ought to have a matron for this lady, too. It's a long story and I'd like to get the cuffs off her."

231

"Just give me a grasp of what we've got and we'll work out the niceties as they come up. I'm holding regular court in less'n an hour."

Longarm shrugged, fished the key from his pants, and tossed it over to Timberline. "Unlock her and sort of stand over there by the door, will you? I reckon Mabel knows enough to be a good girl, but we gotta do things proper, court in an hour or no."

He waited till Timberline had carried out his instructions before he began to tell the whole story from the beginning. After a few minutes he started to describe the sniping in Bitter Creek. "Hold on, now," Hawkins cut in. "Did you *see* this lady firing at you from across the street?"

"Not exactly, but we found high-heel prints and a .30-30 is a womanly rifle, Your Honor."

"Hmmph, I've seen many a cowboy in high heels, and as for a .30-30 being womanly, I hunt deer with one myself! Are you saying I'm a sissy or that I took a shot at you in Bitter Creek?"

"Neither, Your Honor. I'm saying it's circumstantial evidence."

"Damn *slim*, too! Keep talking."

Longarm told the rest of it, with a few more interruptions from the judge. When he got to the part about the Mountie stealing the corpse of Raymond Tinker the judge laughed aloud and said, "Hold on! Are you saying that fool Canadian, backed by them rascals in the State Department, is packing the wrong man all the way back to Winnepeg in high summer?"

"Yessir, he seems to take his job right serious."

"By jimmies, I can't wait to tell the boys at the club that part. But you lost me somewhere. Deputy Long. You say it looks like this lady killed at least two, maybe three men. What have you to say for yourself, ma'am?"

Mabel Hanks said, "He's full of shit! This whole thing's nothing but—a lovers' spat!"

"A lover's *what*?"

"You heard me, Your Honor. He's just mad at me

232

'cause I wouldn't leave my husband for him. I'll admit he turned my head one night. He is good-looking and, well, I'm a poor, weak woman. But I saw the error of my ways in time and went back to my true love. He *said* he'd fix me for spurning his wicked advances, and as you see, he's trying fit to bust!"

Longarm found something very interesting about his fingernails to look at as the judge raised an eyebrow and observed, "Now, this is getting interesting! What have you to say for yourself, Deputy Long?"

"I'm a poor, weak man? The question before you ain't no morals charge, Your Honor. So I'll save a lot of useless talk by offering no defense to her wild allegations. I brought her in for killing folks, not for . . . never mind."

Hawkins stared at the woman thoughtfully for a long, hard moment. Then he nodded and said, "I've known Deputy Long long enough to suspect he wouldn't hang a lady for spurning his wicked advances, ma'am. However, since you aren't represented by an attorney, it's the duty of this court to cross-examine in your behalf."

He turned to Longarm and said, "Leaving aside your improper reasons for arresting this lady, what in thunder do you have on her?"

"I'll admit it's mostly circumstantial, Your Honor, but—"

"But me no buts. If she killed Kincaid and that other lawman, where are the damned bodies?"

"Your Honor, you can see we'll never find body one, 'less the killer tells us where they're hidden. We do have the body of Sailor Brown, and this woman and her late husband were in Crooked Lance when somebody gunned him."

"As was a whole valley filled with folks, damn it. What on earth is wrong with you? Where did you leave your brains this morning? Don't you remember Sailor Brown was a wanted man with papers on him? Hell, anyone who did kill him could come forward to claim the reward!"

Longarm looked surprised and asked the prisoner, "How about it, Mabel? As you see, there's no charge to the bushwhacking of the old man. Can't you 'fess up just a little and help us clear things up a mite?"

"Oh, go to hell! You'll not trick me again. You told me you'd marry up with me in Bitter Creek, remember?"

"Now, that, Your Honor, is the biggest lie she's told so far, and since we first met, she's told some lulus!"

"Let's get back to the murders she's accused of. Frankly, I'm surprised at you, son. You've never brought a prisoner in with such flimsy evidence to back your charges."

"I'll allow the killer was tricky, Your Honor, but I'm doing the best I know how."

"This time your best isn't good enough. Holding her for killing folks we can't even say for sure are dead won't keep her overnight! You got anything, anything at all, you can *prove*?"

Longarm looked uncomfortable as he suggested, "Maybe if we sent her into another room to be searched for evidence . . . Miss Kim might be willing to help."

Timberline, leaning against the door, spoke up, "We patted her down for shooting irons, remember?"

"I know, but we never really stripped her down for a proper search. Why don't we send the two of 'em in the next room? There's no other way out of here and who knows what we'll find stashed in her corset?"

The judge frowned and said, "Deputy Long, you are starting to tread on the tail of my robes! What are you up to, son? You know I can't order a search unless I order this other lady to search for some *thing*."

Longarm said, "What I'm hoping Miss Kim will find on her will be, uh, documentary evidence, Your Honor. She and her husband were bounty hunters. There were no reward papers or telegrams in their packs when I arrested 'em both."

"That's better. What am I to tell this other lady to look for in the way or papers?"

"Letters, telegrams, anything tying 'em in to someone in Missouri. Maybe someone named James or Younger."

The judge nodded and Kim got to her feet, saying, "Let's go, Mabel. It'll only take a minute."

"Damn it! I don't have nothing on me!"

"That may be so, dear. Why don't we get it over with?"

The judge got to his feet and opened the door to his dressing room. The two women went in, with some grumbling on Mabel's part, and Hawkins shut the door. His voice was ominous as he said, "Now that we are alone, let me tell you something, Deputy Long. I think you are wasting my time! You've been a lawman too long to bring a prisoner in on such flimsy evidence! Have you just gotten dumb, or was there anything at all to that fool women's story about you bedding down with her?"

Longarm grinned and said, "Hell, she's just a no-account adventuress, Your Honor. She did take that potshot at me in Bitter Creek, but you're right. It'd be a waste of time to prove it and her midget husband probably put her up to it. He was the dangerous one of the pair. Without him, she'll likely end her days in some parlor house. Not that she won't give right good service in bed."

Judge Hawkins looked thunderstruck as he almost roared, "You *knew* you didn't have the evidence to hang her?"

"Sure." Longarm said, "She never gunned them lawmen. *He* did." He pointed to where Timberline stood, stiffened against the door, slack-jawed. Longarm added, conversationally, "Don't do anything foolish, Mister Younger. We both know I can beat you to the draw nine times out of ten!"

Timberland gasped, "What are you saying, damn it! I thought I was your deputy!"

"Oh, I deputized you as the easiest way to bring you in without having to fight a score or so of your friends,

235

Mister Younger. You might say the nonsense with Mabel Hanks was a ruse. It was you I wanted all the time. Your Honor, may I present the Right Honorable Cotton Younger from Clay County, Missouri, and other parts past mention?"

Just then the door flew open and the two women sailed out, fighting and fussing. Mabel had a firm grip on Kim Stover's red hair and Kim was holding firm to the corset around her otherwise naked body as they landed in a rolling, spitting heap between Longarm and the man against the door!

Longarm muttered, "Damn!" as Timberline opened the door and crashed backward out of the chambers.

Longarm drew as he leaped over the cat-fight on the rug and came down running. As he left the room, a bullet tore a sliver from the jamb near his head and he fired across the deserted courtroom at the smoke cloud in the far doorway.

He ran the length of the courtroom and dove into the hallway headfirst, landing on his belly and elbows as he slid across the marble floor beneath the first shot fired his way at waist level.

He rolled and fired back at the tall, dark figure outlined by the window at the end of the long hallway. The target jacknifed over its gunbelt and feinted sideways for the stairs—still trying, with a .44-40 slug in the guts!

Longarm leaped to his feet and ran to the stairway, hearing a series of bumps and the clatter of metal on the marble steps.

The man called Timberline lay on the landing, sprawled like an oversized broken doll. His gun lay beyond, still smoking.

As Longarm went down two steps at a time, a bailiff appeared on the steps, coming up. Longarm snapped, "Go down and bar the doors. He's got a score of friends outside!"

Federal bailiffs were trained to obey first and think later, so this one did as he was told. Longarm knelt to feel for a pulse. Then he stood up again and began reloading his warm double-action, muttering, "Damn it to hell! Now we'll never know where Jesse James is hiding!"

Chapter 27

It seemed simple enough to Longarm, but Judge Hawkins made him repeat the whole story in front of a court reporter and Kim Stover and a few of the more stable folks from Crooked Lance he'd decided to let in.

The hearing was held in the outer courtroom, with Timberline—or rather, Cotton Younger—stretched out under a sheet on the floor. The coroner said it had been the fall down the steps that finished him with a broken neck, though he'd have died within the hour from the bullet wound.

As the court reporter put it down on paper, Longarm explained, "The late Cotton Younger rode into Crooked Lance five or six years ago, wanted dead or alive in lots of places and worn out with running. He took the first job offered him, at the Rocking H, and discovered he had a good head for cows. They promoted him to foreman and he became a respected member of the valley community. He had a fine lady he was interested in, and maybe, if things had gone better for him, he'd have stayed straight and we'd have never known what happened to him."

Kim Stover cut in to insist again, "Timberline *couldn't* have been Cotton Younger! He doesn't answer those wanted-poster descriptions at all!"

"That's true, ma'am. He's a head taller now than his army records showed. But you see, he ran off from Terry's Column as a *teenager*. It sometimes happens that a boy gets a last growing spurt, along about twenty or so. He was tall when he rode into Crooked Lance. Taller

238

than most. The rest of you probably didn't notice another saddle tramp at first. By the time it was important just how tall he really was, he was five or six inches taller. Must have been some comfort to him, when his real name came up in conversation, but as you see, he still dyed his hair."

"Where would he get dye like that?"

"It wasn't easy. He likely used ink. His hair was too black to be real. Not even an Indian has pure black hair. Natural brunettes have a brownish cast to their hair in sunlight. His was blue-black. I noticed that right off. Noticed a couple of slips, too. He knew the old man I found on the mountain had been shot, before I said one word about his being dead. Another time, he referred to Sailor Brown as the old tattooed man. I don't remember mentioning what I found under his beard to anyone in Crooked Lance, but a boy who'd ridden with him would have known about Brown's tattoos."

Judge Hawkins said, "I'll take your word for it you shot the right man, Deputy Long. Finish the story."

"All right. Cotton Younger was hankering after the widow Stover, here. Don't know if he had anything to do with her being a widow, so let's be charitable. Kim Stover and her friends liked to play vigilante when the cows were out minding themselves on the range. So when they spied the late Raymond Tinker just passing through, they grabbed him, searched him, and found him with a running iron.

"Cotton Younger was just showing off as usual and there's no telling what they'd have done with the cow thief, if the poor stranger hadn't answered to the old description of Cotton Younger!"

"That's the corpse you pawned off on the Mountie, right?"

"Yessir. Had to. Once word was out that a sidekick of Jesse James was being held in Crooked Lance, every lawman in creation converged on the place to claim him for their own.

"While I was whittling away some of the competition,

the other dead man, here, was sweating bullets. You see, he didn't *want* lawmen sniffing around. Sooner or later, any one of us might have unmasked him as the *real* Cotton Younger. He got word by wire that Kincaid and another lawman from Missouri were riding in. He busted up the wire and laid for 'em. He knew anyone from Missouri might recognize him on sight, and by now, he was trying to pass the cow thief off on us as the real article."

"What about Sailor Brown? I thought he was a *friend* of Cotton Younger."

"He was. Or, that is, he used to be, in another life. Brown rode in with me, pretending to be some crazy old French Canuck, and aiming to get his old pal out. He never got to *see* the man in jail, but it didn't matter. When a bunch of us rode over to talk to this lady here about the fool notions her friends had on holding Tinker for the reward money, Sailor Brown took one look at what everybody called Timberline and knew what was up. He was also wanted himself, and the Mountie rattled him some by talking French to him. Brown didn't savvy more'n the accent. So Brown was riding out, likely laughing about how his young friend had slickered us all, when said young friend put a bullet in him."

"To make certain no one in the outside world would ever learn of his new identity, right?"

"There you go, Your Honor. That takes us to the midget, Cedric Hanks, and the lady being held over in that jail cell as a material witness. They were what they said they were—bounty hunters. They knew they didn't have the weight to ride out with the prisoner. They only wanted him to tell 'em where the James Boys were, so they could collect on that much bigger bounty. They were playing their tune by ear, pumping the rest of us for information, obstructing us as best they could. Sort of like a kid tries to fix a stopped clock by hitting it a few licks and hoping."

240

"You say the midget was the more vicious of the pair."

"No sir, I said the smartest and most dangerous. I've sent a few wires and gotten more on 'em to go with what the railroad detective first told me. Little Cedric had a habit of collecting his bounties the easy way and was probably in on more killings than we'd ever be able to prove. So it's just as well he made things simple for us by acting so foolish. He was at least a suspect when he got killed trying to escape, so my office says I'm not to worry about it overmuch."

"I intend to hold his wife seventy-two hours on suspicion anyway, before we cut her loose. She said some mean things about this other lady and she'd best cool off until Miz Stover's out of Salt Lake City."

Longarm turned to the redhead and said, "I've been meaning to ask about that set-to before. I went to all that trouble to get Cotton Younger in here peaceable, pussyfooted to get you gals out of the room before I announced his arrest, and there you two were, rolling and spitting like alley cats between us, and he was able to make a break for it!"

Kim Stover blushed and looked away, murmuring, "If you must know, she passed a very improper remark and I slapped her sassy face for it. I suppose I shouldn't have, but she sort of blew up at me. After that, it's sort of confusing."

"I'd say you were winning when the bailiffs hauled you apart. You're gonna have a mouse over that one eye by tonight, but she collected the most bruises."

"She bit me, too. I daren't say where."

Judge Hawkins took out his pocket watch and said, "I think we've about wrapped this case up, and damned neatly, too, considering. By the way, Deputy Long, do you know a Captain Walthers, from the Provost Marshal's office?"

"Yessir. They've heard about this over at Fort Douglas, have they?"

"Yes. I just got a hand-delivered message, demanding Cotton Younger as an army deserter."

"You reckon they'll get him, Your Honor?"

"Justice Department hand over *spit* to the War Department? I turned the fool message over and wrote, 'Surely you jest, sir!' "

"They won't think that's funny, Your Honor."

"So what. I thought it was funny as all hell!"

Chapter 28

The train ride from Salt Lake City to Bitter Creek took about nine hours—a long time to go it alone and far too short a time sitting across from a very pretty redhead with a black eye.

They'd wound up things in Salt Lake City by midafternoon. So the sunset caught them more than half way to where Kim Stover and the others were getting off. They'd had dinner in the diner alone together, since the others were considerate, for cow hands, and Kim had stated that she was mourning Timberline's demise, and was ready to forgive and forget where Longarm was concerned. He'd asked a friendly colored feller for some ice for her eye, but all it seemed to do was run down inside her sleeve, so she'd given up. He thought she was as pretty as a picture in the evening light coming in through the dusty windows, anyway.

She was studying him, too, as the wheels under the Pullman car rumbled them ever closer to the time when they would have to say goodbye.

She licked her lips and said, "Your cigar is out again."

"It's a cheroot. I'm trying to quit smoking."

"Don't you allow yourself any bad habits?"

"Got lots of bad habits, Miss Kim. I try not to let 'em get the better of me."

"Is that why you never married?"

He looked out at the passing rangeland, orange and purple now, and said, "Soldiers, sailors, priests, and such should think twice before they marry. Lawmen should think three times and then not do it."

"I've heard of lots of lawmen who've gotten married."

"So have I. Knew a man who let 'em shoot him out of a circus cannon for a living, too. Didn't strike me as a trade I'd like to follow. He left a wife and three kids, one night, when he missed the net."

"A woman who thought enough of a man might be willing to take her chances on widowhood."

"Maybe. More to it than that. A man in my line makes enemies. I've got enough on my plate just watching my own back. Could run a man crazy thinking of a wife and kids alone at home while he's off on a mission."

"Then you never intend to settle down?"

"After I retire, maybe. I'll be pensioned off before I'm fifty."

"Heavens! By the time *I'm* fifty we'll be into the twentieth century!"

"Reckon so. These centuries do have a way of slipping by on us, don't they?"

"You mean life, don't you? I'm staring thirty down at medium range and there's so much I've missed. So much I never got to do. My God, it does get tedious, raising cows!"

"Well, the price of beef is rising. You'll likely wind up rich and married up with someone, soon enough."

She suddenly grimaced and marveled, "My God, if you hadn't come along when you did, I might have married Timberline, in time! There's not much to choose from in Crooked Lance, and a woman does get lonesome."

"I know the feeling, ma'am. Reckon we were both lucky, the way it all came out in the wash."

"You mean *you* were lucky. You must be pretty pleased with yourself, right now. You got the man they sent you after, solved the murder of your missing partner, and made fools of your rival law officers. I'll bet

244

they're waiting for you in Denver with a brass band!"

"Might get a few days off as a bonus. But I got a spell of travel ahead, first. This train won't be in Cheyenne till the wee, small hours. This Pullman car is routed through to Denver, but we'll likely sit in the yards for a spell before they shunt it on to the Burlington line. Be lucky if we make Denver by noon."

She looked up at the ornate, polished paneling and said, "I never rode in a Pullman before. How do they fix it into bedrooms or whatever?"

"These seats sort of scrootch together over where our legs are, right now. A slab of the ceiling comes down to form an upper bunk, with the stuff that goes on this bottom one stored up there. They run canvas curtains around these seats. Then everybody just goes to bed."

"Hmm, it seems a mite improper. Folks sleeping all up and down this car with only canvas between 'em."

"The wheels click-clack enough to drown most sounds. I mean, sounds of snoring and such."

"Be a sort of unusual setting for, well, honeymooners, wouldn't it?"

"Don't know. Never had a honeymoon on a train."

"I never had one at all, damn it. What time do you reckon they'll start making these fool beds up?"

"Later tonight. Maybe about the time we're pulling into Rawlins."

"That's a couple of stops past Bitter Creek, ain't it?"

"Yep. We'll be getting to Bitter Creek before nine."

"Oh."

The train rumbled on as night fell around them and the porter started lighting the oil lamps. Kim Stover rubbed at a cinder or something in her good eye and said, "I reckon I'll walk up to the freight section and see to my pony."

Longarm rose politely to his feet, but didn't follow as she swept past him and out. And likely out of his life, forever, a bit ahead of time.

He sat back down and stared out at the gathering darkness, wondering why he didn't feel like dancing.

He'd pulled off a fine piece of work, with no loose ends worth mentioning and no items on his expense voucher they could chew him out for, this time. Not even Marshal Vail would blanch at paying for that horse he'd lost, considering the laugh they'd had on the War Department. So why did he feel so let down?

It wasn't on account of shooting Cotton Younger. He'd been keyed up and braced for it ever since he'd noticed that funny blue shine to that too-black hair.

"Come on, old son," he murmured to his reflection in the dirty glass. "You know what's eating at you. You can't win 'em all! This time, you got into damn near ever skirt in sight. Includin' some you'll never know the who-all about! So just you leave that redheaded widow woman alone. She's the kind that needs false promises, and that ain't our style!"

The train ate up the miles in what seemed no time at all. Longarm couldn't believe it when the conductor came through, shouting, "Next stop Bitter Creek! All out for Bitter Creek!"

He glanced around, wondering if she was even coming back to say goodbye. It didn't seem she was. But, what the hell, mebbe it was better this way.

He got to his feet and walked back to the observation car as the train slowed for Bitter Creek. He was out there, puffing his cigar, as the train pulled into the station.

He stared over at the winking lights of the little cow town as, up near the front, the sounds of laughter and nickering horses told him they were unloading from the freight section. He started to lean out, maybe for a glimpse of red hair in the spattered, shifting light. But he never.

Someone fired a pistol into the air with a joyous shout of homecoming. Even though they had a long, hard ride ahead, the Crooked Lancers were a lot closer to home than he was. Then again, he didn't have a home worth mentioning.

As laughter and the sound of hoofbeats filled the air, the train restarted with a jerk. He stood there, reeling backwards on his boot heels as they pulled out of the place where it had all started. Some riders waved their hats and a voice called out, "So long, Longarm!"

He didn't wave back. He threw the cheroot away and watched the lights of Bitter Creek drop back into the past. As they passed a last, lighted window on the edge of town, he wondered who lived there and what it was like to live anywhere, permanently.

Then he shrugged and went inside. The observation car was dimly lit. The bartender had folded up and closed down the bar for the night. He walked the length of the train back to his own seat, noticing that they'd started making up the Pullman beds and that the centers of each car were now dim corridors of swaying green canvas that smelled like old army tents. After a short while he got up and went to his own berth and parted the curtains to get in.

Then he frowned and asked, "Where do you think you're going, Miss Kim?"

The redhead was half undressed on the bunk bed. So she just smiled shyly and said, "We'd best whisper, don't you reckon? I'm sort of spooked, with all these other folks outside these canvas hangings."

He sat down as she moved against the window side to make room for him. He took off his gunbelt, saying softly, "You got lots of cows expecting you, Kim."

"I know. They'll keep. You warned me when we met I was destined to get in trouble with the law."

"Before I take off my boots, there's a few things you should know about me, honey."

"Hush. I'm not out to hogtie you, darling. I know the rules of the . . . *game* is sort of wicked-sounding. Let's just say I was hoping for at least two weeks with you before I go back to punching cows. You reckon we'll last two weeks?"

"Maybe longer. Takes most gals at least a month before they've heard all a man's stories and start nagging

247

him about his table manners. I reckon that's why they call it the honeymoon."

"You must think I'm shameless, but damn it, I'm almost thirty and it's been lonesome up in Crooked Lance!"

"Don't spoil the wonder by trying to put words to it, honey. We got lots of time to talk about it between here and Denver."

And so they didn't discuss it as he took off his boots, removed his clothes, and finished undressing her in the swaying, dimly lit compartment while she tried not to giggle and the engine chuffed in time with their hearts.

A good two hours later, as the night train rolled on for Cheyenne, Kim raised her lips from his moist shoulder and murmured, "Will you tell me something, darling?"

He cuddled her body closer and asked, "What is it, kitten?"

"Am I as good in bed as that hussy, Mable Hanks?"

He didn't answer.

She raked her nails teasingly through the hair on his chest as she purred, "Come on. I know you had her. She told me something about you that I thought at the time she had to be making up."

"That why you tagged along?"

"Partly. But I'm afraid I might be in love with you, too. But, yeah, it pays to advertise. I thought she was just bragging, but I'm glad she was right about you."

He decided silence was his best move at the moment. But she moved her hand down his belly and insisted, "Come on. 'Fess up. Am I as good as Mabel?"

"Honey, there ain't no comparison. You're at least ten times better."

"Then prove it to me. Let's do it some more."

So they did. But even as her lush flesh accepted his once more, he found himself wondering. Did this make it Kim Stover and her mother-in-law, Kim Stover and her sister-in-law, or all *three* of the Stover women?

SPECIAL PREVIEW

Here are the opening scenes
from

LONGARM ON THE BORDER

second novel in the bold
LONGARM series from Jove

Chapter 1

Even before he opened his eyes, in that instant between sleep and waking, Longarm knew it had snowed during the night. Like the hunter whose senses guide him to prey, like the hunted whose senses keep him from becoming prey, Longarm was attuned to the subtlest changes in his surroundings. The light that struck his closed eyelids wasn't the usual soft gray that brightens the sky just before dawn. It had the harsh brilliance that comes only from the pre-sunrise skyglow being reflected from snow-covered ground.

Opening his eyes, Longarm confirmed what he already knew. He didn't see much point in walking across the ice-cold room to raise a shade at one of the twin windows. The light seeping around the edges of the opaque shades had that cold, hard quality he'd sensed when he'd snapped awake.

Longarm swore, then grunted. He didn't believe in cussing the weather or anything else he was powerless to change. He was a man who believed swearing just wasted energy unless it did something besides relieving his own dissatisfaction.

Last night, when he'd swung off the narrow-gauge railroad after a long, slow, swaying trip up from Santa Fe to Denver, he'd noted the nip in the air, but his usually reliable weather sense hadn't warned him it might snow. It was just too early in the year. It was still fall, with the Rocky Mountains' winter still a couple of months away.

Longarm hadn't been thinking too much about the

251

weather last night, though. All that had been in his mind was getting to his room, taking a nightcap from the bottle of Maryland rye that stood waiting on his dresser, and falling into bed. On another night, he'd probably have followed his habit of dropping in at the Black Cat or one of the other saloons on his way home, to buck the faro bank for a few cards until he relaxed. He'd started to cut across the freightyard to Colfax instead of taking the easier way along Wynekoop Street. What he'd seen happen in New Mexico Territory had left a sour taste in his mouth that the three or four drinks he'd downed on the train couldn't wash away.

There was little light in the freightyard. The acetylene flares mounted on high standards here and there created small pools of brightness, but intensified the darkness between them. Longarm was spacing his steps economically as he crossed the maze of tracks, sighting along the wheel-polished surface of the rails to orient himself, when he sensed rather than saw the man off to his left. He couldn't see much in the gloom, just the interruption of the light reflected on the rail along which he was sighting.

"Casey?" Longarm called. He didn't think it was Casey, who was the yard's night superintendent, and more likely to be in his office, but if it was one of Casey's yard bulls on patrol, using the boss's name would tell the man at once that Longarm wasn't a freightyard thief.

A shot was his answer. A muzzle-flash and the whistle of lead uncomfortably close to his chest. Longarm drew as he was dropping and snap-shot when he rolled, firing at the place where he'd seen the orange blast. He didn't know whether or not he'd connected. He hadn't had a target; his shot was the equivalent of the warning buzz a rattlesnake gives when a foot comes too close to its coils.

Faintly, the sound of running footsteps gritting on cinders gave him the answer. Whoever had tried the bushwhacking wasn't going to hang around and argue.

For several seconds, Longarm lay on the rough, gritty earth, trying to stab through the darkness with his eyes, straining his ears to hear some giveaway sound that would spot his target for him. Except for the distant chugging of a yard-mule cutting cars at the shunt, there was nothing to hear.

Longarm didn't waste time trying to prowl the yard. Being the target of a grudge shot from the dark wasn't anything new to him, or to any of the other men serving as Deputy U.S. Marshals in the unreconstructed West of the 1880s. Longarm guessed that whoever had been responsible for the drygulching attempt had been skulking in another car of the narrow-gauge on the trip up from New Mexico. God knows, he'd stepped on enough toes during his month there to have become a prime target for any one of a half dozen merciless, powerful men. Any of them could've sent a gunslick to waylay him in Denver. The attack had to originate in New Mexico Territory, he decided, because nobody in Denver had known when he'd be arriving.

Brushing himself off, Longarm had hurried on across the freightyard and on to his room. Bone-tired, he'd hit the sack without lighting a lamp, dropping his clothes as he shed them.

On the dresser, the half full buttle of Maryland rye gleamed in the light that was trickling in from the window. Its invitation was more attractive than the idea of staying in the warm bed. Longarm swung his bare feet to the floor, crossed the worn gray carpet in two long strides and let a trickle of warmth slip down his throat. As he stood there, the tarnished mirror over the dresser showed his tanned skin tightening as the chilly air of the unheated room raised goosebumps.

Crossing the room to its inside corner, Longarm pulled aside a sagging curtain to get to his wardrobe. Garments hung on a pegged board behind the curtain. He grabbed a cleaner shirt than the one he'd taken off, and a pair of britches that weren't grimed with cinders from his roll in the freightyard last night.

He wasted no time in dressing. The cold air encouraged speed. Longjohns and flannel shirt, britches, woolen socks, and he was ready to stamp into his stovepipe cavalry boots. Another snort from the bottle and he turned to check his tools. From its usual night resting place, hanging by its belt from the bedpost on the left above his pillow, Longarm took his .44-40 Colt double-action out of its opentoed holster. Quickly and methodically, his fingers working with blurring speed, he swung out the Colt's cylinder, dumped its cartridges on the bed, and strapped on the gunbelt.

He returned the unloaded pistol to the holster and drew three or four times, triggering the revolver with each draw, but always catching the hammer with his thumb instead of letting it snap on an empty chamber, which could break the firing pin. When Longarm had returned the Colt to its holster after each draw, he made the tiny adjustments that were needed to put the waxed, heat-hardened leather at the precise angle and position he wanted, just above his left hip.

Satisfied now, he reloaded the Colt, checking each cartridge before sliding it into the cylinder. Then he checked out the .44 double-barrelled derringer that was soldered to the chain that held his railroad Ingersoll on the other end. He put on his vest, dropping the watch into his left-hand breast pocket, the derringer into the right-hand one. Longarm always anticipated that trouble might look him up, as it had in the freightyard last night. If it did, he intended to be ready.

Longarm's stomach was growling by now. He quieted it temporarily with a short sip of rye before completing his methodical preparations to leave his room for the day. These were simple and routine, but it was a routine he never varied while in civilized surroundings. Black string tie in place, frock coat settled on his broad shoulders, Stetson at its forward-canted angle on his close-cropped head, he picked up his necessaries from the top of the bureau and stowed them into their accustomed pockets. Change went in one pants pocket and his jackknife in the other; his wallet with the silver federal badge pinned inside was slid into an inside breast pocket. Extra cartridges went into his right-hand coat pocket, handcuffs and a small bundle of waterproof matches into the pocket on the left.

As he left the room, he kicked the soiled clothing that still lay on the floor out into the hallway ahead of him. He'd leave word for his Chinese laundryman, Ho Quah, to pick it up and have it back that evening. He closed the door and between door and jamb inserted a broken matchstick at about the level of his belt. His landlady wasn't due to clean up his room until Thursday, and Longarm wanted to know the instant he came home if an uninvited stranger might be waiting inside: for instance, the unknown shadow who'd thrown down on him last night. Anybody who knew his name was Custis Long could find out where Longarm lived.

Not only the rooming house, but the entire section of the unfashionable side of Cherry Creek where it stood was still asleep, Longarm decided, after he'd moved on light feet down the silent hallway and stopped to look over the street before stepping out the door. The night's unexpected snowfall, though only an inch or less, made it easy for him to see whether anyone had been prowling around. He took a cheroot from his breast pocket and champed it in his teeth, but didn't light it, while he studied the white surface outside.

There was only one set of tracks. They came from the house across the way, and the toes were pointed in the safe direction—for Longarm—away from the house, toward Cherry Creek. Just the same, he stopped on the narrow porch long enough to flick his gunmetal-blue eyes into the long, slanting shadows. He didn't really expect to see anyone, though. The kind of gunhand who'd picked the safety of darkness once for his attack would be likely to wait for the gloomy cover of hootowl time before making a second try.

His booted feet cut through the thin, soft snow and crunched on the cinder pathway as Longarm walked unhurriedly to the Colfax Avenue bridge. He turned east on the avenue; ahead, the golden dome of the Colorado capitol building was just picking up the first rays of the rising sun.

George Masters's barbershop wasn't open yet, and Longarm needed food more than a shave. He didn't fancy the cold free-lunch items he knew he'd find in any of the saloons close by, so he went on past the barbershop corner another block and stopped at a little hole-in-the-wall diner for hotcakes, fried eggs, ham, and coffee. He stowed away the cheroot while he ate. The longer he held off lighting it, the easier it would be for him to keep from lighting the next one.

Leaving the restaurant, twenty-five cents poorer, but with a satisfactorily full stomach, Longarm squinted at the sun. Plenty of time for a shave before reporting in at the office. He walked at ease along the avenue, which was just coming to life. The day might not be so bad in spite of the snow, he decided, feeling the warmth from his breakfast spreading through his lean, sinewy body. He grinned at the bright sun, glowing golden in a blue-crystal sky. Deliberately, he took a match from the bundle in his pocket, flicked it into flame with his thumbnail, and lighted his cheroot.

Smelling of bay rum, his overnight stubble removed and his brown mustache now combed to the angle and spread of the horns on a Texas steer, Longarm walked into Marshal Billy Vail's office before eight o'clock. It gave him a virtuous feeling to be the first one to show up, and even Vail's pink-cheeked, citified clerk-stenographer wasn't at the outside desk to challenge him. The Chief Marshal was already on the job, of course, fighting the ever-losing battle he waged with the paperwork that kept coming from Washington in a mounting flood. Vail looked pointedly at the banjo clock on the wall.

"This'll be the day the world ends," he growled.

"What in hell happened to get you here on time for once?"

Longarm didn't bother answering. He was used to Vail's bitching. He felt his chief was entitled, bound as he was now to a desk and swivel chair, going bald and getting lardy. Desk work, after an active career in the field, seemed to bring out the granny in a man, and Longarm felt that he might bitch about life, too, under the same circumstances.

Vail shoved a pile of telegraph flimsies across the desk. "I guess you know you raised a real shit-stink down in New Mexico. You'd better have a good story to back up your play down there. I've got wires here from everybody except President Hayes."

"Chances are the word ain't got to him, yet," Longarm replied mildly. "Don't be feeling disappointed. You might get one from him, too, before the day's out. You want me to tell you how it was?"

"No. In fact, I'm not sure I want a long report in the file telling exactly what happened. Think you can write one like the one you handed in after that Short Creek fracas a few years back?"

Vail was referring to a report Longarm had turned in about his handling of another political hot potato that had consumed a month of time, resulted in eight deaths, and upset a hundred square miles of Idaho Territory. The report had simply read, "Assigned to case on May 23. Completed assignment and closed case July 2."

"Don't see why not." Longarm considered for a moment before he went on. "I figured things might be hottening up down around Sante Fe, at the capitol. Some gunslick tried to bushwhack me when I got off the narrow-gauge last night."

"The hell you say." Vail's tone showed no surprise. "You get him?"

"Too dark. He ran before I could sight on him."

"Well, keep your report short. I won't have to explain things I don't know about. Besides, I want you out of this office before that pot down there boils over clear to Washington."

"Suits me, chief, right to a tee. There's snow on the ground and a smell of more in the air, and you know how I feel about that damned white stuff."

"If it'll cheer you up any, the place you'll be going to is just a little cooler than the hinges of hell, this time of the year." Vail pawed through the untidy stacks of documents on his desk until he uncovered the papers he was after. "Texas is yelling for us to give them a hand. So is the army."

"Seems to me like they both got enough hands so they wouldn't need to come running to us. What's wrong with the Rangers? They gone to pot these days?"

Vail bristled. As a one-time Texas Ranger, he automatically resented any hints that his old outfit wasn't up to snuff. Huffily, he said, "The Rangers have got more sense than to bust into something that might stir up trouble in Mexico. Here's what Bert Matthews wrote me from Austin." He read from one of the papers he'd uncovered. "He says, 'You see what a bind we're in on this, Billy. If one of my boys sets foot across the border and gets crossways of Diaz's Rurales, we'd risk starting another war with them. Whoever goes looking for Nate Webster's got to have Federal authority back of him and can't be tied to Texas. That's why I'm looking to you to give us a hand.' "

Longarm rubbed his freshly shaved chin and nodded slowly. "I hadn't looked at it that way. Makes sense, I suppose. What'd this Nate Webster do?"

"As far as Bert knows, he didn't do anything except drop out of sight somewhere on the other side of the Rio Grande. So did two black troopers who deserted from the 10th Cavalry, and a captain from the same outfit who went off on his own to bring them back."

"Wait a minute, now. That Rio Grande's a damn long river," Longarm observed. "It's going to take a while, prowling it all the way down to the Gulf of Mexico. I got to have a place to start looking."

"You have, so settle down. I wouldn't be so apt to send you if it wasn't that all four of them disappeared from the same place. Little town called Los Perros. Dogtown, I guess that'd translate into. You ever hear of it? I sure as hell never did, but it's been a spell since I left Texas."

Longarm shook his head. "Name don't ring a bell with me, either. Where's this Los Perros place at, in general?"

"It's supposed to be close to where the Pecos River goes into the Rio Grande."

"Rough country in that part," Longarm said. "If it's there, I reckon I can find it, though. I aim to circle around New Mexico instead of going there the straightest way. If I show my face in old Senator Abeyeta's country before the old man wears his mad off, I'd have to fight my way from Santa Fe clear to El Paso."

"You steer clear of New Mexico Territory, and that's an order," Vail agreed. "You've stirred up enough hell there to last a while."

"Now, don't get your bowels riled up, Chief. I'll figure me out a route. Just let me think a minute." He leaned back in the red morocco-leather chair, the most comfortable piece of furniture in the marshal's office, and began thinking aloud. "Let's see, now. I take the KP outa here tonight and switch to the MP at Pueblo. That gets me to Wichita, and I'll make a connection there with the I-GN or the SP to San Antone. Pick me up a horse and some army field rations at the quartermaster depot there and ride to Fort Stockton. That'll beat jarring my ass on the Butterfield stage, and it'll get me to spittin' distance of the border a lot faster."

"Tell my clerk," Vail said impatiently. "He'll write your travel vouchers and requisition your expense money. Here. Take these letters and read them on the train. They'll give you the whole story as good as I can. Now, get the hell outta this office before I get a wire from the attorney-general or the president telling me to suspend you or fire you outright."

"Which you can't do if I ain't here." Longarm grinned. "All right, chief. Time I cose this case and get back, things ought to've cooled down enough to get me off the political shitlist."

During the three train changes and four days and nights it took Longarm to reach his jumping-off place deep in Texas, he spent his time catching up with lost sleep and studying the letters Marshal Vail had gotten from the Texas Ranger captain and the post adjutant at Fort Stockton. He was looking for some sort of connection that might tie the four disappearances together, but couldn't see any.

Ranger Nate Webster had been working on a fresh outbreak of the style of rustling along the Texas border that had come to be called the "Laredo Loop." Cattle stolen from ranches in central Texas were hustled across the Rio Grande's northern stretches, their brands altered, and with false bills of sale forged to show that the steers had been Mexico-bred and bought from legitimate ranchers in the Mexican states of Chihuahua, Cohuila, or Nuevo Leon. Then, driven south, the rustled herds were taken back across the river at Laredo and sold there to buyers. Laredo was the only point along the Texas-Mexico border where railroad shipments crossed; it had long been a center for livestock sales. Even with Mexican cattle selling well below the market price for Texas beef, the profits were huge. Nate Webster's investigation had led him to Los Perros, where he'd been heading when he reported to ranger headquarters in Austin. That had been in July. He hadn't been heard from since.

About a month before the ranger made his last report, the two troopers from the all-black 10th Cavalry—the "buffalo soldiers," as they'd been named by the Indians, who saw in the blacks' hair a resemblance to buffalo manes—had deserted from Fort Lancaster.

Lancaster was an outpost of Fort Stockton; it was one of a string of such small posts dotted along the El Paso-San Antonio road. The men had left a trail that the Cimarron scout summoned from Fort Stockton had no trouble following. He followed it to Los Perros. Captain John Hill, the Charley Troop commander, had gone with the scout. The captain had sent the Cimarron back to report and had himself followed the deserters' trail across the Rio Grande. Like Webster, like the deserting troopers, Hill had vanished on the other side of the river after leaving Los Perros.

"Dogtown," Longarm muttered to himself, drawing on four-year-old memories of the last case that had taken him to Texas. "Los Perros. Mouth of the Pecos. Wild country. Big enough and rough enough to swallow up four hundred men, let alone four, without much trace left. Hope I ain't forgotten what little bit of the local lingo I learned."

Then, because it was his philosophy that a man shouldn't cross rivers before he tested them to see how deep and cold they ran, Longarm ratcheted back the rubbed plush daycoach seat, and went to sleep again with the smell of old and acrid coal dust in his nostrils. A little stored-up shuteye might come handy after he hit the trail on horseback from San Antonio to the Rio Grande.

At the I-GN depot in San Antonio, Longarm swung off the daycoach and walked up to the baggage car to claim his gear. He'd left everything except his rifle to the baggage handlers, but it would have been tempting fate to leave a finely tuned .44-40 Winchester unwatched in a baggage car or on a depot platform between trains. The rifle had ridden beside him all the way from Denver, leaning between the coach seat and the wall.

As always, he was traveling light. He swung the bedroll that contained his spare clothing as well as a blanket and groundcloth over one shoulder, draped his saddlebags over the other, and picked up his well-worn

McCellan saddle in his left hand. Then he set out to find a hack to carry him from the station to the quartermaster depot.

"To the quartermaster depot?" the hackman echoed when Longarm asked how much the fare would be. "That's a long ways, mister. Cost you 15¢ to go way out there. It's plumb on the other side of town and out in the country."

"We got to go by Market Plaza to get there, don't we?" Longarm asked. When the hackman nodded, he went on, "I'll pay the fare, even if it does seem a mite high, provided you'll stop there long enough for me to eat a bowl of chili. I got to get rid of the taste of them stale butcher-boy sandwiches I been eating the last few days."

"Hop in," the hackman said. "It's my dinnertime, too. Won't charge you extra for stopping."

Counting time taken for eating, the ride down Commerce Street and then north on Broadway to the army installation took just over an hour. The place was buzzing with activity. After more than five years of debating, the high brass in Washington had finally decided to turn the quartermaster depot into a large permanent cantonment, and everywhere Longarm looked there were men at work. Masons were erecting thick walls of quarry stone to serve as offices, others were busy with red brick putting up quarters for the officers. A few carpenters were building barracks for the enlisted men on a flat area beyond the stables, where the hackman had pulled up at Longarm's direction.

Not until he'd been watching the scene for several minutes did Longarm realize that there was something odd. There was only a handful of soldiers among the men working around the quadrangle the buildings would enclose when all of them were completed. The hackie lifted Longarm's saddle and saddlebags out of the front of his carriage; Longarm got out and paid the man. He stood with his gear on the ground around his feet until the hack drove off. Then he slung his saddlebags and bedroll over his shoulders, picked up the saddle, and started for the nearest uniforms he saw, a clump of soldiers gathered around a smithy's forge a few yards away from the stable buildings.

Longarm singled out the highest-ranking of the group, a tall, lantern-jawed sergeant. "I'm looking for the remount duty noncom," he told the man.

"You found him, mister. Name's Flanders."

"My name's Long, Custis Long. Deputy U.S. Marshal outta the Denver office. I need to requisition a good saddle horse for a case I'm on."

"Well, now. You wanta show me your badge or something, so I'll know you're who you say you are?"

Wordlessly, Longarm took his wallet from the pocket of his frock coat and flipped it open to let the sergeant see the silver badge pinned between its folds. The sergeant studied it for a moment, then nodded. He measured Longarm with his eyes.

"How far you gonna be travelling?"

"To the border."

"You're a sizeable man, Mr. Long. You plan to pack any more gear than what you've got here?"

"Nope. This is all I need."

"Follow along, then. I guess we can fix you up."

Longarm followed the sergeant around the stable to a small corral where a dozen or so horses were milling. The rat-a-tat of carpenters' hammers nearby was obviously making a few of the animals nervous; they were walking around the corral's inner perimeter. The others stood in a fairly compact group near the center of the enclosure. Most of them were roans and chestnuts, but there was one dappled gray a hand taller than the rest who stood out like a peacock among sparrows.

"Don't try to palm off any of them walking ones on me," Longarm warned the sergeant. "Last thing I need's a nervous nag."

"Maybe you'd rather do your own picking, Mr. Long?" the sergeant suggested.

"Maybe I better, if it's all the same to you."

263

Longarm was still carrying his Winchester. He tilted the muzzle skyward, levered a shell into the chamber and fired in the air before the sergeant knew what he intended to do. Two of the horses at the corral's center reared, three others bolted for the fence. Most of those that had been fence-walking either reared or bucked. The gray was among the handful that had not reacted to the shot. Longarm studied the dapple through slitted eyes. A light-coated horse made a man stand out more than a roan or chestnut would, but he told himself that could be both good and bad. He pointed to the animal.

"I'll take the gray, if he stands up to a closer look. Bring him over and let me check him out," he told the sergeant.

"Well, now, I'm sorry, Mr. Long. That's the only one I can't let you have."

"Why not? Is he officer's property?"

"Well, yes and no."

"Make up your mind, Flanders. Either he is or he ain't."

"He ain't exactly officer's property, Mr. Long. Thing is, Miz Stanley, that's Lieutenant Stanley's lady, she's took a liking to Tordo, there. Rides him just about every afternoon. She'd be mighty riled if I was to—"

"This lieutenant don't own the horse?"

"No, sir. Except, we was going to ship Tordo up to Leavenworth for their bandsmen, seeing we got no band here, and the lieutenant stopped us because his lady'd took a shine to the nag."

"I suppose Miz Stanley'd be just as well off if she got her exercise on another horse, wouldn't she?"

"No, sir. Begging your pardon, Mr. Long, she'd want Tordo."

"Happens I want him, too. He's the best-looking of that bunch out there. Bring him here and let me check him over. You can give the lieutenant's lady my regrets next time she wants to ride."

Longarm's tone carried an authroity that the sergeant was quick to recognize. He opened his mouth once, as

264

though to argue further, but the deputy's steel-blue eyes were narrowed now, and the soldier knew he was looking at a man whose mind was made up. Reluctantly, the sergeant walked over to the gray and put a hand on its army-clipped mane. He walked back to where Longarm stood waiting. The horse, obedient to the light pressure of the man's hand on on its neck, walked, step for step, with the sergeant.

"Seems to be real biddable," Longarm commented.

"Tordo's a good horse, Mr. Long. Can't say I blame you for picking him out."

Longarm checked the gelding with an expert's quick, seemingly casual glances. Teeth, eyes, spine, cannons, hooves, were all sound. His inspection lasted barely three minutes, but when it was completed Longarm was satisfied with the choice he'd made.

"He'll do, sergeant. Make out the form for me to sign while I'm saddling him. Or is this the kind of post where I got to find a commissioned man for that?"

"No, sir. Most of the officers are out on a field exercise, anyhow. I've got the papers over yonder in the stable. I'll have 'em ready by the time you're ready to ride. If you don't want to bother saddling him, I'll call a trooper to do it for you."

"I'd as soon do it myself, Flanders. You take care of the requisition form."

Longarm saddled the dapple with the same economy of motion that marked all his actions. He'd finished cinching the girth and had sheathed his Winchester in the scabbard that angled back from the right-hand saddle fender and was knotting the last rawhide string around his bedroll when a woman's voice spoke behind him.

"I don't know who you are, but that's my horse you're saddling."

Without turning around, Longarm replied, "No, ma'am. It's the U.S. Government's horse."

"Don't be insolent! Take that saddle off at once and

find yourself another mount! I'm ready for my afternoon canter."

Longarm finished knotting the saddle-string and turned around. He doffed his Stetson as he spoke. "Beg pardon, ma'am, but I ain't about to do that. I need this one in my work."

"Really? Just who are you? And what sort of work do you do?"

"I'm Custis Long, ma'am. Deputy U.S. Marshal from Denver. And I'm on a case, which is all I need to say, I guess." Longarm realized he was speaking arbitrarily, which wasn't his usual way with a woman, but this one was being just too damned high-handed.

His abrupt manner surprised and puzzled her; that was clear from the expression on her face. Longarm took the moment of silence to inspect her. He wondered if she kept one full black eyebrow higher than the other when she wasn't angry. But she wasn't what you'd call pretty, he decided; her features were just a mite too irregular. Her nose arched abruptly from the full brows down to wide nostrils now flared with displeasure. Her lips were compressed, but that didn't hide the fact that they were on the full side. Her chin was thrust out aggressively. Her eyes were dark, and her hair was dark, too. It was caught up in ringlets that dropped down the back of her neck to her shoulders.

She was wearing a cavalry trooper's regulation campaign hat, although it didn't have the regulation four dents in its crown. A soft, plain white blouse was pulled tightly over upthrust breasts. Her feet, in gloss-polished riding boots, were spread apart to show that she was wearing a split riding skirt that dropped nearly to her ankles. Her hands were planted on her hips, and from one wrist a riding crop dangled by its looped thong.

Longarm's unconcealed inspection didn't cause her to drop her eyes or seem to embarrass her. When she found her voice, she said firmly, "Mr. Long, there are ten or fifteen other horses over there in the corral. One of them will be just as satisfactory as Tordo for your use."

"I'm sorry if it makes you mad, ma'am, but the plain fact of it is, where I'm heading for, my life might depend on me having the best horse I can throw my saddle on."

As though he hadn't spoken, she went on, "I'll find Sergeant Flanders and tell him to get you another horse. Meanwhile, you will take that saddle off Tordo at once!"

"I ain't about to do that, ma'am. Let's see, you'd be Lieutenant Stanley's wife, I guess?"

"What difference does that make?"

"Not one bit, Miz Stanley. Except it ain't goin to do you no good to call the segeant. He told me you'd be mad, when I'd made up my mind which horse I wanted. It didn't matter to me then, and it don't matter none to me now."

She stamped a booted foot. "Mr. Long, if you don't take that saddle off Tordo right this minute, I'll—"

"You'll do what?" Longarm had held his temper, but he was getting angry now. "I need this gray for my business. You just want him for funnin'. It's a government horse, and I figure my claim to it's just a lot better'n yours is. Now, I can't waste no more time arguin' with you. I got my job to tend to."

As Longarm turned away to mount the gray, she moved cat-quick, raising the riding crop to slash at him. As fast as she acted, Longarm reacted faster. He caught her arm as it came down and held it firmly while he took the crop off her wrist and tossed it on the ground. She brought up her free arm, to slap his face, but Longarm grasped it before the blow landed. For a moment, they stood there with arms locked, anger flowing between them like an electric current where flesh touched flesh. Then she relaxed, and Longarm released her.

They were glaring, eye to eye, when Sergeant Flanders came hurrying up. His arrival broke the tension. He said, "Now, let's don't you and Marshal Long go having words, Miz Stanley. I hope you ain't blaming me. I told him—"

"It's all right, sergeant," she broke in. "Mr. Long's explained that you tried to tell him I laid·claim to Tordo."

"I've convinced the lady my claim's better'n hers, sergeant," Longarm said. "Now if you'll give me that form you got, I'll sign it and be on my way." He took the requisition Flanders had in his hand, rested it on the saddle skirt and scrawled his name on the proper line. Handing the form back to the sergeant, he said, "Now, if you'll show me where the commissary's at, I'll swing by there and pick up some rations and be on my way."

Flanders pointed to a sprawling warehouse-type building a short distance away. Longarm nodded and swung into the saddle. Touching his hatbrim to the woman, he rode off, leaving them looking at his back as he made his way to the commissary. He didn't turn to look back at them.

Chapter 2

Following the directions he'd gotten at the commissary while waiting for the rations he'd drawn to be assembled, Longarm rode due west from the quartermaster depot. The houses of San Antonio lay to his left; the city was just beginning to push northward. The line of closely settled streets stopped nearly two miles south of the army depot, although there were a few scattered dwellings, most of them marking small truck farms, between the bulk of the town and the military installation.

Longarm was taking his time, getting acquainted with the habits of the gray horse. Tordo had been well trained. The animal responded to the pressure of a knee and the touch of a boot-toe with as much readiness as it did to the rein. For the most part, after he'd satisfied himself that the dapple was the kind of mount he could trust, Longarm let the horse pick its own way across the grassy, tree-dotted plain that sloped gently to the banks of the San Antonio River, half a mile ahead of him, now.

He'd reached the riverbank and was looking for signs of a ford when thudding hoofbeats caught his attention and he turned to look behind him. Mrs. Stanley, mounted on a roan that must have been her second choice of the horses in the corral, was overtaking him fast. Subconsciously, Longarm noted that she sat on the horse well, holding to the saddle easily as the roan loped toward him. He reined in and waited. She drew alongside and brought her mount to a stop.

"If you're looking for a ford, the best one's only

about two hundred yards upstream," she said. "If you don't mind company, I'll ride with you a little way."

"If you're scheming to talk me into swapping horses, you'll just be wasting your time," Longarm warned her. "Otherwise, I'll be right pleased to have you ride alongside me, Miz Stanley."

"I promise that I won't try to persuade you." She seemed to have gotten over her fit of anger; her voice was light and pleasant. "I really rode after you to apologize for the way I acted back at the depot. I don't usually behave so thoughtlessly."

"Wasn't no need to come apologizing, ma'am. I don't hold grudges over things that don't amount to a hill of beans."

"Just the same, it was childish of me. I understand why you'd need the best horse you can find, in your job. It must be a dangerous one."

"I reckon it is, sometimes." Longarm wasn't given to dwelling on the dangers of his work. In his book, a job was a job, and you did it according to your best lights.

"Here's the ford," she said, pointing to the spot where the river's green water took on a lighter hue as the stream spread out to run wide and shallow over a pebble-covered underwater limestone shelf. Turning their horses, they splashed across through water only inches deep.

"Guess you must ride this way pretty often," he suggested after they'd covered a few hundred feet on the west bank of the river.

"Almost every day. Riding's about the only relaxation I have in this dull little town. Especially now, when my husband's away on a training exercise."

"Funny. I never figured San Antone was so dull."

"I don't suppose it would be, for a man. You've got the gambling places and the dance halls and saloons. But all I've got is the company of other army wives, and we get bored with one another after a few gossipy afternoon teas. At home, now, it's a different thing."

"Where's home to you, Miz Stanley?"

"New York. It's never dull, there. There're the Broadway shows, musicals or dramas, tea dances at most of the big hotels."

"I can see there'd be a difference. Can't rightly say much about New York. I never visited back there, myself."

"You should, some time. It's worth the trip." She pointed to a thickly-wooded area that lay just ahead of them, where trees in closely spaced clumps spread across a wide stretch of grassland that ended on their right at the foot of a high, white bluff. "Of course, you won't find places like that in New York. The nearest thing to open country there is Central Park. Though it's very much like that stretch ahead of us. Perhaps that's why I feel at home when I see it."

"I recall this place from when I was here a few years back. They call it San Pedro Springs, don't they?"

"Yes. It's one of my favorite spots. On Sundays and holidays it's overrun with families having picnics, but on days like today, in the middle of the week, it's as deserted as the Forest of Arden."

"Can't say I been there, either. Matter of fact, I never even got to prowl around that stretch of woods up ahead except once, when I was in San Antone before."

Mrs. Stanley seemed compelled to talk. "Sometimes I bring my lunch out here and stay most of the day. I've found arrowheads and pieces of old Mexican army equipment from the Texas-Mexican war of fifty years ago."

"You interested in history, then, Miz Stanley?"

"Not especially. But it gives me something besides garrison gossip to think about."

They were approaching an especially large growth of hachberry and pinoak trees bordered by low-branched chinaberry trees that formed a wide belt around the taller growth. Longarm kneed the dapple to turn it and skirt the edge of the motte, but the lieutenant's wife was reining in.

"There's a beautiful spring in the middle of this

271

grove," she said. "I just can't pass by it without stopping for a sip of water."

Longarm thought the excuse was flimsy, almost as thin as her story of having ridden after him to apologize. His work took him to army posts quite regularly, and he'd met bored, restless army wives before now. Almost from the time they'd crossed the river he'd been getting the groin-twitches that he felt whenever he was with an attractive woman who was obviously making herself available to him. He pulled rein and swung out of his saddle before she was quite ready to dismount.

"I'm pretty thirsty myself. We'll go get some of that spring water together."

He moved to help her from her horse. She was riding sidesaddle, with her right leg hooked over the horn, and had to swing the leg high over the pommel to free it. Longarm caught her booted foot in one hand and steadied her to the ground, his free arm pressing up the back of her thighs, over the soft bulge of her buttocks to her waist. She was beginning to tremble even before both her feet were on the ground. The trembling increased as he pulled her to him and sought her lips. They locked together, tongues entwined. Longarm felt himself growing erect as she rubbed her hips across his crotch.

She felt the swelling beneath his jeans, pulled away, and panted in a half-whisper, "Hurry! Let's go into the grove! I want you right now, this minute!"